Goode Vibrations of
the Wresting Place

Amy Safford

Saco River Books

ISBN: 979-8-9903619-0-4 (paperback)

ISBN: 979-8-9903619-1-1 (e-book)

ISBN: 979-8-9903619-2-8 (hardcover)

Cover design: Marissa Joly

First edition 2024

Author's Note

In 1911 and 1912, the racially diverse settlement on Malaga Island in the eastern Casco Bay of Maine was exiled by the state and then-governor Frederick Plaisted. A combination of racial prejudice, yellow journalism, nativism, political corruption, and the popular eugenics movement of the time led to the unraveling and expulsion of the mixed-race community, which had been on the island for nearly seventy-five years.

About forty-five residents were forced to dismantle their homes and were then set adrift on the New Meadows River. The final expulsion was the removal of the cemetery on Malaga. Roughly seventeen bodies were exhumed and reinterred at the Home for the Feeble-Minded in New Gloucester, Maine, in a mass grave.

Apart from recorded historical facts, the names, characters, places, and incidents portrayed in this work are either the products of the author's imagination or, if real, are used fictitiously.

Foreword

As a tribal historian and indigenous woman from the Penobscot Tribe, I have ancestral roots that run deep in this place now called "Maine." I personally have experienced intimate connection with the landscape and waterways and have often stated that my vast historical knowledge can be both a blessing and a curse. It is a blessing to stand before vistas like Katahdin and know its stories, and know my Ancestors stood there in a similar manner taking in the mountain's grandeur. Balancing barefoot on ledges at ancient fishing sites along the Penobscot, I wonder how many of the Ancestors have stood in this same spot?

At these times I know and feel I am in direct alignment with generations and generations of Penobscot people who have gathered here since time immemorial, fishing, living, and being in these spaces. Being steeped in the history of my Ancestors can also feel like a curse, like when I am standing on contested grounds and know the trauma endured there. Places like The Pines of Norridgewock, Indian Point at the confluence of the Mattawamkeag and Penobscot Rivers, and countless other places in the state. This novel introduced me to another such place of deep history, connection, and loss: Malaga Island.

Masterfully woven into this modern story are feelings, perceptions, and intuitive senses important to bring into the open for people to connect with and know they are not alone. My professional path has provided me ample opportunities to engage in conversations with people who share secrets with the land. Perhaps it is because I am Native American that they feel they can divulge feelings or experiences they fear may sound too farfetched to others. I know there exist many people who feel mysteriously connected to spaces and places but remain sheepish to reveal that side of themselves. Like humans, the land is a sentient, living entity experiencing loss and trauma the same way people do; that trauma can get stuck in places.

How does the land feel when suddenly the people who once belonged to that place are gone? People who loved and cherished the happiness of the land in all its glory and abundance. Ours is the generation that stands to bridge the gap of understanding this intimate and real connection between people and place. This story is a liberation of hidden history. It shines a light of truth into the darkness so that we may begin to find our way out and move toward healing our relationships with each other and the land. Here is the type of book I can imagine fellow history buffs curling up with during a snowy Maine winter weekend or taking to read on the beach and then wondering, "What of this beach? What happened in this place?" It is easy, interesting reading with substance, intellect, and a story that flows.

—Maria Girouard, M.A. History, University of Maine, Orono
Penobscot tribal member and tribal historian

New Meadows

The river dividing the island
from the mainland looked easy
to cross with our limbs, nimble
as we navigated in and out of faded dinghies,
along mossy granite fingers
slick with seaweed and sunshine

But the swim was hard
in the chilly summer waters. The river
pushed up our noses and in our eyes
with its soft slap of waves,
lobster boats rumbled nearby with the chorus
of gulls at each trap haul - pulling to the surface
what lay beneath

Our breath caught, but the thick hush of the deep
whispered us on to shallow waters ahead. And you
said you heard the shore gasp for air.

—*Kristin Rieff, MFA*

This book is dedicated to my father (1936–2023)
and to the people who lived on Malaga Island and their descendants.

"Reconciliation starts with the acknowledgement of the truth about what happened, not to lay blame, but just to say yes, this happened, and what are we going to do about it now. To me, reconciliation is a continual process of learning how to be in the same space together."

—*Esther Anne, MS, member of the Maine tribal-state Indian Child Welfare Act (ICWA) workgroup*

Contents

Chapter 1
Lucky Thirty

Cloudy memories of last night moved through Pennie as she lay in bed. Vague images of the dark clear sky, of the stars so close, tugged at her shallow soul. The early birthday celebration blurred her consciousness of people she thought she knew but was not quite sure she saw. When did Dani and Mali show up at the Painted Pony? Everyone wanted to buy her a shot. Mistake number one: downing that dirty rotten no-good boilermaker.

She stared up at the A-frame ceiling, at a brown water stain shaped like a three-legged dog. Memories of tainted lovers swirled before her, an eddy of failed relationships. Each one took a little piece of her.

She rolled over in bed, naked. The flannel sheets smelled like the boy lying beside her, innocent and intense. Twenty, maybe, little patches of black hair on his tender face. Mistake number two. Still, she wanted to see his smile again, the lopsided one that seemed full of tragic secrets, alluring her until it felt like melting wax between her legs. Or perhaps it was the blanket of whiskey that enveloped her last night.

She stepped out of bed onto damp, forgotten clothes and remembered more of the night before. A snowball fight with Tita on the plunge down the mountain, the sharp ice, their drunken, cloudy breath. Mistake number three. She winced, spotting the beginning of a purplish bruise on her translucent thigh and faced the regret lying on the sheets behind her, the White Stripes from last night's jukebox ringing in her ears. Her woolen long johns hung on the back of an old wooden rocker, and she slipped them on.

Coffee. She followed its aroma to the kitchen where her cousin Tita sat, waking up, a veteran of the back snowfields on a hangover. Tita had made the pot strong and plucky, adding a shot of Baileys to her cup. Pennie joined her and sipped a little hair-of-the-dog, feeling a tinge better, though her head still felt like the inside of a foggy goggle. Time to push past it, pull those bootstraps up and face the day. They were Maine girls, after all, and Maine girls can handle anything, anywhere, anyhow. You name the place; they'll name the time and the rules.

"Keeping it real, sister." Tita downed her second gritty cup. "Who's the pup that followed you home last night?"

"Ski patrol."

"Ah, so he's got to be at least eighteen."

Pennie groaned. "Like I don't have enough self-loathing already." They heard rumblings from the stranger in the back bedroom, then all fell quiet inside the warm cabin except for the woodstove roaring. What was his name? Ian or Ethan or Eli? Pennie found her bibs, zipped them up, and sat down to buckle her ski boots. Time to exit this scene. "And when's *your* lover boy coming home?" Lars was Tita's on-again, off-again high school boyfriend.

"*Former*, you mean." Tita yanked on her polar fleece. "Lars flies in next week. Promised to show me his progress on the film when he gets here."

He fancied himself a director and came up with the idea of making a documentary about Tita's rise to Olympic stardom. Tita had told Pennie that it seemed like a silly idea. Who would want to see a film about her brief rise to a silver medal in freeskiing ten years ago? Then Lars had shared his "vision" of highlighting the history of the women's freestyle competition with Tita as the poster child of overcoming adversity in a male-dominated sport.

"Did he meet any famous Hollywood types out there? Any good money connections?"

"No mention of it, but we haven't exactly been in sync lately." Tita grabbed her helmet before locking the closet with her extra skis and other gear. They'd done this before, leaving the condo with a stranger behind. It was safe enough, but beginning to get old.

Outside, meeting the beautiful, bright skies, an ache behind Pennie's eyes made her stop to breathe in the cold, exhilarating air. She followed her cousin to the bottom chairlift that scooped them up, the March winter sun waking their insides. They didn't say a word during the short ride to the base. Tita beelined for the lodge, and Pennie caught a glimpse of her own bloodshot eyes and crow's feet in the frosty window of the outside ticket counter. The cruel clarity of another year gone by staring back at her. Age. But what was age? Better to burn out than to fade away as Neil Young sang, as Kurt Cobain wrote in his suicide note.

A familiar face crystallized behind her in the window's reflection, a ghost from the past. *Spirits help me now.* Tracy came up from behind in his flannel shirt, hanging suspenders and bright pink snowboard boots, that ski-bum grunge thing. Another giant swirl of diversion from her life.

"Hey, Pennie, what up?"

She steadied herself, greener than green around the gills, meeting his fist bump. "I live to die another day." She tried to sound convincing, become someone in control of her life instead of an out-of-work grad school dropout.

"You skiing alone?"

"I'm here with Tita and some friends." Her voice cracked and fell in the bone-chilling air. "You?"

"Same here. We're meeting up at the Pony for lunch. Join us?"

"Sure." She'd feel better by then, just needed to ski things off, soar away to that happy place of complete and utter escape.

Tracy gave her a look. "You okay, Pen?" Clearly her face wasn't reflecting her optimism.

"You know, a little rough around the edges."

"Roger that. Skiing it off myself. Little fresh air and sunshine's all we need." He turned away, waving the peace sign.

Stumbling her way up to the lodge, Pennie found Tita surrounded by groupies. From the time she joined the Olympic circuit, she'd been an attention whore, always looking for an audience. The locals loved her for the very rebelliousness that led to her public downfall. It was her carousing and partying with the men on the US Ski Team that sullied her reputation as a role model for young female athletes. The press had a field day with her, and she'd lost sponsorships, but she'd put Coos Canyon on the map with her daredevil freestyle attitude.

Pennie squeezed through, giving the fan club her best *back off bitches* stare-down before taking a seat on the bench. "You aren't going to believe who I just ran into."

Tita waved away the crowd. "The suspense is killing me."

"Tracy Bayer."

"Wow, that's a blast from the past. I haven't seen him since Vancouver when he fell in the snowboard cross." Tita took great enjoyment in pointing out anyone else's screw-up, especially during a competition.

"He's meeting us for lunch at the Pony."

"You didn't invite him to ski with us?"

"Are you kidding? I don't think I can even snowplow down the mountain this morning."

"I've never known you to take it easy. Let's go, Lucky Pennie." Tita had been calling her that since they were kids. Uncle Alfie and Aunt Aggie brought them up like sisters, even though Pennie felt like an outsider, especially after her aunt had kicked her out when she was nineteen. And Tita hadn't helped, throwing her under the bus for the tattoos they came home with. But no one knew her better than her cousin. Knew personal things like the crush she'd had on Tracy since middle school.

Tita raised her eyebrows. "Maybe you two will rekindle the flame after all these years."

Penelope swallowed the bile and stale beer that threatened to come up. She remembered sitting in the movie theater with Tracy, holding hands, on their first and last date. "Actually, it was more like a flicker, and he's not interested anyway."

"You're right. He must know what a *weirdo* you are!"

Some things about Tita never changed: the glee at having an old wound opened, the cruelness of youth, the harsh words exchanged when they were teenagers testing one another. Before Pennie could toss back an insult, Tita took off laughing out the lodge's front door. Pennie chased after, reaching for her long curly braid, but Tita had grabbed her old-fashioned K2s before she could catch her.

Out in the frosty mountain air, a white husky crossed Pennie's path, stopping her short and conjuring up her own dog, Boone. It'd been a week since his road accident. An unexpected pain grabbed her and winched tight in her stomach—the regret of letting him out that icy morning. She lingered on the husky bounding down the slope toward a mother helping her daughter with her ski boots. The little girl laughed in the sunshine, hugging the dog.

Pennie skied her way to the lift, past the chalkboard with the temp: 33 degrees on March 3. Perfect spring skiing. She joined Tita beside her friends Dani and Mali, identical and preternaturally beautiful twins. While Tita and Pennie complained about their mutual degrees of head throbbing, the twins shook their heads, laughing. They had seen too many lives ruined by drinking and swore off the stuff from an early age. Lucky them.

"Thank God that bartender cut you off last night," said Dani. Pennie flashed back to the gray-bearded tapster who'd taken a shine to them early on, barking at the too-friendly guys who mostly swarmed around the twins with their dusky complexion and deep brown soulful eyes, the eyes that made them so unforgettable. But Dani and Mali were both married now, only making Pennie more desperate about her own stalled life.

"If I never drink a shot of schnapps again, I'll be happy," said Tita.

Pennie leaned forward on her ski poles. "Try a boilermaker."

Tita shook her head. "Always trying to keep up with the young hellions."

"*You're* one to talk," Pennie laughed.

Mali inched forward. "Yeah, what happened to that hot young ski patrol?"

"From the sounds of it last night, he put up a good fight," said Tita.

Pennie's squeamishness surfaced again.

"Pennie," said Dani. "You better ski that hangover to hell."

Once the humming chair brought them into the sunshine, Pennie returned to a sense of self. The new snow sparkled, eye-watering but beautiful in the sunlight. This was her favorite place in the world, the only place she didn't feel disconnected from herself.

Tita and Mali looked down at Dani and her from the chair above. "Right or left?" yelled Mali.

"Go left. Last one down buys lunch!" Dani beamed with the sun. She was Pennie's best friend, the introverted twin, always ready to take on a fresh snowfall. Always the one to push Pennie to assert herself. Maybe the day had promise after all.

She scraped the snow from the top of her old Dynastars. "I ran into Bayer the Slayer."

Dani clicked her ski poles together. "No shit? I saw him last weekend. The first thing he did was ask about you."

"Really?" Maybe there was a chance after all these years. Maybe he was coming off a bad romance. Maybe she could help him heal.

Maybe she was still hungover.

"I didn't see a ring on his finger. I think you still got a shot!"

"He's too cool for someone like me."

"Getting way ahead of yourself. Besides, it's been a minute since Kush left."

Dani had to bring him up, the only boyfriend she'd ever managed to keep for more than three months. But she was right. Pennie had to stop overthinking everything, concentrate on the here and now, the moment, the steady humming of the chair, the cloudless sky. At the top, they waved to the yellow-bearded fellow in the warm shack with his feet up, waving back. He knew all about the mountain madness ahead.

Tita took the lead, starting the day off with a double black D.

"No warm-up run?" yelled Mali.

"This *is* the warm-up!" Tita cut into the headwall, a little ball of dynamite. The memory of Joan Jett's "Bad Reputation" followed her, the track that replayed over and over during her famous mogul run at the Vancouver Olympics, the one that won her a silver medal and forever a place among Maine's legendary badasses. Among poor role models for young women.

Pennie fell in line, flying fast, her boards scraping with every icy turn. Her brain froze, the hangover making its reappearance with grand force. No choice but to ski through it, into it, past it, to let go and feel true liberation from the chaos of her life. She followed the tree line and mounds of snow, skimming the top, carving out small turns in the new powder, floating in the rhythm. She was a child again, skiing the tree line at Pleasant Mountain, laughing on the inside all the way down, immersed in the moment of being.

Soaring down and testing her own limits, she caught the sight of a group merging from a trail to the right. She kept her rhythm, moving through any fear, any unknowing. Another group of skiers glided in and stopped in a bunch, blocking her way. As she ran out of room, flying on the out-of-control side of life, a harsh reality sank inside. She dug in her right edge to slip around the stalled skiers but found herself veering grossly close to the trail's edge. Nowhere to go, her mind screamed in horror. She caught her edge on packed ice, flipped, slid at breakneck speed into a spray gun, bounced off, and slammed backward into a tree.

Nothing. White silence. No pain, only a stark numbness. Her mind hiccupped, her heart thumped, pulsing in panic. Gruesome stories about ski accidents and paralysis flooded her mind. Then her legs moved. Her legs moved! Her mind floated back to the night before, Tita tackling her, grinding her into the snowbank, pushing her into the drunken night with the close stars above, pinpricks in a black emptiness. She thought of Boone licking her face, moaning low, consoling her with those dark eyes, nuzzling.

A voice broke through, and she looked up.

Dani peered down between the white birches, the sun encircling her head. "Are you alright? Pennie, are you okay?"

"Yeah, I'm okay." Sitting, she tried to drag herself up. "I don't know if I can get out of here."

"Don't move! A ski patrol is coming, I can see him."

Her pounding heart reminded her she was still very much alive in this deep pocket of snow. A shadow moved over her, and as she looked up a great winged bird sailed just above the firs, an overseer casting its presence from another world. She took deep breaths. She was okay, no reason to panic. The ski patrol appeared—not the boy from the night before, thank God, but a man—telling her to stay where she was.

Somehow this calm, serious patroller with the red jacket managed to make his way down to her and help her out of the icy hole. She made it back up to the trail, where he and another patroller, a soft-spoken woman, guided her into the sled. She couldn't feel much but her legs moved—she saw them moving.

She was there on the slope, on her thirtieth birthday, being hauled off the mountain in a sled. On her first run of the day, as if she had broken through a dream and headed straight into a nightmare. In a state of icy shock—every bump under the sled a reality check on her upended life—she caught sight of Tracy working his way up to the lift line. "Pennie? Is that you?"

She smiled, a million regrets. "I'll be fine. See you at the Pony!"

As if nothing had happened. *See you at the Pony!* Like she was skiing along, singing a song instead of lying in a sled wondering if her life would ever be the same again.

Dani, Mali, and Tita skied close behind the sled. The ski patrol came to a halt in front of the first-aid clinic, where others came out to help. There he was, the boy from her bed, all serious now, helping lift her inside the clinic. "You'll be okay, Pennie, don't worry. You're in good hands." As the responders checked her vitals, she remembered his soft beer kisses, his groping hands.

The look on Tita's face made her wish she could sink away. "Don't worry, Tita. I'll be fine." But it was a lie. The nurse made Dani and Mali leave, but Tita stayed by her side, helping her puke into a bag. She couldn't get warm, even with the heated blankets draped over her. The patrol called for an ambulance to Rumford, the nearest hospital. Her body alternated from hot to cold to hot to cold to wishing she would die.

In the ambulance, clear bags from the IV swinging, her rib cage screamed in a vice of distress, her left side sore. She couldn't stay still enough. The paramedic spoke into a radio: "Left upper quadrant. Blunt abdominal trauma. Possible hemorrhage, vitals dropping." Her cousin, the hellion who'd seen her own share of close calls, took her hand. But Pennie couldn't stop shaking, couldn't help thinking about Boone after he was hit by the pickup, when she'd wanted to save him, dragging him off the road as he tried to bite her arm off. She knew exactly how he'd felt. If someone had tried to pull her, she would have lashed out with everything she had.

Tita had her phone out calling Aunt Aggie, always the first person Tita ran to in a crisis. Pennie grabbed her arm. "Tell her I'm fine." Then she threw up yellow bile as an icy chill took hold again.

Shaking so hard the cot rattled, she sank deeper into a hole. Boone was beside her now, she was sure, and they were back on the road where he tried to breathe, his eyes pleading with her. She heard her own choking cry, *Don't go! Hold on, buddy. Hold on…* Watching him take his last breath on the roadside, oblivious cars flying by as he foamed at the mouth, a blue cloud escaping, saturating the air, surrounding her, a warm feeling, an absolute peace, and she knew deep inside his soul had left. The cloud passed up to the clear gray above, into a fine mist. Her eyes wet, she blinked to see the bright light turn to a hanging dome fixture overhead, masked white strangers hovering.

"Are you with us, Pennie? That's a girl. Easy deep breaths. You really gave us a scare there. Pulse is returning to normal. That's a girl. You're gonna be just fine."

When she awoke, her eyeballs hurt. She blinked at the digital clock: 3:33. She remembered skidding down the icy slope, bouncing off the snow gun into a tree.

Tita was at the bedside. Her smile was a kind of grimace. "Jesus, you know how to ring in a birthday. From now on, leave the racing stunts to me."

Her throat hurt. She wanted to tell her all about seeing Boone again, his soul, how incredible it was to finally know he was still with her somewhere, somehow.

Tita saw the effort, raised a hand as if to say *stop*. "Don't talk. Just rest."

Pennie slept on and off. She had a ruptured spleen and fractured rib, but her spine was okay. They gave her some good drugs. The doctor said they'd keep her for a few days. She was a lucky girl. They kept telling her how lucky she was.

Tita stayed at the mountain and drove back and forth to visit, even though Pennie told her not to. But she never complained, never mentioned the thought of returning to Portland without her. Uncle Alfie had wanted to drive to Rumford to get them, but Tita had insisted he and Aunt Aggie stay at home. What with his diabetes and all, long car trips were bad for his circulation, not to mention the matter of his four dogs.

Her second night at the hospital, alone, Pennie stared out the dark window at the parking lot, plow trucks under the streetlights picking up the relentless loads of snow. Funny thing: all she could think about was skiing, of lovely mounds of white stuff falling on the mountain and the back snowfields. She hoped Tita was taking advantage of the virgin powder before the snowcats got to it, to at least make something good out of it. Pennie cursed herself again and again before resigning to her predicament. "If the day wasn't your friend, it was your teacher," Uncle Alfie liked to say.

After the third day, they released her from the hospital. Tita picked her up in the VW bus, nicknamed the Jan Van, for the long drive back home to Portland. Pennie fell into a trance, listening to Tita's tape of *The Lion and the Cobra*, Sinead O'Connor's voice echoing true, watching big wet flakes melting as they hit the windshield, memories of Boone running through her mind.

"Do you believe in the afterlife?" Pennie asked.

Tita accepted the random question as perfectly normal. They'd talked like this for years. "I believe in this life. And wanting to stay in it."

The funny thing was, after the whole episode, Pennie wasn't afraid of dying anymore. More than ever, she wanted to confront life, to face it head on, in the winter of her thirtieth birthday. Despite the dismal outlook of early March, knowing her skiing days were over for a while, her spirit was expectant, the formidable clouds overhead shifting, slow and steady.

Chapter 2

Omen

TITA PUT A KETTLE on the stove for tea. Pennie settled into the couch and kicked on the television, happy to be home in her own apartment. She would have to call the clinic in the morning to delay the start of her job as a vet tech. After flunking out of veterinarian school a year before, she'd managed to get certified as a technician and land a decent job. But now she had even screwed that up. Her less-than-stellar life stalled again. She secretly breathed a sigh of relief.

"Where are the cookies?" Tita called out, rummaging around the kitchen.

"Lazy Susan, bottom shelf." The TV was on, but Pennie stared out the dark window instead, watching the nothingness.

Tita walked to her, balancing two mugs and a box of ginger snaps. "Here we are. Nothing like hot tea on a dreary night."

"Where would I be without you?"

"Hmmm, probably lying in a ditch somewhere."

"I feel kind of guilty that I haven't called Uncle Alfie and Aunt Aggie."

"Call them tomorrow. Mum would just insist on dragging you to the house."

That was the real reason Pennie hadn't called them. She wanted to sleep in her own place. Ever since her aunt had kicked her out eleven years ago, she'd been determined to make it on her own. The steam rose from the tea mug, clearing her mind. She sank into the couch.

"What am I going to say when I call work tomorrow? 'Hello, this is supposed to be my first day, but I won't be coming in today or any day this week because I skied into a spray gun, bounced off, and wrapped my body around a tree. Don't worry, I'm on the mend! Just ruptured my spleen, cracked a rib, nothing serious. Give me a week.'"

"I'm sure you're not the first person to miss their first few days of work."

"Not exactly a stellar first impression."

"A week won't make or break you. You've got your whole life to work."

"You haven't seen my checking account." How was she going to pay rent and a hospital bill that was sure to be astronomical, not to mention the ambulance? Her school insurance ended weeks ago. The world had closed in; another door was abruptly slamming shut. "I've gone two years without anything more than a cold, and *this* happens. Days from starting a job with health insurance."

"You can always move back in with the family. And it would take some of the focus off me."

"I could never move back home." She recalled the sight of her belongings piled on the townhouse front lawn, her regret at staying out all night partying, yet again. But it was the tattoo that really did her in with Aunt Aggie. She eyed the running wolf on the inside of her forearm. Tita, Dani, and Mali had all done it with her that night—all on their forearms with their favorite animal. But it was Pennie's idea. She happened to be dating a tattoo artist back then, James, who was biracial and referred to himself jokingly as "half-cracker." This always made her laugh, especially knowing Aunt Aggie did not approve of his profession or his mixed race, puritan that she was.

Tita set down the mugs, her owl tattoo showing. "Ever since Lars left for California, they've been on my case about finding a *healthy* relationship. I'll barf if I hear that one more time."

Pennie had to hold herself back from sharing that she never liked Lars. His cockiness, the way he blathered on about himself and his moviemaking career and his great artistic achievement, a film about the underground punk scene in Boston. He seemed to gravitate toward stories about rebels.

Inside, Pennie wished she still had the same defiance she once had. Her aunt accused her of "swimming against the tide," especially when she was dating James. But like most of her romances, it was short-lived.

Tita crunched another gingersnap as she surfed channels, scanning reality shows, rom-coms, and crime dramas. "Don't worry. Once you start your new job, you'll get back on your feet. Besides, we'd probably kill each other if we lived under the same roof again."

By the time Tita graduated from high school, a year ahead of her, they weren't speaking. Pennie couldn't even remember what the big fight was about. Maybe it was because Tita got to move out to the carriage house, while she had to stay in the big house under constant surveillance. But as soon as Tita moved out, off to college and the ski circuit, there was a dull void in her life. While her cousin was out making a name for herself, she was lost, struggling to stay focused on something, anything.

Pennie looked around her small place. The bookshelf in the corner stacked with biology textbooks mixed with grimy crime novels, the desk looking out onto the roof terrace of the building next door. She'd spent hours trying to study, to keep her mind from its constant wandering, Boone by her feet, his quiet eyes. It had all seemed so empty a few days ago, but now something was different, as if his presence was still...there. She shifted her weight.

Tita stood and stretched. "I should probably head back to the home-stead. See what trouble the old folks have gotten into."

"I'm sorry I kept you up here for a week."

"Good thing I've got an understanding boss."

She conveniently ran Uncle Alfie's real estate practice, had been there ever since she left her competitive skiing days. He kept pushing her to get her paralegal degree, but she dragged her feet. Tita never finished college because it was "a waste of time," as she liked to put it. Even in high school, she and Lars loved to talk about how real smarts came from the streets. They'd compare themselves to people with natural talent like Quentin Tarantino. *Sure, Tita, Lars is just like Tarantino.*

Her tougher-than-nails cousin yawned when her phone rang. "Oh, it's Mum." She pressed it to her ear. "Don't worry, I'm on my way home. What do you need?" The baritone of her aunt's voice was serious. Tita looked at Pennie. "She's doing fine—and no, she won't be coming home with me. She wants to sleep in her own bed."

Pennie felt a vibration move through her, a small tremor on her tender side, a sense of doom overwhelming her in a wash of sudden worry. "Is Uncle Alfie okay?" Pennie asked, urgent. "Can you ask her if he's alright?"

Tita scrunched her face, annoyed. "Yes, I'll get the lights when I come home. Pennie wants to know how Pop is doing." The silent television images reflected against the dark window. "Okay, good, see you soon." Hanging up, she tossed her phone in her bag. "He's fine and sound asleep snoring in his old ratty recliner. I'll probably have to wake him up to send him to bed, which is where you should be."

"I'm sleeping right here on the couch."

"Don't be afraid to call me if you find yourself on the floor in a puddle of tears."

Pennie held her side. "Don't make me laugh."

Tita slammed a pair of muscle relaxants and a bottle of water on the coffee table in front of Pennie. "And stay away from the booze."

Pennie saluted her, pulling the comforter up to her neck. The strange sensation about her uncle still nagged at her as she drifted off to sleep. She dreamed that Boone was still there at her feet, staring through her with those immense dark eyes, the blue mist of his soul circling around.

THE PHONE RANG FROM her purse, startling her awake. In her delirium, Pennie forgot about her cracked rib and tried to move in the dark. The sudden pain twisted her in two. By the time she was able to shift her weight up off the couch, the ringing had stopped. With baby steps, using the furniture for support, she reached for her purse hanging by the door. Tita. It was 5:01 a.m. This couldn't be good.

Her cousin picked up on the second ring. She was at Mercy Hospital where Uncle Alfie had just been admitted. Heart attack.

"I woke up from a loud thud, like a tree had fallen through the floor. I found Pop sprawled out in the kitchen, the dogs all around him, of course. I nearly fell on top of him trying to yank them away."

"Was he conscious?"

"Sweaty and pale, but he was awake. Then Mum came in screaming. What a zoo. The ambulance came fast, thank God."

"I've got to get down there."

"No you don't. Just stay put. He's doing fine now and sleeping."

She thought about the feeling of dread she'd had just hours before. "He's working too hard. Puts in way too many hours."

"You know what they say about an old dog. Sometimes it takes a wake-up call."

She'd had her own wake-up call on the mountain. "What can I do? I feel helpless."

"You *are* helpless. Seriously, I'm going to check on things at the office. I already got a call on my cell this morning from a crazy woman who thinks her soon-to-be ex-husband is trying to kill her. Can't say I blame him. You'd think we were divorce attorneys by the calls we get."

"Maybe I can help you return some calls for him."

"Maybe you should just stay put and rest. I'll stop by to see you later, make sure you haven't shriveled away to nothing."

"Can you pick up some soup at that Vietnamese place?"

Tita breathed deep, put out. "Anything else?"

If there was anything or anyone she needed right now, it was Boone. "No, that'll do it. And bring the dogs here if you want."

"The last thing you need are those mongrels all over you."

AWAKE NOW, PENNIE LOOKED at the picture on the end table of her uncle with his four dogs: rottweiler Teddy, Labrador Casco (or more often Cassie), cairn terrier Fella, and English bulldog Daisy. They went with him everywhere. They must be stressed out.

Popping a muscle relaxant and antibiotic, Pennie dressed in her favorite jeans and a Black Keys T-shirt given to her by her ex-boyfriend, Kush. The hot and heavy relationship had lasted a little over a year, until the IT firm offered him a promotion in Philadelphia. He'd wanted her to go with him; it was an opportunity he couldn't pass up. But she couldn't see herself in Philadelphia, the City of Brotherly Love. No, Portland was her city. But Kush was the closest thing to love she'd ever felt. He wasn't afraid to be silly around her or to show gentle kindness. Everyone urged her to make the long-distance relationship work, but she broke it off.

Sometimes she pictured their life together, still in a safe, steady, and frighteningly healthy relationship. The way he always checked in with her, even insisted on picking her up to take her out to dinner and a show or a concert at the Merrill or the State. He even surprised her by buying a jacket that she'd tried on but couldn't afford. When he showed up with it, she was so touched she briefly considered marrying him then and there. But she wasn't moving to Philadelphia. She couldn't imagine leaving Maine and the unpredictable ocean, the formidable mountains, the dependable change of seasons.

AFTER THE RAIN THE night before, the temperature was hovering around freezing. A thin slick coat of tricky ice covered the brick walkway in front of Aunt Aggie and Uncle Alfie's townhouse near the Old Port where she'd grown up. The Paysons lived in the house on the left, the Thompsons on the right, most townhouses in families for generations. Everyone knew one another.

She could hardly fathom that invincible Uncle Alfie had suffered a heart attack.

Fishing out her key, she opened the giant mahogany front door to the sounds of happy, frantic barks. They knew it was Pennie before she entered the hallway, greeting her with relief. All except Daisy, of course. The white bulldog strolled in behind the line of wagging tails as if to say, "I'll let these guys get this."

Sensing her precarious condition, none of the dogs jumped on her, just rubbed against her instead. Cassie even groaned in sympathy, moving alongside her down the long hallway. "I bet you're hungry," Pennie said. "Something tells me you never got breakfast this morning."

In the kitchen, dried spaghetti sauce radiated a splatter on the white cupboards, pieces of a broken plate strewn across the old blue tiles. She pictured Uncle Alfie in the dark kitchen enjoying his late-night snack, then picked up the pieces of blue willow plate, one of the same ones from when she was growing up.

The dog food sat in the bin under the pantry cupboards. They waited patiently while she put one scoop in each dish, marked with their names, until she said, "Okay, have at it."

They fell in line, arranged by height: Teddy, Cassie, Fella, and Daisy. Their tails wagged in unison, snuffling and wolfing the food down like they hadn't eaten in days. Teddy, the rottweiler, was the first to finish. He came to sit at Pennie's feet. Even though he wasn't the brightest of the lot, he had a sweet disposition, always eager to please and protect. She scratched his block head and he leaned against her. Cassie nuzzled her way in between them to get her share of attention. "Hey, Mama Cass, how's my favorite girl?"

The Labrador, Boone's mother, licked her hand. Pennie was filled with a surge of loneliness and despair for the loss of her closest companion, but she had these four to help her through. Fella walked to the back door and barked, and Daisy lay down by her dish. "I guess you all deserve a special treat for taking such good care of Uncle Alfie last night."

She found the dog biscuits in the top cupboard and made each one sit quietly while she handed them out. Daisy needed no guidance, never moved from her position beside the dog dish until she was called, exerting tremendous effort to walk over. They followed her outside to the backyard. There was a glint of ice melting on the bird feeder where a black-capped chickadee ruffled its feathers into a puffy ball, small but magnificent. She said a silent prayer for Uncle Alfie, remembering the doom she'd sensed about his safety the night before. Was this some kind of sign? She believed in her own internal resolve to change her fate. Maybe this was a moment to reassess.

Her uncle would understand what she was going through. When she'd told him about Kush moving to Philadelphia, he'd said, "Go or stay where your heart takes you. One thing about it, you can take the girl out of Maine, but you can't take Maine out of the girl." He'd always encourage her without making the decision for her.

The well-kept brick carriage house at the end of the driveway sat quiet and sturdy. This was where Tita lived on the second floor, the same studio where Pennie's mother once lived. A deep ache sunk into her at the loss, again, the emptiness of losing her so long ago she could hardly remember her face anymore.

She was calling the dogs back inside when the kitchen phone startled her. It rang three times before she finally decided to answer it.

"Hello."

"Hi, ah, is Alfred Goode home?" The man's voice was soft but determined.

"No, I'm afraid he isn't. Can I ask who's calling?"

"This is Stan Lewis, over at Heritage Acres. I left a few messages at his office but didn't hear back, so thought I would try his home number. Sorry for the imposition."

"Is this about a title?"

"Not exactly. I need to speak with him about a development."

"What kind of development?"

"If you don't mind, I'd like to speak with Mr. Goode about the details." His tone grew impatient.

"I'm afraid he's in the hospital."

"Oh, no. Sorry to hear that."

"I'm sure he'll call you when he's feeling better."

Pennie took down his information and placed the receiver in the cradle, intrigued. Heritage Acres was the horse farm that used to be an institution for people with disabilities. Now she had to deliver this message, a good excuse to go to the hospital. Her side felt fine. She looked around for something she might bring to her uncle. Across the hallway in the dining room, a partially finished puzzle covered the oak table. He was usually working on one, though maybe that wasn't the best activity for him in a hospital bed.

The dogs clustered around her as she walked to the front hall. Little Fella had his leash in his mouth. "I'll be back to take you out," she said, scratching the terrier between his perky ears. "Go lie down." The dogs collectively sulked, walking to their beds in the den, Daisy pulling up the rear. Teddy laid his dark head between his paws and sighed, Fella sat on his bed at attention with his head cocked, leash still in his mouth, and Daisy fell on her side and wheezed. Cassie still stood, watching Pennie with distress. Pennie scratched her velvet ears, telling her not to worry.

A book sat on her uncle's favorite old recliner, so she grabbed that. Something about the history of the Scots. She considered grabbing the knitting basket beside Aunt Aggie's wingback, but thought better of it, knowing she would have her travel bag with her. This den was one of Pennie's favorite rooms in the house, though she and Tita were allowed there only right before bedtime for a story when they were children. She remembered them all: *White Fang* and *Little Women*, *The Secret Garden* and *James and the Giant Peach*, *Watership Down* and *Charlotte's Web*. All those extraordinary books that intensified her childhood dreams.

Locking the door behind her, she walked slowly down the icy brick walkway. Sensing a presence nearby, she turned and waved to old Mrs. Payson, sitting in her usual seat by the front window next door. They never had to worry about their house being left unattended with old eagle-eye Payson around.

Pennie's 1971 blue Karmann Ghia coupe started right up. Uncle Alfie had bought it for her years ago, the same one he helped her load up with all her belongings, her clothes and sneakers, stuffed animals and rock collection, notebooks and novels, the morning they were piled on the front lawn. After her aunt's clear message to get out and grow up. Uncle Alfie sympathized with her when she knew she didn't deserve it.

THE HOSPITAL ELEVATOR DOOR opened, and she immediately heard Aunt Maude's high-pitched laughter. Pennie turned the corner to find her in the waiting room with Aunt Aggie sitting next to her, her knitting needles busy.

"Pennie, dear, how are you?" Aggie asked. She looked over her glasses in usual fashion, the surveyor.

"Just fine," she said, though her side was beginning to ache again.

"I'm surprised to see you here." Aunt Maude kept things upbeat. "Aren't you supposed to be resting?"

"You know me. Can't sit still for too long."

Aunt Maude pressed on. "Sounds like you had quite a fall. I don't know why you girls ski like that. It was bound to happen, especially with that crazy cousin of yours tearing down the mountain."

"Oh, Maude, the last thing she needs is a lecture," Aggie interjected. This, from somebody who spent years delivering nothing but.

"Someone's gotta talk some sense into these kids."

"I'm just glad you're okay, dear." Aunt Aggie patted Pennie's arm. "Next time, take more caution trying to keep up with Christina. She can ski circles around everyone."

Christina the Great, the same old thing. "How's Uncle Alfie?"

"Better. He's as strong as an ox, you know. Doctor says it was mild, but he'll need some recovery time."

"Can I see him?"

"He's across the hall. Don't stay too long. The nurses want to make sure he gets plenty of rest." Aunt Maude pointed to the room on the left.

She walked over. Door 33. Pennie didn't believe in superstitions, but what was up with threes everywhere? Past the curtain divider, she found him sleeping, his heavy frame now looking fragile and gaunt under a single sheet. A monitor pulsed silently with his heartbeat. His arm twitching, his boney knuckles soft. Those hands, gentle and sure and comforting.

She was a kid again, sitting on his lap, playing that game where she had to lay her hands on his giant palms and try to move them quickly before he slapped her knuckles. The quick sting, all in the fun of the game, teaching her quick reflexes. Even though Aunt Aggie insisted they stop when tears sprung in her eyes, Pennie egged him on, ignoring the smarting pain. When she managed to give him a good whack in return, it was all worth it, seeing the look of surprise and delight on his face.

His wrinkled eyelids fluttered open. He gave her a weak smile, and she covered his kind, generous hand with hers, holding back her sadness.

"Geez, I just left the hospital and now you've got me back here," she said, trying to keep things light.

The skin folded around his tired, earnest eyes. He breathed hard, rasping, eyes closed.

"Don't worry, I fed your dogs this morning and Tita's checking on the office. We've got it covered." She didn't know what she'd do if anything happened to him. No matter how much of a little shit she had been, he was always there for her, was always encouraging her to do better. To be a better person. Remembering the book, she laid it on his bedside table. She thought about the name and number in her pocket, the strange phone call, but now wouldn't be the time.

A noise from behind startled her. Tita walked in with a paper bag from the Vietnamese restaurant, a puzzled look on her face. Pennie pointed to the hallway and met her there.

Tita shook her head. "What the hell are you doing here?"

"I had to feed the dogs. And then I thought, since I was out…"

"Those dogs are just fine. That was my next stop."

"See, I saved you some time."

"How're you feeling?"

"A little stiff, but fine." Pennie took the Styrofoam soup container Tita was handing to her.

In the waiting room, the two aunties chattered away, Aggie's needles moving as if by magic, Maude concentrating on a crossword. "A four-letter word. Believed to portend good or evil."

"Pretend good or evil?" asked Tita.

"No *portend*." Pennie took a mouthful of soup. "Like foreshadow."

"How do you know this shit?"

"Is he still asleep?" Aunt Aggie looked up, needles never missing a beat."

"He opened his eyes for a minute to smile."

"See, he knew you were here."

"What did the doctor say?"

Tita slurped between her own mouthfuls of soup. "She doesn't think there's any lasting damage. Angioplasty is scheduled. Probably needs a few stents."

"Christina, can't you sit down and eat like a human?" Aunt Aggie gave her the look.

Pennie let the steam hit her in the face, breathing in the spicy broth. "Yummm. Thanks again for getting this. I'll share if anyone's hungry."

"I don't know how you can eat that spicy stuff." Aunt Maude put down the paper. "Aggie, let's go down to the cafeteria, I could eat a horse."

"Now that you mention it. Can you watch our things, girls?" Aunt Aggie stuffed her knitting needles into her travel bag.

"We'll be right here." Pennie sat down in a pleather chair. Aunt Maude rubbed her shoulder and kissed her cheek. She always seemed to know when Pennie needed a kind gesture of comfort.

The sisters-in-law grabbed their purses, Maude about half the height but equal the girth, complaining about the prices the cafeteria charged for a hamburger. Pennie waited until they were out of earshot to tell Tita about the call.

"Hey, someone called for Uncle Alfie at the house. Something about a development at Heritage Acres."

"What kind of development?" Tita tipped her cup, finishing the soup.

"He wouldn't say. But it's the horse farm where they had the old institution, right?"

"Oh, yeah. Never been there. What else did he say?"

"Not much. He wasn't exactly forthcoming."

"Sometimes we get the strangest calls. You'd think we were a legal advice hotline, especially for estates."

Pennie slurped the last drop of her soup, her insides now pleasantly warm. "*Omen*," she said.

"What?"

"Foreshadowing good or evil. Four-letter word."

Tita picked up Aunt Maude's crossword and penciled it in.

Chapter 3
Three Brigids

A GRAY SKY HOVERED over Baxter Boulevard. As soon as Pennie and Tita parked in the lot beside the Back Cove Trail, snow began to sift onto the tidal basin of Casco Bay. The three-and-a-half-mile trail was the dogs' favorite walk, no matter the season. Pennie let Cassie and Fella out of the backseat of the Karmann Ghia and leashed them. Tita unloaded Daisy and Teddy from the Jan Van and cursed the rottweiler for pulling, always a challenge with his bullish personality. But Tita loved him for it. He was hers. Ever since he'd stumbled into their house on Pine Street as a little pup, she had claimed him and named him.

Already wrapped in a hand-knit scarf, Pennie pulled on the matching hat and mittens. As ever, she and Tita were adorned in Aunt Aggie's collection of homemade outerwear all winter long, the yarn a strong thread of shared family history. Cassie could hardly sit still in anticipation and barked at Pennie to hurry up. Of all the dogs, she was her favorite. Pennie wondered if Cassie forgave her for the accident. The first time she showed up at the house without Boone, only a week before her ski accident, Cassie stared at her balefully, looking for some hint of his whereabouts. Today she was different, though, upbeat and wagging her tail. Almost as if Boone was there with them again.

Winter was their favorite season to walk on the boulevard, the Portland skyline in the distance. Not many souls were out on the loop trail, an almost perfect circle around the bay. Snow geese settled in the iron blue water, extending their white wings outlined in rich black as if dipped in ink. Cassie watched them, ready to give chase, and Fella pulled on the leash.

Pennie's left side ached, despite her earlier claims of recovery. She wished now she'd taken more pain meds. "Fella, heel!"

Tita yelled at Daisy to hurry up, trying to keep up with Pennie. "Maybe we shouldn't do this."

"No, I'm fine. I need the fresh air after being on the couch for two days."

The dogs stopped to relieve themselves on any tree or dry bush poking through the snow. The woolly flakes falling made the day solemn as they walked the mild incline up to Tukey's Bridge, alongside the buzzing traffic of I-295. Pennie thought about losing her mother. The suicide happened such a long time ago, her mother only in her thirties then, jumping to her demise. There it was again, the number three. The water swayed and rolled, an intense darkness.

Their boots crunched, the dogs' tags tinkled, the sound crisp and eerie. A car flew by spraying slush, and in an instant reflex she jumped back and stumbled against Tita.

"Easy there. Are you alright?"

"Sorry, not sure what's the matter with me lately."

"You're awfully jumpy. You calling the vet clinic in the morning to tell them you need more time?"

"I think I've stalled them long enough. Not sure what they'll say if I ask for more time."

"What did the doctor say—another few days off?"

"Something like that."

"Good, you can help me field some calls at the office, if you're up to it."

They reached the other side of the bridge, Fella pulling on the leash toward a golden retriever running beside a woman. Cursing him, Pennie felt her side twinge in pain, filling her with resentment toward the runner for simply being there. "I'll need something to keep me occupied. And I'm dying to know more about the Heritage Acres development."

"That guy better not be looking for free advice. Pop hates that."

"I don't think so. He was hesitant, like he didn't want to talk about it over the phone. Not with me, anyway."

Tita yelled, "Heel, Teddy!" The rotty was pulling her down the path toward an invisible scent. "Pop gets calls about disputes gone nasty sometimes. Maybe the title is in question."

"Anyway, I'm curious."

"I wonder how long he'll be able to keep working."

"I can't imagine Uncle Alfie not working. He loves it and he's only fifty-nine."

"This heart attack will certainly slow him down."

"You'll have to pick up the slack, maybe take on more responsibility," Pennie said, trying to sound positive.

"That's just it. I don't want more responsibility." Tita shivered in the quiet cold. "I don't even know what I want to do with my life. I'm thirty-two, only eight years from forty and old. My sponsor contract with Coos Canyon will be up next year so my days of being paid for skiing will soon be over, and the last thing I want to be is a paralegal sitting in an office all day."

"Uncle Alfie will only lean on you until he's back on his feet."

"Like you said after your accident, maybe this is a wake-up call."

Pennie missed the mountain already. "Did you ever see Tracy at the mountain while I was in the hospital?"

"No, why?"

"I don't know. I thought he still lived in Rangeley, and you might have seen him during the week."

"Forget about him, Pennie. He's a ski bum. He hasn't changed, still hanging around with the same potheads and slumming around the mountain."

"Wow. Sounds like you've got something against him."

"I just think you could set your sights a little higher."

The heavy snow covered the dogs' coats now, their eyelashes hooded. Cassie's breath came out in clouds, and she looked up at Pennie, the sides of her mouth back, wide open. Little Fella jogged happily behind her, his little ears pricked in expectation. Daisy shuffled behind Fella. Teddy moved around all of them on surveillance, much to Tita's frustration. Cassie trotted out, deliberately in front of Pennie, her gait turning stiff legged, and her neck bristled. Pennie looked for a sign of anyone in the distance, the visibility poor in the waning light. "What is it, Cass?"

Teddy gave a quick warning bark, moving alongside Cassie. A man's thin, dark form appeared, walking toward them, slumped over, head down, wearing a canvas contractor's jacket and heavy black work boots. As he passed with lumbering footsteps, a cold draft swept between them, a lovely swirl of snow like a mini squall stirring the air. The dogs moved around in a crouching position, their ears back. She caught the man's eyes for a brief second, a penetrating slate blue sadness. "Did you see that?"

Tita lagged, lost in her own thoughts, the snow piling on top of her floppy pink wool hat. "See what?"

"That swirl of snow beside that guy?"

Tita looked back at the thin dark figure disappearing in the gray light. "I saw an old guy walk by."

"Didn't you see the dogs move out of the way like that? That was bizarre."

"They always make room."

"No, they really moved back, and their hair was up."

"I think you're seeing things. Are you losing it? And what was it the other night that made you ask about Uncle Alfie, the night he had his heart attack?"

Pennie shook all over and felt her face flush. "I don't know."

"You don't look so good. I knew this was a bad idea."

They passed the three-mile marker. Cassie, close by her side, looked up to make sure Pennie was okay. The truth was, she was beginning to feel a little lightheaded. The wind picked up and she wondered about seeing things. In the distance, another tall shadow figure walked toward them. The dogs slowed their gait and stiffened again. Teddy wagged his tail and barked at the man coming into focus.

"Hey, Lars!" Tita ran toward him, unable to contain her excitement.

It only took a moment to realize it wasn't a coincidence, though Tita hadn't even mentioned he'd landed back in Maine.

"Hey!" He gave Pennie a friendly nod and bent down to scratch Teddy behind the ears. The dogs sniffed him all over to see where he'd been, who he'd been with, and what he'd had for lunch.

He hugged himself to stay warm in his flannel-lined denim jacket. Tita touched the front of her boot to his. Obviously, they were repairing any relationship troubles they'd had while he was away. Daisy lay down between them, exhausted. They all laughed.

"It looks like someone's pooped," said Tita.

Cassie pulled gently on her leash and they all moved toward the parking lot. Lars put his arm around Tita, enclosing her short, stocky frame. "Can I buy you a hot chocolate?"

"Yeah, I'm freezing!" She looked up at him with delight, then back to Pennie. "You wanna join us?"

"I should probably get home and rest." The last thing she needed was to be in the middle of their make-up session. She'd seen this scene before.

Tita opened the hatch and ordered all the canines into the van. Fella hopped in first, then Teddy and Cassie before Tita picked up Daisy's back legs to hoist her in. "Don't push yourself too much, Pen," she said.

Inside her Karmann Ghia, she watched Lars and Tita drive off in the van, the snow spitting off the tires. In the distance, giant white neon numbers shone 33 degrees on the top of the Time and Temperature Building. It occurred to her that Tita must be banking on Lars and his documentary about her pioneering rise in freeskiing. Just as Tita thought her skiing career was ending, Lars offered a new opening, one that could resurrect her reputation as a groundbreaker in a man's sport. Maybe Tita was putting too much stock in Lars to save the day. But Pennie reproved herself. What about her own pathetic, stalled life? She fired up the cold car, wishing she had taken Cassie to keep her company.

Sitting at her old Mac, the trusty laptop that'd gotten her through undergrad over nine years ago, she looked up the significance of the number three. Websites about numerology popped up, bunk about your life number, your expression number, your birth number. Then she came across sites about symbolism and spirituality. Three: the power of the trinity. The beginning, middle, and end. The mind, body, and spirit. The past, present, and future. The three primary colors. The more she read, the more her curiosity grew. The first, second, and third person; the sun, moon, and stars; the id, ego, and superego. The Celtic mother, or goddess, known as the female triad, three Brigids, the solar deity, the beginning of spring.

Brigid. That was her mother's name, her grandmother's name, and her own middle name. A shudder moved through her. She found her way back to a numerology site and pulled up a simple chart with the numbers one to nine matching up to letters of the alphabet. Adding up the corresponding numbers to her name, Penelope Brigid Goode, she came up with $7 + 4 + 1 = 12$, then $1 + 2 = 3$. She closed the cover on her Mac, thinking she must be crazy, and checked her phone. It was 6:33. The frigid winter night seeped through the old paned window, her reflection an ambiguous outline of memories of her mother.

The pressure of a vague fear gripped her, and she reached for Boone. He was here now, here with those clouded memories of a distant mother, of the three Brigids of her soul—the maiden, the mother, and the crone. Like Tita, she was obsessed with age lately, with birth, life, and death like the phases of the moon: waxing, full, and waning. Her mother had died when she was about the same age. Never reaching middle age, never a waning moon. A deep void, worse than any ache in her side, settled inside her. As heavy as loneliness.

The voice of her Aunt Maude came to her. The only voice she really trusted during those tumultuous teenage years, when Pennie was trying to make sense of the world and her unresolved grief. "You were only six years old when your mother jumped off Tukey's Bridge that winter night." A younger Aunt Maude stroked her hair and sighed. "She never stayed in contact with your father after they tried living together for the first few months of your life. He was a talented musician who never really had a home. A troubadour, through no fault of his own, and he just didn't have it in him to settle down. When your mother died, Uncle Charlie and I were living over in Scotland, and that's how you

came to live with Uncle Alfie and Aunt Aggie. They felt blessed to take
you in, Pennie, to raise you like a sister to Christina. Believe it or not,
your opposite personalities provided some balance in the household.
While you were quiet and almost delicate, Christina was as rebellious
as a badger, with a personality to match. They found a channel for that
boundless energy at the ski slope. And you, why, you were always happy
to spend time on the mountain, or anywhere outside for that matter.
You're so much like your mother. Strong, intuitive, smart. There isn't a
single day goes by I don't think about Birdie."

Pennie didn't fight the sadness of her memories, Aunt Maude's voice
in her head. She let sleep envelop her in a blanket wound tightly around
her like a compress. The sky darkened as she fell into wintry dreams. She
was back on Baxter Boulevard, the dogs at her feet, barking furiously, the
wind whipping. She made out the shape of her mother in the distance on
the bridge, leaning over the railing, her hair wild in the dark winter gale.
Running, the dogs still at her heels, she slowed until she found herself
paralyzed, her feet unmoving despite her terror, her internal pleading,
her side throbbing. In slow arduous motion, the dogs barking incessant-
ly, she finally reached her mother. Close enough to grasp her coat, only
for her mother's shadowed figure to slip through her hands and fall into
the abyss.

Chapter 4
Cipelahq

UNCLE ALFIE SAT AT the large oak dining room table, working on a puzzle. His black reading glasses were perched on his nose, a cold cigar clenched between his teeth. Memories of the vibration she sensed the night before his heart attack stirred inside her. "I don't think the doctor would approve," Pennie said.

"Hello, my Lucky Pennie." He reached out to squeeze her hand. "Doc told me to relax and get into my old routine. Just following his orders." He had been home three days now. His face gaunt, shoulders smaller, his long fingers pushing the puzzle pieces into like-colored piles. She picked up the box cover with the picture of the windjammer, a sailboat with three masts, square-rigged. "This looks like a tough one." Five thousand pieces. "Might take you all spring."

"Keeps my mind on something other than work."

"Did Tita tell you that a man called here asking for you? Something about a development over at Heritage Acres?"

"Yes, and thanks for offering to help Tita out at the office."

He fit a piece into the hull of a boat, a blur of gray and brown hues only a discerning eye could lock into place.

She got the feeling he wanted to drop the subject. "Do you know what he wants?"

"Oh, you know. Title work, probably." He chewed on the soggy cigar, rolling it over in his mouth, concentrating, snapping another gray piece into the plank of the ship's prow.

"He didn't say much about it. Quite evasive."

"Tough to nail people down sometimes. I suppose I'll give him a call tomorrow." He drummed his fingers on the table with one hand, moving the azure pieces of sky into a pile blended with purple-gray clouds.

"Well, that's kind of what I wanted to talk to you about. I know this is going to come out of the blue, but I've been thinking I'd like to maybe help you with your business, you know, until you get back on your feet."

He peered over his glasses to give her his full attention, scratching the new growth of white whiskers. "I thought you were starting a new job?"

"Supposed to start tomorrow, but I'm having second thoughts. I don't know. Lately I've been thinking about my future and don't know if working in a clinic is right for me. If my heart is really in it." Cassie stretched and groaned under the table, as if uneasy with the decision.

"I'm not going to tell you to put your career on hold, but I could use the help. Tita's got the office covered, but I need a field researcher and she doesn't want to take that on."

Pennie felt her pulse quicken at the thought of working with her uncle. "I promise I can help you. Even though I don't know a lot about title searches, I like to work with people, and love research." She recounted her job at the university library and how she had to remember that the customer was always right, even when they were unmistakably, horribly wrong.

"Tell you what. You help me get back on my feet for the next few months and I'll give you a paycheck. After that, I'll be back to full steam, and you should go into the animal sciences like you've been studying for. Follow your dream."

She wanted to tell him about the accident and how things had shift-ed inside, how the world was somehow sharper and more vibrant and different. But she didn't know how or why. "I'm really not sure what I want to do with my life."

He reached over and squeezed her hand again. "You know that your mother was a hell of a dog trainer."

Pennie looked down at Cassie, those all-knowing eyes. "You said it was a calling. I'm still searching for that thing." She needed time to consider her options, and this gave her the perfect excuse to put her life on hold again. The back door slammed and Fella jumped up from under Uncle Alfie's chair. Barking soon filled the house.

"Your aunt's home with the groceries."

"I'll help her."

Cassie followed her into the kitchen, where Aunt Aggie was unpack-ing the bread. Pennie saw the strain in her face. Maybe it was because of Alfie's heart attack. Maybe Pennie herself, the motherless child, made her uncomfortable.

"I'll get the rest of the bags," Pennie said.

"Hello, Pennie dear. Thank you, I could use the extra arms."

Out the back door, she followed the brick path to the carriage house. The second-floor studio was dark, Tita nowhere in sight. It was only Tuesday, so she wasn't at the mountain. Sun melted the March ice, warming the chickadees and their mates in the early spring air. Skiing was over this season for her, so the snow couldn't melt soon enough. A shadow moved over her, and she watched a flock of bluejays scatter like buckshot. Above, the giant wingspan of a brownish bird soared only four or five feet overhead, silent as a phantom. A sharp chill slid into her bones, bringing up the memory of lying in the pocket of snow after skidding and bouncing off the snow gun, her heart thudding like a demon. She grabbed the bags from the car and hurried back to the house, using her foot to wedge open the storm door to the kitchen, shivering.

Aunt Aggie helped her in. "I forgot about your side. Are you supposed to be carrying these?"

"I'm fine. Doctor gave me the okay."

"You look a little pale, dear, have a seat here. Maybe you could find Christina. I'll need help with dinner."

"She never came home last night?"

Aggie shook her head, annoyed.

"I was surprised to see she and Lars back together again," Pennie said. She felt guilty as soon as she'd said it; no need to throw any kerosene on that fire.

"One thing about it, she'll have to figure it out. You know your cousin. She takes the most difficult path down the hill."

And I'm always swimming against the tide.

Dogs barking, the click of their nails on the hallway floor moving toward the front door, Pennie heard Tita's voice, shooing them and saying hello to her father before breezing into the kitchen, bringing the smell of spring, her wild curly hair shining, eyes like deep marbles. She kissed her mother. Despite Aunt Aggie's best attempt at annoyance, it was obvious that love bubbled under her skin.

"Where were you last night?"

"Stayed in town." She grabbed a clementine from the bowl on the kitchen table and peeled it in a few quick motions.

"Don't eat too much. Aunt Maude and Uncle Charlie are coming over for dinner tonight."

"What're you making?"

"Boiled dinner."

Tita scrunched her nose. "St. Patrick's Day is next weekend."

"Well, it's your father's favorite, and this is his celebration dinner for coming home."

"Can I invite Mali?" She sucked down the last wedge of the clementine.

"Why not."

"Then we have to invite Dani," Pennie stated the obvious.

Aunt Aggie peeled potatoes at the sink. "I know the twins don't *drink* but we should pick up more wine. I've only got a bottle here."

Pennie grabbed her coat, wanting to remove herself before getting dragged into her aunt's judgment session. "We'll run to the store."

Tita followed. "I'll be back soon, Mum." On their way out, they peeked in to check on the patient. He'd never taken his eyes from the puzzle. A solid hull was forming.

Fella and Teddy skipped at their heels. Shutting the dogs behind them, they loaded into the blue Karmann Ghia. Pennie revved the engine and pulled out, excited to share the news of working together at the practice.

"He agreed to that?"

"I thought it was going to be a lot harder to convince him, but he was all for it. Said he needed help with field work."

"I can't believe he's trusting us to work together. It's almost like he sees us as adults now."

Pennie laughed, happy to have to call the clinic to un-accept the position. "Maybe not adults yet, but at least responsible teenagers."

They pulled up to the corner of the West End Market. "Are you and Lars officially back together?"

"No, and stop asking. We just went to a concert last night. Not a big deal. It was late and he let me crash at his place."

"You seemed like you were rekindling when he met us on Baxter Boulevard."

"Yeah, until I found out about his STD."

"What?"

"Had a little too much fun out West. It's over." She flung open her door and promptly slammed it shut. Conversation ended.

Inside, the market smelled like fresh bread and chocolate. Tita grabbed a box of homemade Needhams from the case, the traditional Maine candy, a mixture of coconut and mashed potatoes covered in dark chocolate. Pennie headed to the basement stairs in search of good wine. Down in the cellar stood an older bald man with thick black rims, stooped over stocking the place, wearing a loud plaid vest and matching trousers. He'd been working here as long as Pennie could remember but she didn't know his name. It seemed he always had a glass of wine in his hand, and never looked up when anyone entered his underground cave. Either he had a very relaxed boss or he owned the place. She perused the bottles shelved along the brick wall and thought of Kush and his good taste in wines. They used to stop here for a nice bottle of port on their way to her aunt and uncle's place. The Goode family had an affinity for a nice tawny port.

She picked out two bottles of pinot noir and was grabbing one port when a draft blew up under her coat. Looking up at the doorway, there was no one. "Did you feel that?" she said to the hunched gentleman.

"Funny how the drafts blow in these old buildings, especially when someone buys the port. It's like the spirits around here don't like it. You know it must be good." He chuckled, then went back to unpacking a new carton.

Tita called after her and Pennie ascended the stairs, an icy hand up her spine. "That cellar is always so chilly."

"Not any different than any other old building around here." Tita paid for everything, and they were out the door.

PENNIE PICKED UP THE twins at their loft apartment near the Maine College of Art where they had majored in visual arts. When Mali and Peter started dating, he introduced his best friend, Max, to Dani. The four became inseparable. Now they ran a silk-screening business out of the loft, making T-shirts and sweatshirts, greeting cards and posters. Pennie climbed up the stairway to the second floor where gangly Peter, splattered in pink and black ink, answered the door. "Hey there, Pen. Mali can't wait to lose me for the night."

"That's right," said Mali. "If I have to eat hot wings one more time, I'm going to turn into a chicken."

"I hope you don't mind a boiled dinner."

"Beats freezer food," said Dani, descending the spiral staircase from the third floor living space. All around the giant second floor studio were screen-printing presses of differing sizes, worktables so spattered they looked like works of art themselves, cans of ink piled high, canvases drying in every available space, T-shirts and cards with tribal designs pinned to a wire that extended the length of the studio. The twins transformed stories from their Wabanaki culture—the Maine Penobscot, Mi'kmaq, Passamaquoddy, and Abenaki tribes—into amazing graphics.

One of Pennie's favorites was the legend of Glooskap, the hero who created the People and taught them how to survive. He had the power to transform beasts and plants for the People's survival. Dani had drawn illustrations of Glooskap changing the moose into a benevolent beast and making syrup run from the maple trees.

Pennie admired the sketches as Max emerged from the darkroom, blinking like a bear coming out of hibernation. "Leaving us already? What'll we do about dinner?"

Dani grabbed her wool coat and blew him a kiss.

"Don't wait up for us," said Mali. Peter tried to grab her as she ducked away, and she practically ran down the echoing stairs. Outside, Congress Street sparkled in the twilight, the sunset casting a warm ancient glow on the brick buildings and remaining crests of gray snow, smelling as if spring lay in wait around the corner.

When they arrived in front of the old townhouse, Uncle Alfie stood at the front door to greet them, dressed in his favorite green checked flannel and Bean's slippers. He looked rested and cheerful.

"Well, if it isn't my favorite ladies. Aren't you a sight for these sore old eyes." He planted a kiss on each cheek of his extended family.

"How're you feeling, Uncle Alfie?" asked Dani.

"Better than I did a few weeks ago."

"Staying off your feet, I hope," said Mali, always the practical one.

"I've got around-the-clock surveillance here." He winked, looking toward the kitchen.

Pennie gave him the bottle of port, which he accepted delightedly. "Ah, your aunt's favorite. We'll save this for after dinner." The dogs stood patiently behind him, barely able to control their glee at their friends' arrival.

The twins had been in and around their house throughout high school because their own home life was a little chaotic after their parents divorced. They never complained about the different boyfriends their mother entertained in the small apartment during their teenage years. What Pennie admired most was how candid they were about their family; their parents had both been born at the Pleasant Point reservation, had both gone into the Maine foster care system.

Dani and Mali had relied on each other when their parents separated, were even a bit fierce, together against the world, until Tita and Pennie managed to break through. Dani crouched down to scratch the dogs, greeting them each by name, and Mali scooted them toward the kitchen. The house smelled of cabbage mixed with salt pork, carrots, turnips, and onion. The piano of Helen Jane Long, eerie and melancholy, played from the speaker on the kitchen counter. Tita set the table in the homey kitchen, placing the nice linen, silver tableware, and china plates like Aunt Aggie had shown her. Aunt Maude gave them big hugs. Uncle Charlie handed out kisses before exiting the room to share a bourbon with Uncle Alfie in the den.

"Smells delicious!" Dani said. Tita plugged her nose. All that cabbage.

Aunt Aggie smoothed her apron. "I'm so glad you girls are all here. It's been too long since I've seen you now that you're old married gals. The husbands didn't mind you leaving for the night?"

"Are you kidding?" said Mali. "They can drink beer, belch, and fart to their heart's content while we get a real grown-up meal."

Aunt Maude poured glasses of pinot noir. "Everyone okay with red?"

The twins refused, as always, happy to drink water or tea. Aunt Aggie put the kettle on for them and Pennie grabbed a glass of wine. "Here's to a new business venture."

The twins turned to her, slightly puzzled.

"I'll be helping Uncle Alfie and Tita at the practice for a while."

"I didn't hear about this," said Aunt Aggie.

"Just decided today. Only until he gets back on his feet."

"What about your job at the clinic?" asked Dani.

"I'll call them tomorrow, say I'm taking some time to help out my uncle." An awkward pause settled, all the women considering this sudden career move. She felt a little dejected that they were not supportive of her decision.

"Oh, you've got to take some chances in life!" said Aunt Maude.

Aggie moved toward the stove. Pennie sensed her disappointment, her judgment—just another impulsive decision Pennie made. "Christina, aren't you going to change for dinner?" All eyes moved to Tita, dressed in jeans and a black Solomon tee.

"Leave the girl alone, Aggie. You look fine," said Aunt Maude.

"I won't hear the end of it unless I change."

"Pen, that's a big change," said Dani.

"I've been thinking about it for a few weeks. Ever since the accident. When Uncle Alfie had the heart attack, it all started to make sense. Even though I know nothing about real estate law."

"Your uncle must be happy to have the help," said Mali.

"I think so. He won't let on too much because he wants me to do it for me, not—"

From outside came a loud crash. They all spun toward the window and the darkening backyard. The dogs ran to the kitchen in a fury, all except Daisy.

Pennie followed them to the back door to look out. "It's probably the Payson's cat in the garbage cans." She stepped outside but the dogs hung inside, hesitant. "What's the matter with you?" she said to them, surprised at their restraint.

Shutting the door behind her, she walked toward the carriage house. An icy gust moved through her, almost inside her, ever so briefly. Hearing a noise, she looked up to the second-floor dormer where her mother once lived, where Tita now lived. A giant owl hovered. She spotted the rodent in its beak, the owl's yellow eyes staring through her, striped feathers puffed and ominous. She stumbled back and fell on the garbage can, shaking, watching the great bird fly overhead, as silent as a specter, just like the shadow that had passed over her earlier that day.

Her breath came out in a fog, and she raced to the back door where the dogs whimpered inside. Dani closed the door behind her. "Are you alright?"

She sucked in, trying to catch her breath.

Dani took her arm. "What was out there?"

"A huge owl with yellow eyes and ears that stood straight up, with a mouse or something."

"Really, an owl?" Mali looked through the glass toward the darkness.

Pennie stamped her feet to get the circulation back and Cassie licked her hand. Fella circled around her feet, and Teddy barked at her until she scratched his head to say it was all going to be fine. "It's gone now, flew away when it saw me. I've never been that close to an owl."

The cheery old men came in with their glasses of bourbon. Pennie asked if they wouldn't mind pouring her one. Her uncle looked perplexed, but promptly left the room to get her a glass. She gratefully took the amber liquid on ice and sat down, catching her breath. Soon everyone was gathered around the fine kitchen table with talk about the owl, a visitor from beyond. Pennie remembered the same uneasy sensation she'd had at the wine cellar. The dogs sensed it, too, all looking toward the back door with their hair up.

Tita came in, wearing a proper sweater, and sat beside Mali, pouring herself a large glass of wine. "What's going on?"

"Pennie's a little spooked," said Uncle Alfie.

"Alfred, she saw an owl, that's all," said Aggie.

"An owl, now that's a rare sight in Portland," Uncle Charlie said.

"It was a great horned owl, I think, a very large one," Pennie said.

"They're supposed to be spirit guides," said Mali.

Tita took a drink of wine and pulled up her sleeve. "You told us all about it that night when we got these." She pointed to the inside of her forearm. "I knew I wanted the owl when I heard about its special powers in the air."

Pennie shifted in her chair. "If I remember the legend right, they're superhuman, like a deity, right?"

Dani nodded. "That's right."

Pennie could remember every legend that Dani and Mali had shared with her, a window to their past, the wisdom of the tribes, the ancient history before Maine was even a state, the history not told in textbooks.

Aunt Aggie placed a large platter on the table. "Something tells me you're going to tell us more."

Dani smiled. "Have you ever heard the Passamaquoddy and Maliseet legend of Cipelahq, the great horned owl?"

Pennie's insides turned warm for her friend's knack of relating their lives to their heritage. The only downturned gaze around the table was from Aunt Aggie, a traditional French Catholic who was never a fan of what she thought of as frivolous lore. But Pennie and the others around the table always loved the stories of good prevailing over evil.

Aunt Maude clapped her hands together in encouragement. "Why I love a good legend. Do tell!"

Dani nodded and smiled, looking around to her captive audience, their glasses or forks suspended. "One day there were two young Passamaquoddy girls walking in the woods when the great owl, Cipelahq, pronounced 'Chebellock' by anglophiles, swooped down to carry them to his world high in the sky. In this special place, the owl loved them and bestowed his special powers of protection upon them. But after several days, the girls became homesick and pleaded to go back to their people on Earth, so Cipelahq agreed. He flew them back down to the forest, but his wings were so large he could not reach the forest floor for the towering trees. Instead, he left them on the magnificent treetop of a hemlock.

They were so high up the tree they could not climb down. After several days, a young man finally came along and they called to him, begging him to help them down. He agreed only on one condition: that one of them would consent to be his wife."

Everyone passed around dishes in silence, except for the clink of a fork or spoon. Even the dogs and Aunt Aggie gave their full consideration to Dani, her soft voice reciting the childhood story. "They agreed to his bargain, and he began to climb the tree. With one eye on him, the young maidens untied the eel skins binding their hair and double knotted them to the top branches of the tree. He finally reached the girls and one by one brought them down to safety. On the forest floor, he stepped toward the Passamaquoddy maidens in expectation, but to distract him, they told him they had forgotten their hair ties on the treetop and that he had to climb back up to get them."

"Just like a woman," said Uncle Charlie, chewing on his corned beef, grease dripping on his chin. "Always one more thing."

"Shush," said Aunt Maude, drinking her wine, eyes smiling.

Mali jumped in. "So he went back up the tree and—"

"Do you mind?" said Dani, glaring at her sister before continuing the story. "With a great deal of disapproval, he started back up the tree, and as he did, the girls began to build him a special wigwam. It took him so long to untie the knotted eel bands from the top branch that when he finally came back down, they had finished the beautiful wigwam. And upon seeing his stunning new home, he went immediately blind from the dramatic sight. Then the girls, knowing full well he was blind, called him to come. He followed their voices until he fell into a pool of water, soaking himself. Then, getting up, he walked toward them again, only to fall into a bed of porcupine quills. When he finally freed himself, he was exhausted and dropped into a deep sleep." Dani looked around the table.

Mali jumped in. "And when he awakened, the girls had vanished."

All mouths around the table stopped mid-chew. "That's it?" said Uncle Charlie. "Those girls left that poor boy like that after tricking him?"

"You always have to steal my thunder, don't you?" said Dani.

Mali ignored her and said, "The owl is stronger than the wind and genius of the air. He loved those girls so much he gave them his superhuman powers of protection."

Dani took a sip of tea. "According to the legend, Cipelahq does not have a body, but a heart, a head, wings and long legs."

Aunt Aggie motioned to Uncle Alfie. "Pass the rolls and let's move away from these *silly* legends." She threw her arms in the air. "It's just an owl, they're everywhere, and poor Pennie just happened to catch one eating a mouse in our garage. I, for one, hope that bird sticks around to catch all the rodents out there."

Pennie gripped the sides of her seat and held her breath. How could her aunt be so disrespectful of their culture? Dani and Mali looked around, afraid to speak out of turn. They had all learned to bite their tongues over the years, growing up in and around Aggie's kitchen, to keep the peace instead of ruining the meal for everyone. They passed around more potatoes and turnips, corned beef and onions, carrots and spicy mustard, a feast in friendly company. "Your grandmother Brigid used to collect owl statues," Aunt Maude told Pennie. "Good omen."

Aggie shot her a warning look for continuing the nonsense.

"My grandmother collected mouse traps," Uncle Charlie chimed in. "There was one in every cupboard when I was growing up."

"I grew up with barn cats," said Aunt Aggie. "We used to name them until there were too many to keep track of. That's about the time my father would put them in a pillowcase and toss them in the river."

The table turned quiet.

"Aggie, you don't have to give away *all* your family secrets," said Uncle Alfie. "Those were different times."

The chatter moved to talk of domesticated cats and how they preyed on the wild backyard birds. Calmness soon settled with the lively conversation, but Pennie couldn't stop looking out the back window for the mysterious creature who'd paid her a visit twice today. Maybe the owl had a nest nearby.

The diners sopped up the salty grease on their plates with the yeast rolls and finished up the wine. Uncle Alfie opened the bottle of port to go with their carrot cake for dessert.

Pushing herself from the table, plump Aunt Maude said she would bust if she had one more thing. "Honestly, Aggie, how am I going to fit into my bikini this summer?"

The mood grew rowdy among the aunts and uncles as the four young women cleared the table and loaded the dishwasher, filling the sink to clean up the pots and pans. Cassie would not leave Pennie's side, even after they'd finished drying the dishes and talked about their week's plans.

Feeling exhausted, Pennie asked the twins if they wouldn't mind heading home. They followed her to the hall closet, Cassie a close companion.

"Looks like you've got a friend for the night," said Uncle Alfie.

"Would it be okay to take her with me?"

"You could use the company. Besides, I don't want any owl swooping in to take you tonight." They all laughed at his amusement with the

Wabanaki legend. He thanked the twins for coming and watched them walk to the car. "I'll see you at the office tomorrow. Get some rest."

Aunt Maude and Uncle Charlie shuffled out behind them as Tita shooed the three dogs back into the house and turned off the outside light of the solid brick family home.

Chapter 5
Ghost Croquet

THE OFFICE OF ALFRED Goode was a thirty-minute walk from Pennie's apartment. She and Cassie rose early to enjoy the stroll now that the temperature hovered above freezing. They could see the ocean from the top of the Western Promenade. They cut through side streets to take the quickest route by the low-income housing, the neighborhood bar with overflowing trash cans in the back, the abandoned warehouses. The Old Port area down the hill by the harbor swelled with pedestrians, bikes, and cars on cobblestone streets. She and Cassie made their way to Commercial Street on the water and toward Standard Bakery, which had the best croissants. Despite her dwindling cash, she bought coffees and pastries for Uncle Alfie's return and her first day at the office.

The old wooden sign for *Alfred Goode, Esquire* hung above the doorway on Exchange, across the street from F. Parker Reidy's, a favorite local bar. Pennie waved to old Mrs. Bernstein, the lady who sold eyeglasses on the first floor of Uncle Alfie's building. It'd been a few months since she had visited the second-floor office. Tita had transformed the space from tacky seventies paneling and pleather couches to funky sixties decor with a burnt orange carpet, gleaming round coffee tables, Jetsons-style couches, and abstract art. The only thing missing was lava lamps.

Teddy met them at the door while Tita talked on the phone. Pennie gave her a coffee and turned to see Uncle Alfie in his office, reading the paper, waving her in. She handed him a decaf and a low-fat croissant.

"I didn't realize they made low-fat."

"Just pretend it's good. Love what you've done with the office."

"That's all your cousin. Trying to liven up the place. I think the brown paneling was getting to her."

His office was still exactly the same as she remembered it growing up: paneled walls and his old heavy wooden desk, Fella underneath. Family pictures sat on the wall shelves beside the legal volumes and filing cabinets. "No updating in here?"

"Nope, told her this is off-limits."

"Whatever's comfortable, right?"

"What about you? Where are you setting up?"

She looked at Tita in the middle of the office, still on the phone. "I guess over there." She pointed to a table across the room by the window overlooking the street.

"It's either that or the file closet, which could get a little claustrophobic."

Tita hung up the phone to join them, looking efficient and sporty in her tight black slacks and V-neck sweater. "Welcome, and thanks for the coffee!"

"Trying to make a good impression on my first day."

Tita grabbed a croissant and took a bite. "What do you think?"

"Love it, very retro! Now I just need a desk."

"I found the perfect one online. But a little business before we get to that. Pop, that was Jeannette McCarthy on the phone. She's still insisting her dead husband is on her property and he's trying to tell her something. Crazy lady wants to know if you can get out there to assess the situation *very* soon."

"Now, now. This is your cousin's first day. We don't want her to think all our clients are crazy," he said, chuckling.

Tita raised her eyebrows at Pennie.

Her uncle ate the second half of the croissant in one bite. "Grab their old file from 1999. I think that was the year they bought the place. What else?"

"I spoke to the guy who called the house when you were in the hospital, the one Pennie talked to. He works at the stables out at Heritage Acres and wants to talk to you about a development. Wouldn't go into any detail."

"That has some potential. What else is on the burner?"

"That developer in Kennebunkport is looking for more title work for free. And you got a call from Bath Savings and Camden National looking for help on deeds."

"Alright. You get the ball rolling with the banks. Line up something for next week. That'll give me a chance to clean up my desk. Don't return the call to the Kennebunkport guy. Eventually he'll get sick of trying to get a rise out of me. Pennie and I'll take a ride out to see Mrs. McCarthy and then up to the horse farm in Fairview."

Pennie swiveled toward her cousin. "You want to come along?"

"I'd much rather stay in the office, far from the insane clients, thank you. It works for me and Pop. It's enough I get to talk to these people on the phone all day."

Uncle Alfie's car, a good old American Packard Mayfair, didn't go above 75. But he never rushed to get anywhere anyway, and the car was, after all, dependable despite the cost of maintenance. Tried and true was always his mantra. When they pulled up to Mrs. McCarthy's cast-iron gate on Falmouth Foreside, it magically opened to a long winding driveway leading to an oceanfront mansion.

"She likes it when you call her Jeannette, but only after she gives you permission," Alfie cautioned. "I haven't seen her for years, but I'll bet she still has little dogs who are spoiled rotten and will take your finger off if you give them a chance. She gets new ones like buying shoes." Cassie was wagging her tail from the backseat. He reached back to scratch her. "Right, old girl?"

"What are we doing here exactly, other than looking for her dead husband?"

"Checking her property boundaries. Seems her late husband's son is building a colossal house right beside her. Even though I've explained where the property lines are, we'll check the perimeter to make sure they're clearly marked and that her husband's ghost is nowhere to be found. She's paying me nicely, so I don't mind setting her mind at ease. Plus, she knows I'll contact her stepson's lawyer to make sure everything is copacetic."

He parked the car in front of the white mansion, its giant red front door flanked by pillars. "This looks like it belongs on the coast of South Carolina," Pennie said.

"You'll soon find out why."

Cassie hopped out of the backseat and roamed freely, sniffing around. A middle-aged housekeeper with fried blonde hair wearing lime green stretch pants and a tight Donald Trump T-shirt greeted them at the door, then escorted them to the front room. As she left them, Jeannette came in, yapping Pomeranians by her side.

"Hello, Alfred, so nice to see you after all these years," she said in a refined Southern drawl. "And sorry to hear about your medical scare. Been there a few times myself, but somehow, we keep on ticking."

"Hello, Jeannette. Thank you, I'm doing just fine. The doctors expect a full recovery. May I introduce my niece, Penelope? She'll be working with me for a while, helping out. "Hello, Penelope. I see you've got your uncle's handsome genes."

Was this aging debutante flirting with her uncle? She shook the woman's soft, cold, diamond-clad hand.

"Jack and Ginger, enough!" Jeannette called to the dogs. They scurried around her feet before quieting down. She looked at Penelope. "That was my late husband's favorite beverage: Jack Daniels and ginger ale."

"How long has your, um, husband been gone?" she asked, wondering if this was too forward.

"Oh, Colin's been dead over a year now. And don't be afraid to ask questions. We don't hold any pretense around here. Just ask your uncle. I'm a straight shooter, aren't I, Alfred?"

"You can depend on that. What was this about your late husband's ghost?"

"You can't even imagine how frazzled I've been lately with this noise keeping me and the doggies up all night. It sounds just like Colin is outside playing croquet. That was his favorite game in the summer. We used to set up the course on the front lawn so he could play whenever the whim struck him. So, I'm lying in bed and hearing the clack of the mallet against the balls and of course it's dark and no one's there. It's the darndest thing. You must think I'm just crazy, Penelope."

Pennie smiled warmly, doing her best to act as if nothing seemed further from her mind.

Her uncle looked out the window to the south. "There's got to be a reasonable explanation. Did you say your stepson is putting up a house next door?"

"Yes, I'd really like you to look at that property line for me again. That foundation area looks awfully close, and I know that Colin wanted to keep our view unobstructed. Otherwise, I'll have to look at their swim dock all day long, not to mention the noise from the kids and the motorboats. It's all changing now. My peace and quiet will soon be gone."

"Why don't we look at the boundaries again?"

"Do you mind? It would put my mind at ease knowing they weren't deliberately pushing the envelope."

He turned to look at the gorgeous vista of Casco Bay north of Portland. "You've got a hell of a spot here, Jeannette. I haven't been out here since you and Colin bought the place."

"We did make the right decision when we decided to buy back in '99, especially with your work on the deed." The yappers jumped up on the upholstered window seat, barking at Cassie. "Oh, look, there's your beautiful Labrador. Will she be okay with Jack and Ginger?"

"Absolutely, we'll take them out with us."

"Thank you, Alfred. I'll be in the living room when you get back."

Outside, the orange powder puffs chased Cassie, but she ignored them and kept her nose to the ground, following Uncle Alfie through the pine grove. He found the stake that marked the property's southerly border. From there, he paced out the area until he reached the hole for the foundation on the adjoining property with the same gorgeous ocean views. *What a life it must be to belong to the lucky sperm club*, Pennie thought. *All you have to worry about is your father's crazy widow next door.*

Alfie jotted things down in his pocket-sized notepad, wetting the tip of the pencil with his tongue.

"Ever thought about a smartphone to take notes?" she said.

"I prefer the old-fashioned way. I've got it in my hand and it's not going anywhere."

"Any problems with easements?"

"Paced out fine but not much wiggle room for decks or porches. Some people try to get away with inches. Probably just to test her. Can you run to my car and get the wheel?"

Pennie and Cassie fetched the long tape measure from the trunk, happy to be of some assistance. Alfie stood beside the dug foundation as Cassie jumped in the hole. Head down, she started to dig until she reached what she was after, popping up with an old muddy yellow croquet ball in her mouth.

Uncle Alfie chuckled and bent down to take it. "Looks like Colin left one of his balls out." He motioned Pennie to walk backward, holding the end of the tape.

She paced back over the last remnants of snow and sensed a small ground tremor. Cassie barked at her. "Do you feel that?"

"Feel what?" He motioned to her to keep walking.

Pennie hesitated. *He doesn't need one more woman possibly imagining things.* Carefully, she continued backward.

"That's it right there. Mark that spot," he said.

The tremor stopped and Cassie barked again. Uncle Alfie placed the muddy yellow ball on the quiet ground beside the foundation hole.

"You didn't feel that tremor?" she said.

He walked toward her, winding the tape. "Look at that," he pointed to the place she'd marked.

Was he losing his hearing or just ignoring her? She decided to drop it. "That's not much room. What'll you tell her?"

"That I've got to check. I'll get a surveyor to come out and measure."

"Uncle Alfie, I felt a ground tremor."

He shrugged, looking out toward the vista. "Tremors happen all the time." There wasn't a cloud in the distant horizon. Jack and Ginger ran around, up and down the wide front lawn where Colin played ghost croquet, his lost yellow ball still resting by the foundation hole.

Inside the house, they found Jeannette in the living room watching a widescreen television on her white chintz couch, a thick-pile bronze carpet under her embroidered slippers. "I just love Judge Judy. She's a straight shooter, doesn't gloss anything over with doublespeak."

He took out his notes and concentrated. "I've paced the boundary and setbacks, and everything looks fine, but I'll have the surveyor come out to double-check."

Pennie stared at a framed picture on the side table—Jeannette with her husband, and a beautiful fair-haired teenage girl standing between them. Noting Pennie's gaze, the Southern belle picked it up and handed it to her. "My daughter, Chloe. You must think I look too old to have one this young, but I had her late in life. A blessing from God."

"What a beauty. She must miss her father."

"Chloe's no longer with us. Died in a car accident a year before Colin passed. She was our only child, together."

Pennie swallowed, staring at the girl in the picture, the stunning smile, wearing a black dress with a lovely sterling silver necklace, a locket that caught the flash of the camera. *How horrible*, she thought. *Your own daughter gone...and to have a stepson building next door*. Her uncle moved closer to Jeannette. "I didn't realize you lost your daughter. Sorry to hear that."

"We kept it pretty quiet. It was hard enough on Colin and me without it being broadcast."

Uncle Alfie nodded, a parent's understanding passing between them. "And as for Colin's croquet matches at night, I suggest you have your own Jack and Ginger nightcap to try to sleep through that racket." He smiled. "Oh, and I'm curious. Is there a shooting range nearby? Don't know why they'd be firing off in the middle of the night, but you may want to check around about that. Sounds like the crack of a mallet."

"I'll say no to the Jack and Ginger. A nice martini is my preferred sleeping aid. But maybe I will make some calls about target practice around here. You never know. I appreciate your time. Nice to meet you, Penelope dear, and good luck learning the ropes. You've got the best in the business here."

"Thank you, Mrs. McCarthy."

"Please, call me Jeannette."

She saw them out the front door where Cassie waited. As they drove through the black gate, Pennie had the strange sensation she was leaving a possessed house.

"I got an eerie feeling from that place," she said. "Maybe because it's right out on the ocean. It's beautiful but stark and almost too perfect."

"She does keep things groomed. Even in the pine grove you get the feeling someone has been in there with a broom sweeping the pine needles."

"And Cassie dug up that ball."

"Dogs have a way of doing that."

Cassie pushed her head out the window, looking at the road behind them, as if she were thinking about the oddness of the place they just left, or how relieved she was to get away from those little dogs.

Alfie drove with his knee against the steering wheel, looking at the directions Tita had printed out.

"You really ought to have a GPS. Makes it safer to navigate and drive at the same time."

"What's the challenge in that?"

He scratched the new growth of whiskers on his chin. Pennie wondered how he was feeling but didn't want to bring it up. He'd been everything a child could want in a father, and it wasn't based on property or inheritance or extravagance but on safety and love. They drove up the interstate to the exit toward Fairview and found Heritage Acres among rolling backcountry roads.

"We're supposed to meet Lewis at the horse stable," he said, turning in, seemingly unfazed by everything that struck Pennie as odd.

Driving onto the property grounds, they passed several *NO DOGS* signs before stopping at the welcome center. Pennie walked inside to get a map. The Lewis family had purchased the two-hundred-acre property and renovated the brick buildings into senior living apartments, the same buildings that had once housed people with developmental disabilities or mental illness, once called the Home for the Feeble-Minded. How gloomy this place must have been before the Lewis family turned it into this senior community with a network of paved walkways, all the buildings restored and buttoned up tight.

"Here's the horse farm," said Pennie, back in the car and reading the map. "Says here, they rehabilitate abused and neglected horses. I guess that's where we're going." She pointed out the sign and Alfie drove up to an enormous barn with gray cedar-shake siding. Rolling hills stretched out on either side, an outdoor arena to the left and horse pasture to the right. When they stopped in front, Cassie stood up in the back seat, awash in horse scents.

"Better keep her in," he said.

Pennie coaxed Cassie's head back into the car and closed the window. They walked through the barn's side entrance and down the wide padded floor, horse stalls on either side, all post-and-beam construction. She spotted a woolly coated roan mare eating hay from a hanging net inside one of the openings. The horse eyed Pennie with curiosity and swished her tail. The stable was nearly spotless, hardly a dropping anywhere, the horses as well kept as Westminster dogs.

A pudgy teenage girl wearing tan riding pants and black boots appeared at the end of the hallway, asking if she could help them.

"Hello, young lady. We're looking for Mr. Lewis."

"Right this way." The stalls went on forever until they walked into an indoor arena with bleacher seats. "He's in there." She pointed to a door on the other side of the riding ring.

Uncle Alfie opened the door and inside sat a man, maybe in his sixties, with a gray beard and thick cropped hair and a ruddy complexion, wearing a checked shirt. He stood up from his unorderly desk and came around to shake their hands.

"You must be Alfred Goode."

"Mr. Lewis. Nice to meet you. This is my niece, Penelope."

"Please, have a seat."

While they settled themselves into black captain's chairs, Mr. Lewis attempted to push the papers on his desk into piles. File drawers sat open behind him, and three half-empty cups of coffee, a rusty horseshoe, and a dirty brush cluttered his desk. A dust-covered computer sat on a corner, shut off.

"Thanks for coming today. Please excuse the mess. I, uh, can never seem to get organized. You find the stables okay?"

"We stopped at the Welcome Center. Pennie found a map."

He smiled at her, deep creases in his eyes. "Penelope, you must be who I spoke to on the phone?"

"Yes, that's right. Good to meet you, Mr. Lewis."

"Please, call me Stan. Have you been to Heritage Acres before?"

"No, can't say as I've ever been out here," Alfie said. "Quite a place."

"My grandfather really transformed it. You probably know this used to be an institution."

"I remember when the state sent crazy people here, or you know, feebleminded."

Pennie shot him a look.

Stan Lewis saw her embarrassment and chuckled. "Yes, that's what it was called. Quite a storied history here. We're lucky those days are over."

"Must have been quite a transformation from the institution to this campus. How many acres here?"

"Originally two hundred, but we added property over the years. Now it's about double that."

"You must turn a good profit then."

"Not me, sir. My grandfather and father bought the land over the years. And some of it's under conservation easement."

"Tough on a town when a large property like this can't bring in any income. Falls on less and less people to bear the burden," her uncle continued.

Stan shifted in his chair. Pennie hoped he would not continue this conservative bent. "You're absolutely right, Mr. Goode."

"Please, call me Alfie. Not to get off on a tangent. I know you've done a good thing with this place."

"We're still working on it. That's why I called you. My sister and I inherited the property from my father about five years ago. We're thinking about selling acreage that's not under the easement to a business developer. To your point, bringing more income to the town. Ward Lewis Properties has proposed a business park development on the north side, about fifty acres, and I wondered if you would set up a meeting to talk about some of the property issues."

"Ward Lewis Properties? New outfit?"

"Fairly new. My son's business. Started it a few years ago and I'm trying to thread this needle."

"You mean between your son's interest and your family's interest."

"That's right. After my father passed, the torch was passed to me. Believe me, I was happy running this horse barn. But now I'm also managing the senior housing and the acreage, and the overhead is killing us. But I will make damn sure things are done correctly and right by my sister."

"So, I'll be working for you and your sister? Anyone else?"

"Nope, just the two of us own it. She retired to Florida so I'm left holding the bag here."

"I can see why you'd want to approach this cautiously."

"You came highly recommended, Mr. Goode. My son has big ideas for the property, and I'd like to make sure he's doing everything by the book. Don't want it to look like I'm giving him any special treatment. He's agreed to keep me involved every step of the way. That's the only way I agreed to this."

"I'll give you my best assessment based on what I find."

"Can I show you and your niece the center? We're proud of the rehabilitation we do here, and we also board horses."

Pennie stood up. All the talk this morning about meddling family members coming in to take control of property made her anxious. Besides, she wanted to see more horses.

Later, at home, sitting on her couch with a cup of chamomile tea, she couldn't stop thinking about Jeannette's daughter. She typed *Chloe McCarthy Maine* into a search engine, and one small news story popped up. She had been found dead, the only person inside her mangled car with an empty bottle of OxyContin on the passenger seat beside her. Images of the girl, wearing that same silver locket around her neck, began to blur when Pennie fell asleep on the couch.

She dreamed about elderly Colin McCarthy whacking a yellow croquet ball on the front lawn under a foggy overcast sky, steady rain coming down, winds and angry waves ripping across Casco Bay. She watched him from the ground, a dog's-eye view, following the ball as the haggard Irishman smacked the mallet against the ball and sent it sailing through the wire U and straight past her to the pine grove, near the new foundation. She felt herself panting like a dog, running through puddles on the lawn, following the ball. She began to dig like a maniac, her claws pulling up the layers of half-frozen mud and needles until her paws bled. And there appeared a silver chain. Grabbing it with her teeth, she ripped it from the ground until it popped loose from its shallow grave. Falling back into a pool of water, she stared down, seeing her reflection and the necklace dangling from a husky's jaw.

Startled awake, breathing in the dark, Pennie lay still, petrified. *What on earth?* Shaking, she sat up and hugged herself, her heartbeat taking its time to subside. Her fingers ached and she looked down at her nails. Some were broken and bloody. Switching on the light, she realized she must have been scratching the couch with everything she had...the dream inside the body of a dog? Who's necklace? Chloe's?

In the bathroom, she washed her sore fingers and took stock of her face. Shocked but unchanged. Picking up the bottle of painkillers on the sink, three or four left, she dumped them into the toilet.

Chapter 6

Sixth Sense

For the first time in three weeks, she woke without pain. Life after the skiing accident was all about second chances. She took a quick shower, put on a wool knit sweater and striped wool socks Aunt Aggie once made for her. Then she realized it was St. Patrick's Day. Examining her copper-colored hair and blue eyes in the mirror, still shocked by the vividness of her dog dream, she wondered about her Scotch Irish lineage and whether, inside her soul, she held some kind of deep-rooted capacity to see things that others could not. On the way out, she found her floppy plaid tartan tam on the door hook and covered her head.

At the office, her desk had arrived. She thanked Tita for her excellent online shopping. "I love the orange. It compliments your pink one."

"Thanks, you can pay me in drinks tonight."

"What's the plan?"

"Lars is meeting us at Brian Boru after work."

Pennie's mood deflated.

Tita turned away. "Why do you have to be so judgy? You're as bad as Mum."

She grew warm under the sweater. "It's just that I wasn't expecting it. That's all. I thought it would be a girls' night out."

Tita thumbed through some papers on her desk. "I wonder if this is going to work out with us in the same office."

"Don't worry, I'll be out most of the time." Pennie looked down from the second-floor window to see Uncle Alfie on the street with the four dogs, none of them on a leash. He was reading a paper with one hand, holding a coffee in the other, and looked up to greet a heavyset man in a peacoat who passed him as he crossed the street towards the office. No one noticed the dogs were untethered, keeping stride with him, even when Teddy or Fella marked a lamppost, lifting their legs without breaking stride. Pennie realized how eccentric he must look to others in his houndstooth overcoat and Donegal tweed cap. Even on St. Paddy's Day.

Whistling preceded him up the stairs. The dogs plowed into the office, stumbling over each other to get to Pennie and Tita.

"Top o' the morning, girls!" Alfie called out.

"Morning," they chimed.

"Got some green-frosted donuts here," said Tita, taking one out of the bag.

Pennie reached over and grabbed the bag. "You didn't offer one to me."

"Thank ya, pretty lass," he said.

"Are we going to have to listen to that all day?" said Tita.

"Who woke up on the wrong side of the bed?" He ate the donut in three bites, licking his fingers. "I guess it's okay to cheat today, but don't tell the home boss. What's on the calendar?" Tita checked her screen. "Only the meeting with Ward Lewis Properties."

"Right. And where are they?"

"Down on Middle Street."

"You coming with me, Pennie?"

"If you don't mind."

"We've got to dig into this thing. Find out what this Ward fella has got up his sleeve. Why don't you do some research on his real estate outfit. Fill me in on the walk down. What time are we expected?"

"Ten o'clock."

"Perfect. That gives me time to do the crossword."

The dogs followed him into his office and he closed the door.

Pennie took a sip of coffee. "He's in a good mood today."

"We're closing shop early. Only happens twice a year—St. Patrick's Day and Christmas Eve."

"I'd better get busy." Pennie opened her laptop on the new orange lacquered desk. Tita had even ordered her a matching swivel chair.

"This is really quite nice," Pennie said. "And I do think we can work together. We shared a room for ten years. I think we can share an office."

Tita's mouth was full of frosted donut. "And we can always get the tape out to mark the boundaries if we have to."

They both laughed, their teeth green, as the phone rang. Tita swallowed and picked up. Aggie. Tita swiveled with her head back, tapping her pencil. "Yes, we'll make sure Pop gets home...I don't know, maybe five or six? Yes, we're working today, you know, most of the day." She winked at Pennie. "See you later."

She hung up the phone and picked up a Harley-Davidson magazine.

"Are you buying a bike?"

"We're thinking about it, after the movie premiere."

Pennie resisted rolling her eyes. "And when is that?"

"Lars has all the ski footage. It's in postproduction now. He's thinking by the fall."

Pennie wondered how many times Tita and Lars would break up between now and then. And whether her aunt would survive it all. "Should we invite Aunt Aggie to meet us at Brian Boru?"

"And hang out with us drunken monkeys? Never. Besides, Friday's her bridge day with the ladies. They'll be soused by two o'clock."

Her browser open, Pennie looked up Ward Lewis Properties, skimming to get the basics on him, then typed in Heritage Acres and scrolled down to the history of the Home for the Feeble-Minded. The institution opened in 1908 on Hill Farm in Fairview for residents who were deemed "idiots, morons, retards, defective, deficient," and other labels that doctors, judges, and town officials chose to stamp on them. As the population grew, more dormitories were built, and the quality of care slid. Judges often sent orphans or destitute children there, whether they had a disability or not. Once there, few left. Unless they managed to escape.

"Listen to this," said Pennie. "In the early and mid-1900s, many considered people with intellectual disabilities dangerous. This was all during the era of eugenics when the common theory was that only people with 'good' genes should reproduce. Mental retardation, promiscuous behavior, alcoholism, and poverty were considered hereditary. In New England, 1,815 people were sterilized in the twentieth century, mostly women and those considered feeble-minded. In Maine alone, between 1925 and 1936, there were 326 people legally sterilized, and 189 of these were at the Home for the Feeble-Minded."

Tita kept thumbing through her magazine, its cover an image of a gleaming red chrome motorcycle with a blonde bombshell lying in front of it. "People are really sick, aren't they?"

"It's all about maintaining the purity of the white race." Pennie closed her laptop and thought about the campus and how it had been completely transformed. Stan Lewis had invited them back to a show in the indoor arena on Saturday. "The horses are in the barn and people are out in the community," he'd said. "Where they belong."

IT HAD STARTED TO sleet outside when they left the office for their appointment. Huddled together under her uncle's wide umbrella, she filled him in. "They advertise themselves as strictly Maine-based commercial brokers, so they're going for that local appeal. I didn't see any Heritage Acres listings on their website, only four or five buildings in town and quite a few lease options out by the mall."

"Stan said his son was just getting on his feet. How long have they been in business?"

"Doesn't say. The site does look a little barren. Very professional, though, like he's got some money behind it."

"Did you find out any background on him?"

"He used to be in residential. I found him on some old Maine Bank and Trust listings. Oh, and it looks like he recently sold his own house in Yarmouth. Nice place, from the pictures I saw. Thirty-five hundred square feet, gourmet kitchen, primary bath with Jacuzzi, radiant-heat floors, the works."

"He could be house flipping, or maybe been through a divorce."

"Wow, I hadn't gone there. Maybe he's just downsizing."

"That's true, too."

They found the unassuming brick office building. A black placard beside the elevator inside listed five floors, with W. Lewis at the top. Uncle Alfie shook the umbrella. "He's got the prime space in here."

They rode the old elevator to a large open office space. An ostentatious crescent-shaped mahogany reception desk faced them, *Ward Lewis Properties* printed in gold letters across the front. A young man in a button-down wool sweater sat behind it. "May I help you?"

"We're here to meet with Mr. Lewis. Alfred Goode here."

"He's expecting you, Mr. Goode. Please have a seat." He fanned his right hand toward a leather couch. Alfie pointed to a magazine on the coffee table: the broker's shining face graced the front cover with the headline, "Ward Lewis Ventures into Commercial Properties." What a charming smile, Pennie thought. Something so familiar about him, something she couldn't put a finger on.

She felt her uncle rise beside her and looked up to see the man from the cover approaching. "Please don't read that," he said, smiling, and reached out his hand to her. "My assistant Bethany arranged for that article, but I don't normally do that sort of thing. I'm Ward."

"Pennie, uh, Penelope Goode."

"You two must be related. Mr. Goode, so glad you could make it."

"Same here. This is my niece. She's here to catch anything this old brain misses."

"From what I hear, you don't miss much, Alfred." He walked them around the office, carpeted in gray Berber, the interior walls painted a nautical blue with white trim, the exterior walls exposed brick. Ward wore jeans and a green sweater, his face clean-shaven. "I hope you don't mind my appearance. It's casual Friday and everyone chips in a dollar to dress down. Every month we give the money to a local charity."

"What a great idea," she said.

"Another idea from Bethany. I don't know what I'd do without her." He pointed to the young woman sitting at a desk outside his glassed-in office. She looked younger than Pennie, with straight dark hair, horn-rimmed glasses, and a toothy smile.

"Beth, please hold my calls."

He offered them the low stiff chairs facing his desk before sitting in his own high-backed one. Behind him, a window looked out onto Middle

Street. "What a gray day. I don't know about you, but I'm ready for spring."

"Not long now," said Uncle Alfie. "Eventually this sleet and snow will turn to rain."

"It's always easier to sell properties when the weather improves. I've got so many clients in a wait-and-see mode right now, it's enough to drive me insane. Patience is everything in this game."

"How long since you opened?" asked her uncle.

"Six months. We've managed to move a few properties to keep us going, but I'm looking for more opportunities."

"How many brokers?"

"Right now, it's just me and my associate broker, Keith, who you met out front covering the reception desk. We're trying to grow slowly. I've got space here to take on more staff eventually. What about you? How long have you been in real estate law?"

"Too long to keep track, really. I guess I've been on Exchange Street for close to twenty years. Before that, I worked out of the house, but my wife got tired of that."

Ward looked at Pennie. "How long have you been working with your uncle?"

"Just started this week. I'm learning the ropes."

"Are you a title lawyer?"

"No, but my uncle was nice enough to offer me a job until I find the right, um, opportunity."

Uncle Alfie placed his palm on her hand. She could feel the pressure on her tender fingernails, rekindling memories of her dream the night before. "Don't let her fool you. She's helping me out more than the other way around."

"Looks like you can handle just about anything," said Ward, slightly raising his eyebrows. Pennie crossed her legs, a nervous laugh giving her away.

Her uncle folded his arms. "Sounds like you have a development opportunity out at Heritage Acres. What ideas have you got?"

"I like your style, Alfred. Right down to business."

"I'm assuming you're a busy young fella. We don't want to take up too much of your time."

"Busy, yes, but not exactly young anymore. As you probably know, my father is managing the estate, so he's being cautious about the development." He reached for a rolled plan behind him and brought it to his desktop. She and Uncle Alfie stood up as he laid it out flat, placing glass seashell paperweights on each side. She thought she could see a white band on his finger where a wedding ring once might have been.

He tapped near the top edge of the campus rendering. "Here's where we're looking to put up an office park. We're in negotiations to buy the property from my father's estate. There's roughly sixty acres of forested area, prime for development. Everything has already been submitted to the planning board. As you probably know, the property has miles of walking trails and a horse stable. It offers everything a business campus needs to attract working professionals. Less than an hour from Portland, it's really an ideal location. I've already started talking to big tech companies like Google and HP about building to their specs. This is exactly what Maine's economy needs to bring businesses in and ensure our future, and our children's future."

"What does your father think about bringing these big businesses to campus?"

"He's a little hesitant, as you can imagine. But he also understands the importance of bringing in the economic growth we need in Fairview right now. And it's the perfect location and setting for a high-tech company. Imagine peaceful natural surroundings, a horse stable and walking tails where you work? That could de-stress any executive and attract those high-wage earners who want the job potential without the rat race and high housing costs of a big city. It's a great place to bring up kids, too. We've got it all."

Uncle Alfie examined the plans and asked a few zoning questions. Ward had an answer for everything and even offered to walk the property with him.

"Let's set something up for next week." Her uncle stood up.

"Perfect, I'll have Bethany schedule it on the way out."

They gathered their coats and her uncle asked for a copy of the plans.

"Of course. I'll have it sent to your office."

They shook hands and Pennie felt him linger for a moment before letting go of her hand, still tender from the dream. "I hope you can join us, too."

"I—I will plan on it." She took a deep breath and stuck her hands in her pockets.

On the elevator down, her uncle cleared his throat. "The best advice I can give you is to not mix business with pleasure," he said. Didn't miss a thing. "And to watch out for people who have an answer for everything."

She tried to object, but he put his hand up. "I won't say another word about it. You're an adult and can make your own decisions. Just keep a clear head when it comes to business." When the elevator door opened, he looked at his watch. "Eleven thirty. Perfect. Where can I take you for a pint?"

THEY HAD BURGERS FOR lunch over several black and tans at Ri Ra Irish Pub on Commercial. He reminisced about growing up with his parents and sisters in Portland. They were quite poor back then. Pennie's Scotch Irish grandfather Patrick Goode worked as a laborer in a shipyard and, according to family lore, he'd acquired the deed to the townhouse on Pine Street from a ship's captain in a poker game. Her Welsh grandmother, Brigid James, worked at a cannery until she got pregnant with Maude, and then Brigid, and then Alfred. Raising the family put an end to her working outside the home. As soon as Alfred was old enough, nine or ten, he found jobs at the fish pier, especially when the big catches came in.

He recounted times on the docks, working for five dollars a day unloading fish and getting to know the fishermen. He wanted to be one of them, to set out to sea for weeks at a time. In his teens he fished aboard a tuna boat in the Gulf of Maine, but it was a rough go, backbreaking and dangerous work. When he met Aggie, she was twenty-one and he was twenty-five, now with a future family to consider.

He was full of promises from their first days of courting. He took her out for dinner and talked to her about his plans of going to law school to make a respectable living. At the time, he was young and full of talk with no serious plans to go to any school. Just something to say to impress this girl before moving on to the next one, his pattern throughout his young adulthood. But he couldn't get Aggie out of his head. She was different. She had a sophisticated way about her, a bit more refined when she spoke and in the way she held her wineglass. By the time he met Aggie's family, she'd already told everyone that he was going to law school, and Aggie's father would not let that go. Every time he saw his daughter's courter, he'd say, "How're those law school applications coming, young man? I'm sure you don't want to be fishing for the rest of your life. Every man needs a good profession so he can settle down and make a proper home for his family."

"To tell you the truth, I never would have gotten into law school without the old man's connections," he said, downing the remainder of the stout. "You know, you and I are not so different, Pretty Pennie."

"How do you mean?"

"The likes of you and me are not afraid to try on something new. We don't shy away from a challenge, do we?"

"No, I guess not."

"That's the Goode in you. I'm glad to have you working with me. It's nice to have the company."

It wasn't often he was so sentimental. Kind? Always. But sentimental? Not unless he'd had a few. She examined her fingers, her broken nails. "I had the strangest dream last night. I—"

Uncle Alfie slapped a $100 bill on the bar. "Hold that thought. Let's head toward the office before it gets any later."

They weaved their way back up the hill in the cold Portland mist. It wasn't sleeting anymore; the sun squinted between the clouds every so often, making shadows on the cobblestones. The right moment to bring up her dream about the dog digging up the necklace had come and gone. When they reached the top of Exchange, he talked her into having one Irish whiskey at Parker Reidy's across the street.

Inside the mahogany bar, her uncle seemed to know every other person. A handsome woman sitting at the bar waved to him. He said, "Hello, Esther. You're looking as lovely as ever." Alfred Goode was a flirt, but a harmless one—and what lady didn't love a compliment from a gentleman dressed in tweed? The bartender poured Jameson on the rocks without asking, and they chatted it up with Jack, a friendly and verbose local surveyor Uncle Alfie often hired. They were soon talking about Jeannette's property, the abutting mansion going up, and her late husband's ghost croquet.

Her uncle looked directly at Jack. "Get this one. Mrs. McCarthy called this morning to tell me that one of her little dogs had dug up a necklace, and it belonged to her daughter."

Pennie grew rimy and stiff.

He went on. "She claims her daughter was wearing that same necklace the night she died in a car accident."

"No shit," said Jack, drunk.

"It was found inside the foundation, same place where my lab dug up the old croquet ball, right Pennie?"

She shifted, white as a sheet. "Right."

"That was her dead husband's favorite game."

Jack looked perplexed. "Sounds like a mystery novel, *Murder by Mallet*."

They laughed before turning quiet. "Poor girl actually died in a car wreck. Happens to too many teenagers, unfortunately." Uncle Alfie ordered another round for the table and Pennie quickly downed it, absorbing the shock. He continued to tell Jack about the police investigation that had already started where the necklace was found. The more they became engrossed in conversation, and the louder the barroom grew around them, the more Pennie visualized the husky with the locket dangling from its mouth, staring through her. There was more to her dream than she dared to think about.

It was early evening when they finally made it back to the office. The dogs barked madly while he unlocked the door. "Okay, pups, we're back. Life is good again. Your mother is going to wonder what's been keeping us, so let's get a move on." Pennie followed them down the stairs and out into the night air, the dogs trotting alongside them in the darkening city streets. "How did you like your first week?" he said.

"Sometimes I wonder what I'm doing with my life."

"If you want to make God laugh, tell him your plans," he said. He twirled his folded umbrella around in a circle. "Let's enjoy today and not worry too much about tomorrow." He whistled as they strolled in the misty late afternoon.

"I feel a little lost lately, as if I'm walking around in a daze. At the same time, I've never felt more alive. Maybe it's just the whiskey talking." She straightened her tartan tam and combed her fingers through her hair. "I have to say I really enjoyed the meetings with your clients this week."

"*Our* clients. If there's anything I'm happy about, it's how independent you and Christina have become. That's the ticket. Curiosity, freedom, not being afraid to take a few risks."

"Uncle Alfie, why didn't you tell me about the necklace found at Mrs. McCarthy's?"

"Oh, I thought I had. I'm sorry, sometimes things slip my mind. Just ask your aunt about that."

"I have to tell you I had a dream last night about being there, and a dog digging up a necklace..." She stared down at the cobblestones, not sure what to say.

He stopped short and took her chin in his gloved hand. "Listen, Birdie. Never be afraid of your dreams. That's your intuition at work." *Birdie.* That was what they used to call her mother and her grandmother. He took her arm and coaxed her along. "Your mother and my mother both had an unusual sixth sense and constant premonitions. I think that's what made your poor mother so ill. She couldn't seem to tame her own thoughts. I would never want you to end up like that."

"I'm not going mad. I'm just a little scared by what I dreamt."

"This is an interesting business we're in, but it can get spooky. Sometimes I find myself knowing the outcome before the evidence is found. You're not alone."

She felt raindrops on her cheeks and tugged his arm. "I'm pretty lucky to have you." Tears formed in her eyes, but she blinked them back, thinking about what life might have been like if her mother hadn't died. Would she still feel like an outsider?

He opened the umbrella, twirling it over them. "I know your mother is looking down on us now and smiling."

They were connected by blood and something more, a knowing. When they came to the corner down near Brian Boru, he bent down to kiss her on the forehead and told her to have a fine time with the band and to bring her sister home safely. Somehow Pennie thought it might be the other way around. She waved to the dogs, and they lingered, especially Cassie, barking at her as she walked away.

INSIDE BRIAN BORU, HER eyes adjusted to the darkness. She searched the first floor for any sign of Tita, of the twins and their husbands. Pushing her way back through the crowd, she wound her way upstairs where a five-piece band played Irish folk music. An old man with long white hair and a beard belted out a Celtic song, the dance floor crowded with drunkards. Pennie spotted tall Lars up at the bar in his black leather jacket, then saw the table with Tita, Mali and Peter, Dani and Max behind him.

"'Bout time you showed up," yelled Dani, wearing a green bowler hat, a shamrock painted on her face.

"Nice shamrock," Pennie shouted above the revelry.

"You missed the face painting! Where've you been?"

"It *is* my uncle's favorite holiday."

"Right, of course. How's everything going at the office?"

"Great." She moved her mind from one case to another. "Especially the meeting I had this morning at Ward Lewis Properties."

"Oh yeah?"

"I've met some hot prospects, but this guy sizzles."

"Tell me more," she said, sipping her soda.

"Let me get a drink first."

Pennie waved to Tita, who was standing with Lars and Mali. When she saw the pint being poured, Pennie got up to throw a five at the bartender.

"So, anyway, *Ward.*" She took a long swig of beer. "Lord, I've got it bad for Ward."

"Where'd you meet him?" Dani's eyes were alight.

"At his office downtown to talk about a development."

"So, he's got money."

"Who knows. Uncle Alfie seems to think he may have gone through a divorce. He didn't have a ring on, and I'm not sure but I think he was flirting with me."

"How old is this dirty flirty?"

"Mmm, maybe late thirties, forties? He's a dirty birdy."

They laughed like loons and Dani choked on her soda. "Pen, sounds like you're smitten."

"Jesus, I know! I only met him today." She gulped her beer, embarrassed by her infatuation.

Dani rubbed her arm, sensing her discomfort. "You ain't getting any younger. Let's dance!" She grabbed her hand, and they weaseled their way into the middle of the floor, wedged between the sweaty bodies shaking and twisting. They busted a move to the Irish Rovers, now that the band added an electric guitar to the mix. Dani, the man magnet on the dance floor, danced with pure electricity. When the song ended, sure enough, a guy followed them to the bar. "Someone behind us wants a piece of you," said Pennie.

Dani wheeled around to face the bearded drunk, about an inch shorter than she was.

"Wanna dance?" he asked.

"Go away."

"What?" he yelled.

"I said get lost." She showed him her ring finger. He gave her his own finger and walked away. She looked around the crowd. "Where's Max? This place is lame. Let's get some food. I'm hungry."

They found Tita, Lars, Mali, Peter, and Max at the bar downstairs. They weren't ready to leave. "Okay, I'll catch up with you later, I'm going to get some food," Dani yelled as Pennie grabbed her to drag her outside.

"Oh, I can breathe," said Pennie. The crisp air made her sweaty body tingle. "Let's go for a slice and then take a cab home. Can you stay at my place?"

"Sure, Max won't care."

They stopped at Portland Pie Company on York Street, sat at the bar, and ordered an entire pizza pie with buffalo chicken and blue cheese drizzle. Dani called Max and left a message that she'd see him in the morning. She had red sauce on the corners of her mouth.

"I'm glad I get to live through you and your hot new romance," she said.

Pennie knew encouragement from Dani when she heard it. Seemed everyone was disappointed when Kush left the scene. "There's no hot new anything right now. It's totally a one-sided affair made up in my head." She dipped her slice into the blue cheese.

"Just call the guy. Tell him you wanna jump his bones."

"He could have any woman, or any*one* on the planet."

"You said he was flirting."

"Yeah, in my own mind he was ready to put a rock on my finger and take me away to an island in the Fijis. Then I woke up."

"Any guy would be lucky to have you," she said.

This was not something Pennie could fathom. Despite feeling more aware of everything around her, a strange unsettledness was creeping in.

They finished the pizza, and Dani belched in contentment. "Oh, I almost forgot," she said. "Max heard from Kush the other night. He's coming home from Philly in a week."

Pennie's heart hurt a little, thinking of her ex. "So?"

"Sooooo, maybe we can all go out, you know, while you're waiting for Mr. Real Estate to make his move." Dani picked up the check. "I got this."

Putting on her coat, Pennie felt an icy chill crawl up her spine, sensing something behind her. She spun around to face a thin, haggard man sitting at the far end of the bar with an untouched beer. She recognized him. And sitting beside him was an apparition. A white shadow of a young girl, not actually touching the stool but floating on it, long hair covering her face and shoulders, talking into the man's ear. The man just stared ahead blankly, as if comatose. Pennie turned to see Dani leaving and ran after her.

"Did you see that guy and the girl sitting at the bar?"

"What're you talking about?" Dani kept walking down the steps and along the brick sidewalk.

Pennie said, "I thought we were getting a cab?"

"I could use the fresh air."

"It was the man on Baxter Boulevard," said Pennie.

"What?"

"That guy in the bar with the girl. He was the guy I saw walking Baxter Boulevard about a week ago." She pictured the dogs again on the snowy walk with their hair up, afraid of something, and the mini squall.

She followed Dani along York Street, her head spinning, wondering if she was going out of her mind. "Have you ever seen a ghost?"

"You're sloshed," said Dani, laughing, and stamped in the icy puddle on the sidewalk to soak her best friend.

"Stop it! I'm totally serious right now! I just saw a girl on a barstool that was floating above it. And I'm not hallucinating. Have I ever joked about something like this?"

Dani stopped and turned toward her under the streetlight, sober. "You're serious right now."

"I couldn't be more fucking serious."

"Okay, so you're crazy *and* you're drunk." She put her arm around Pennie and then slapped her on the ass so hard Pennie screamed and chased her all the way up to the Western Prom, playing in the rain, in the dark, running from what she thought she saw but hoped was simply a beer-induced apparition, an uncanny dream at the end of a very long week.

Chapter 7
Stopping by Woods

THE NEXT MORNING, SHE woke up to a throbbing head protesting last night's St. Paddy's hoopla. Nothing that a day on the couch watching *Seinfeld* reruns wouldn't cure. That's when it hit her: Stan Lewis from the stable had invited her and Uncle Alfie to a show at the equestrian center today. She felt like shit, but the idea of visiting the horses again, smelling their hypnotic scent, hearing the way they talked to one another, filled her with unexpected longing.

Dani had slept on her couch and was awake and ready for a ride home to Max and the comfort of her own bed for a few more hours of sleep. Pennie hugged her best friend. She wondered when Dani would tire of carrying her drunk ass home after so many years in their friendship, but she never complained. At the Congress Street loft, she bid her farewell, and never mentioned their conversation last night in the rain. She turned the car toward Pine Street, wondering if maybe she could talk Tita into going to the show with her. In front of the townhouse, old lady Payson spied out the front window.

The dogs announced her intrusion as she entered without knocking. The smell of bacon and blueberry pancakes filled the house. Her stomach was growling for food of any kind, despite the late-night pizza. Uncle Alfie sat working on the puzzle, the grayish hull now mostly pieced together. Fella ran to greet her.

"Pretty Pennie," he said, without looking up. "Have fun last night?"

"A little too much fun."

"Hungry?"

"Starved. Seen Tita? Left her and the others at Brian Boru."

"Nope." He chewed on the stub of his unlit cigar, turning it absent-mindedly between his lips.

Pennie scratched Fella, who kept trying to get her attention, waiting for the next thing, as if to say, "Where we going today? Huh? What are we doing?"

She leaned against the doorway. "Any interest in going to that horse show that Stan Lewis invited us to?"

He looked up. "I need to lay low today after my first week back."

"You're right. Don't want to overdo it."

"Get your cousin to go with you."

Pennie studied the shape of a glaring hole in the puzzle's hull and thought she saw the absolute perfect piece to plug it. She tried it—no—and felt the sting of failure in front of the master. Maybe Tita *would* want to go. She left Alfie to his puzzle and walked up the stairs to the bedroom she and Tita used to share. It was now a guest room, but still had their twin sleigh beds and matching cedar chests where she used to hide her rolling papers, pipes, and weed. Pennie looked out the window to the front lawn where her aunt had thrown all her stuff, only a month after her high school graduation. Tita was gone by then, off training with the ski team.

On the bookshelf stood her favorite novels from high school: *My Antonia, To Kill a Mockingbird, East of Eden, Their Eyes Were Watching God, The Catcher in the Rye, Beloved.* She pulled out the paperback by Toni Morrison, remembering her aunt picking up the book and asking her what kind of literature they were teaching young minds these days in the public school system and what was the purpose of studying fiction, anyway, when you could read the *real* history. Pennie searched her memory, but couldn't remember if she responded, only a feeling of resentment. She slipped it back quietly between the other books.

She then peered into her aunt and uncle's well-appointed bedroom with the tall four-posted maple bed and matching dressers. The high mattress was still covered in the ivory and green wedding ring quilt that her mother's mother, Grammy Goode, had made as a wedding gift for Alfie and his new wife nearly forty years ago. As the only son, Alfie inherited the Goode family townhouse after Grammy died, under the condition that sisters Maude and Brigid would always be taken care of and have a place in the home until they created their own.

Pennie could hear Aunt Aggie at the kitchen table with Aunt Maude, having coffee. They had spent many mornings here over coffee contemplating the changing world around them, the many friends and family that came and went, the heartaches and celebrations, the family gossip. Hesitating just outside the kitchen door, Pennie remembered overhearing a heated conversation between the two aunts when she was a teen. Aunt Maude had said, "Why don't you let her move out to the carriage house? Tita's gone now."

Aggie replied, "If I let Pennie move out there, she'll probably never leave, like her mother. We all know what a mess that was."

Her headache resurfaced, throbbing, turning her ear to this morning's discussion on the homeless crisis in Portland and all the encampments down on Commercial Street. Aunt Aggie lamented about the immigrants taking all the public housing, living off welfare instead of working for a living. Pennie sucked in and walked directly to the sideboard where a plate of pancakes sat, still hot from the griddle. She grabbed a piece of bacon and waited for the inevitable questions.

"Where's your cousin?" Aggie asked. "Is she back with that *film director*?" She raised an eyebrow at her sister-in-law.

"Not that I know of," Pennie said, half-lying. She loaded her plate up and found the maple syrup in the cupboard. Looking out the back window at the bird feeder with the black-capped chickadees, she remembered the ghostly great-horned owl. She changed the subject. "There's a horse show out at Heritage Acres today."

"A horse show. How'd you find out about this?" asked Aunt Maude, swirling her spoon daintily in her coffee.

"Stan Lewis invited us, the man that Uncle Alfie and I met out there."

"You know, I remember you loved horses when you were growing up," said Aunt Aggie. "Had to have the latest Breyer statues, lined them up in your room. I bet they're still in the attic."

Pennie hated it when they brought up this childhood phase. Tita was collecting boyfriends and skiing medals while she was still collecting plastic horses and nagging her uncle for another dog or cat or hamster. Even today, she somehow understood animals better than people. Cassie nudged her leg, waiting for a piece of bacon or some other fallout from the stack of cakes.

"Well if you find her, can you tell her that her laundry is long overdue? Do you suppose she's sleeping over there?" Aunt Aggie couldn't even say his name.

"I hope not, not with the baggage he brought home from California." Silence filled the kitchen; her aunts stared, mouths open. She wasn't sure why she'd said it, but maybe it was a resentment after all these years of living in a house where she was never considered to be as good as Tita. She braced herself for the interrogation.

"Oh, I hope she's getting laid," said Aunt Maude. "There's nothing like a good stiff one while they're still working like they should."

Pennie choked and laughed. Good 'ol Aunt Maude to the rescue.

"Do not encourage that relationship, no matter how...stiff he is," said Aunt Aggie.

"Your generation takes it all for granted. When you're our age you don't have the luxury of rolling over in the morning to a nice how-do-ma'am," said Maude. "Don't take it for granted, Pennie dear. Get it while you can."

"I'll work on that." She pictured Ward at his desk, laying the plans out.

"Whatever *baggage* he brought home," said Aunt Aggie, "I hope Christina is smart enough to see him for the *opportunist* he is."

Her cynicism had mounted over the years. It had been Lars's habit to honk his horn for Tita outside instead of coming into the house to greet the parents. When Tita moved out to the carriage house her senior year in high school, he'd sneak back there at night and then slip away in the morning.

And here Pennie was again, stuck between Tita and her aunt, trying to wedge herself loose before falling into a trap. Her attention went out the back window to the memory of the owl perched on the roof dormer, the cold chill running through her like ice in her veins, then last night and the shadow of the girl at the bar beside the haggard lonely man. She shivered.

"Are you okay?" said Aunt Aggie.

"Oh, yeah. I'm fine. Just a little foggy from last night is all." She scratched Daisy, who was passed out at Aunt Aggie's feet. "I've got to run. Thanks for the cakes."

As soon as she got in the car, she dialed Tita's number. When she didn't pick up the first time, Pennie called her again until she finally heard a groggy voice on the other end. "Yeah?"

"Come with me to a horse show today?"

"Wha? What time is it?"

"After ten. Time to rise and shine."

Tita groaned on the other end. "I'm not ready for the light of day."

"C'mon. It's work and I need your moral support."

"Like I told you, I don't make house calls."

"Pleaaaaaase!"

A big sigh came across the line. "Oh, all riiiiight."

"I'll pick you up in front of Lars's apartment in half an hour."

Saved from going alone, she drove home to shower and change into something more fitting for a horse show. She put on her favorite jeans and a pair of tall leather boots, a cotton sweater, and jangly bracelets to liven things up. She toweled her slightly dull, long, reddish-brown hair. Hers was a kind of plain look, but different, too. People had told her she looked like a cross between Fiona Apple and Saoirse Ronan. She massaged lotion into the crease that was becoming more apparent between her eyebrows. Blowing her hair dry, she pulled it back with the black silk scarf Aunt Maude had brought back from Scotland.

After checking the time of the horse show, she decided at the last minute to bring the Nikon that Uncle Alfie had given her for high school graduation. She liked taking photos and knew she'd get some good shots of horses today. Heading out into the overcast Saturday morning, she drove to Lars's apartment on Fessenden Street, pulling up in front of the three-story white building with peeling paint, clapboards missing in random sections, and broken mini blinds covering the windows. Impatiently, she called Tita without any answer. She beeped and waited for a long five minutes. Then she texted: *You coming or what?* Another ten minutes and nothing.

She drove away in a tizzy, squealing her tires. Why was Tita still obsessed with that old boyfriend, that film director wannabe? The attention? He wasn't even athletic, more of a marshmallow in black clothing, and he always acted like he was above everyone, like he was in on a little secret to the universe that nobody else could possibly understand. She cranked down her manual window despite the 30 degree weather. Why did she give a rat's ass whether Tita wanted to come or not? Because she was a coward, that's why. She was uncomfortable around strangers, always relying on Tita to break the ice. Her cousin didn't care what others thought of her; that was the difference between them. Pennie was consumed by what others thought, always desperately alone, vulnerable. She stepped on the gas when she hit the interstate.

At Heritage Acres, she drove along the split-rail fence that stretched across the rolling fields, a few gleaming black and brown horses roaming about in their own retirement community. Parking, she checked her reflection in the rearview and grabbed her camera bag before she lost the nerve. Following the signs to the show, she made her way down the wide center aisle between empty stalls to reach the indoor arena full of spectators, the rescue horses prancing, proud with their new lease on life. She tingled with the electricity in the air and made her way to a spot on the benches near the front so she could get some decent shots. Then she saw Stan Lewis near the gate talking with a rugged white-haired woman who looked a little like Bonnie Raitt, wearing red cowboy boots and a black western cowboy hat.

Pennie pulled out the camera and zoomed in to capture Stan smiling, his cheeks ruddy. Then Ward walked into view. She stopped breathing for a moment, her jaw tightening as she zoomed in on his profile, his handsome neckline, a hint of Adam's apple. He laughed with his father and patted the woman's back at some joke. The no-bullshit woman recoiled a little. Ward turned toward Pennie but didn't catch her eye. Bringing the camera down, she watched him survey the crowd around the arena before turning to disappear behind the scenes.

The emcee's upbeat voice came over the speakers, announcing the beginning of the show with the novice riders. Pennie felt more at ease, like she belonged here in the show circuit. The first riders, kids in the ten-to fourteen–year-old group, maneuvered their horses around obstacles and small jumps, the crowd cheering as each child finished a lap around the ring. She snapped pictures of the pretty dappled Appaloosas and the brown chestnut geldings, capturing the small victories of the determined kids in their padded jodhpurs and shiny black boots, their bodies jostling up and down in the joy of their performance.

A procession of different breeds paraded around the oval. She focused on shooting three palomino horses prancing in unison when she was startled by Ward's voice.

"Hello, Pennie." Ward stood in front of her. The familiarity of his smile startled her.

"Hi, h-how are you?"

"Better, now that you're here."

"Your father invited me and I just, on a whim, decided to come and snap a few pictures," she said, still nervous. Pennie held the camera out like she was surprised to find it hanging around her neck.

Ward turned serious. "I didn't know you were a photographer."

"Oh, it's just a hobby. Believe me."

"I'm always looking for someone to get shots of my properties. Maybe I can hire you."

"Like I said, I'm an amateur."

"That's a nice camera."

"Present from my uncle."

"Good 'ol Uncle Alfie."

She picked up the sarcasm. Or was he just trying to be funny? They admired the painted horse with the bareback rider that was in the ring at the moment, a master with the horse.

"Wow," she said, admiring the easy command this rider had over her horse as she rose to a handstand on the saddle.

"Isn't she amazing? I think she comes from a Mi'kmaq tribe up in Canada. She always brings in a crowd. These shows make good money to support Stan's rehab program."

Everyone cheered, mesmerized. Pennie took a few shots of the rider: black hair, bare legs, and a costume of leather fringe moccasins and matching jacket. "What I wouldn't give to be able to ride like that," she said, eying the girl through her lens, the horse stopping short with a command as subtle as a touch.

"Maybe I can give you a lesson."

She laughed. "You don't know what you're offering. I've only been on a horse once in my life and that was a No Baloney Pony at a birthday party when I was eight."

"Sounds like a good time to learn." He smiled that crooked way, one-sided.

Was he toying with her? "To tell you the truth, I've always wanted to learn to ride. I mean, if you really are serious about the offer."

"Of course I'm serious." He touched her hand resting on the zoom lens. "I never offer something I don't come through on."

Shifting her weight, she looked into his olive eyes with specks of black, like the smooth stones on Parsons Beach, where her mother used to take her. Something about him seemed so hidden and complicated. Wearing a bleached white denim shirt and dark jeans, he looked almost too perfect, so unlike his unkempt father who seemed to wear his emotions on his sleeve. She snapped a few more pictures of the acrobat, now doing a headstand on the bare back of the horse.

He said, "Well my daughter's coming up soon, so I should go. Meet me in my dad's office after the show?"

Daughter? "Yeah, sure."

Well, why wouldn't he have a daughter? He was, or had been, married. Not that it mattered anyway. She couldn't believe how jittery she was about meeting him after the show. The fearless bareback rider bounced around to the movements of the horse, able to anticipate its next movement with every headstand or back-bending maneuver before leaving the arena to thunderous applause.

Pennie hoped her hands hadn't shaken too much and that she'd managed to get some decent pictures. Ward was too sure of himself, but somehow she liked that. So different from Kush, who was shy and awkward until you got to know him. Did Dani say he was coming home soon? If she did see him, she'd make it a point to keep things strictly platonic.

A hush fell on the bleachers as a line of teenage girls paraded out, stylish in their English riding gear, the fifteen- to eighteen-year-old group. Propping up her camera, she tried to get a perfect shot of each rider on painted pony, mustang or Appaloosa. Through the lens, she tried to figure out which one was Ward's daughter. Was she the one who sat tall and stiff, smiling in the saddle? Or the petite blonde with the intent concentration? Or the broad-shouldered, sturdy girl who seemed to have command of the ring? Four riders moved to opposing corners and brought their horses to meet in the middle before turning to ride in a perfect tight circle, clockwise then counterclockwise.

Pennie caught Stan Lewis in her lens, standing at the gate watching like a true coach, arms crossed and drumming his thick fingers, completely absorbed. She snapped a few frames of his consternation. Moving to the right, she caught Ward at the base of the stands on the opposite end of the arena. He turned to his right, for a split second, toward a tall slender blonde woman. There was a glance between them, an unspoken exchange that vanished in a moment. Dust flew in the air as the girls trotted around in widening circles. Long red, white, and blue ribbons flew behind them in a lovely crescendo to a perfectly timed show. The crowd cheered for them.

The riders moved in formation toward the gate to leave, as orderly as they'd entered. Pennie put her camera away, tightened the scarf around her hair, and recalled the legend of the owl that Dani had told them about, the Indian maidens tying their eel skins to the tree to trick the young hunter. Summoning the courage to walk down the arena toward Stan Lewis's office, she pictured herself changing her mind. Leaving, hopping in her car, and zooming away, calling Ward later to explain she wasn't feeling well.

But she found her legs carrying her toward the back office, brave enough. The room was just as she remembered it with Stan's cluttered desk, an old dusty neglected computer and coffee cups. She picked up a small framed photograph of a petite blonde girl sitting proudly in the saddle. The same girl she'd seen in the ring moments before, with that same intent focus. This must be his granddaughter, Ward's daughter. Putting the photo back down, she tried to place it exactly in the same dusty spot to look undisturbed.

A door squeaking made her flinch. In walked Ward. "There she is!"

"You know, you don't have to take me for a ride today. You probably have plans with your daughter."

"Not today. She's going home with her mother."

Pennie stared at a picture on the wall of an older woman being nudged playfully by a black and white horse. Ward stood beside her, grazing her elbow. "My mother raised that horse like a child. She and Domino were inseparable."

"Was Domino a rehabilitation horse?"

"He was. She adopted him from a farm up north where he'd been neglected. He's really the reason why this stable got started. My mother had a big heart."

"What happened to Domino?"

"He was over thirty when he died. June 1, 2011."

"You remember the date. He must have been very special to you."

"Not really. I mean, I liked the horse. But I know the date because it was a week after my mother died."

"Oh, I'm sorry to hear that." Pennie swallowed. "What happened?"

"Breast cancer. She was sixty-five. A real tough cookie, too. She put up a good fight for many years, right until the end. Domino seemed to hang on, knew the pain she was in and was there to see her through. Funny how animals can sense things."

She reached out to touch his arm. Ward turned, startled. She said, "I'm so sorry."

"You know what she'd say if she was here right at this moment?"

"What?" Pennie searched his eyes.

"Let's go for a ride!" He extended his arm toward the door.

A stunning landscape emerged before them, an expansive pasture with rolling hills, split-rail fences for miles. Leaning up against the railing, Ward whistled, short and shrill, and three horses looked up from their grazing to come thundering across the pasture. She thought about taking her camera out but didn't want to miss a moment of the amazing beasts bolting toward them. A white horse with black speckles was the first to make it to the gate with a whinny. Ward produced a nugget from his pocket and shook her mane. A pair of mustangs, chestnut coats and black manes, nearly identical in size, nuzzled their way in.

"That's impressive." She reached up to stroke the neck of the white horse, who stared at her.

"Animals and food. They're pretty simple creatures." He watched the white horse nuzzle Pennie. "Wow, I've never seen Sacajawea take to someone so quickly."

"Sacajawea, as in the famous Shoshone woman?"

"That's right. And these two clowns are Lewis and Clark." The stocky mustangs trotted toward the gate, all bravado, swishing their tails. "Looks like they want to get out."

Ward opened the gate to let Sacajawea and one of the mustangs out, the other neighing in protest. "You'll get a turn next time, Clark. Lew's going out today."

Pennie stood back as Ward led the beasts by the halter, one on each side, toward a large sliding door. "Can you hold her?" he asked. "She's fine but has a tendency to run."

Hesitant but game, she took the halter. Sacajawea sputtered, nodding her head up and down. They led the excited horses into the barn and tethered them into place. Ward stroked their necks, preparing the Western saddle and bridle. "We'll go on a trail ride. I'd like to show you the area we're developing."

She relaxed at the thought of riding Western and not that tiny little English saddle. She could even get pictures for her uncle—a productive day—and her headache was almost gone. While Ward saddled Lew, he handed her a brush to run over Sacajawea's coat. The horses leaned into Ward's coaxing, his motions quick and fluid.

Outside, he helped hoist her onto Sacajawea. "Swing that leg around. That's it." He made it look even easier, jumping up on the horse and leading in the direction of the road in one smooth motion. "Don't worry. Sacajawea will follow us. Just relax the reins and rest your hands on the horn."

Pennie felt tall in the saddle, amazed at how easy this horse made the riding. Just a half hour ago she was petrified at the thought of being on a horse. Fear, a constant and almost comforting presence in her life, holding her back, making her overthink, to obsess really. They walked down a hill, the horses dropping into a wide dirt trail that led into the woods. Within minutes, tall pines enclosed them, benevolent sunlight shining down on the trail underfoot. It was a reverent moment, close to peace.

Ward glanced back at her. "Having a good time?"

She felt embarrassed, caught inside herself. "I really needed this," she said.

"Same here." They rode in silence through the quiet woods. The Robert Frost poem came to her, "Stopping by Woods on a Snowy Evening." A poem about death, or possibly rebirth. Little patches of snow scattered along the forest floor, the final vestiges of winter. Spring hung in the air, and she was awakening after a long hibernation, ready to begin anew, even though she wasn't quite sure what that was. Her uncle had given her the space and means to figure herself out.

"When we come out at the end of the trail here, we'll have to cross a road. Just let Sacajawea follow my lead." In the clearing, they stood at the road's edge to let a few cars pass before the horses clip-clopped across. Ward led them up a hill toward the cluster of brick buildings she remembered from her trip here with her uncle. Sacajawea moved up alongside Lew, and Pennie's leg touched Ward's, an intimate exchange without words.

"This was the former Home for the Feeble-Minded," he said.

"I read about its infamous history."

"There was some good, too. The farm gave them work opportunities and a school. But once people entered, they seldom left."

"So it finally closed in the nineties?"

"Right. The state agreed with families that everyone had a right to live in the community."

"Interesting history. Why did your grandfather buy it?"

"He always rode horses growing up in western Maine, so when he saw this farm for sale, he made an offer. He really transformed this place. As you know, my father now manages everything."

They followed another trail into the woods, the wind stirring the branches around them. Sacajawea shook her white mane and swished her tail, the smell of the woods awakening her playful nature. She snorted and Ward said, "What's the matter, girl? Getting a little giddy?"

"She better not giddy-*up*. I'm not ready for anything more than a trot."

He laughed at the chicken in her. "She's a steady girl."

They approached a clearing and Lew picked up the pace. He was ready to run into the open field but Ward reined him in. They stopped to admire the great expanse of rolling fields bordered by tall pines and cedars in the far distance.

"This is it," he said. "We've got about fifty acres here, and there's a road on the other side of the woods. That's where we'll put in the access road to the business park, so it'll have its own entrance. There's ample space here for several large office buildings with plenty of parking. We can keep lots of green space for biking and hiking trails if we can get the town to agree to the project. I've been talking with the business development director in the governor's office, and she thinks it's very feasible to get a high-tech company or a call center here."

Pennie brought her backpack around and took out her camera, but Sacajawea sidestepped and grew unsettled. Pennie grabbed the reins and slid the camera strap over her head. "I think she's troubled about something."

"She's fine. Probably just a little antsy. It's been a long winter, and she hasn't been ridden lately. Be careful. I don't need you falling."

On the green grass alongside the woods, she held onto the reins with one hand and brought the camera up to get some pictures of the wooded area and a path leading to a clearing on the other side and what looked like an old cemetery. The memory of being there, looking at those gravestones with Dani years ago, came back to her.

"Is that a graveyard through the woods?"

"It's the old Home for the Feeble-Minded Patient Cemetery."

"I've been here before," she said, almost to herself. The wind picked up. Out of the trees rose a swirl of white snow, a gust that nearly engulfed them. Sacajawea startled, pulling against the reins. Pennie lost control of the horse, who darted to the left, skirting around Lew and Ward. She could feel herself sliding off the saddle, falling, when Ward caught her under the arms and yelled, "Let go of the stirrup!" She freed her foot just in time, Sacajawea tearing away from them down the hill toward the open spaces.

Hauling her up onto the saddle in front of him, he moved back to make room. "Are you alright? Can you swing your leg over?"

Her foot was wedged underneath her, but she popped it out and brought her leg around to sit facing forward, grabbing hold of the horn.

"Whew!" She breathed deeply. The camera had swung behind her, the strap choking her.

Ward brought it forward, squeezing his arms around her, holding the reins with his right hand. "I don't know what got into her. She's never done that. You okay?"

She rubbed the soreness in her ribs and hot tears filled her eyes. "Just a little surprised is all."

"Hold on. We've got to grab the wild one." With a gentle nudge, Lew trotted down the hill, drawing up alongside Sacajawea, who'd stopped to eat some early green shoots. He made a clicking sound, and when she picked her head up he bent down to grab her reins. "Are you comfortable or squished?"

"I'm just fine." Her heartbeat slowed and they rode along in silence.

A swirl of contrary emotions made her feel almost nauseous, from panicked to protected, abashed to aroused. She leaned back into his arms, riding around the open field, a spiritual place, letting her heart settle.

"Once you put up buildings here, it'll never be the same again," she said.

"You can't stop progress, Pennie. Maine is a poor state, but we can develop it in the right way with the right investments. Like I said, keeping lots of green space."

The wind picked up again and she shivered, pressing against him. Sacajawea let out a high-pitched whinny in protest, her nose flaring.

"Easy, girl. We better head back. It's getting late. Do you mind riding with me?"

"I actually prefer it this way." What was it about him, this stranger, who rattled her and reassured her at the same time?

Ward reined Sacajawea in alongside them until the Appaloosa slowed to a walk, settling onto the trail home. With the mid-March sky darkening, Ward opened his jacket to enclose her.

She breathed in. "That was a weird little snow squall that spooked Sacajawea."

"Is that what it was?" He seemed to be teasing her.

About to defend herself, she stopped. There were more and more things she saw lately that others did not. "Must have been my imagination."

Chapter 8
Crow's Nest

It only took ten minutes to get to Ward's house at the end of a long lonely dirt road. He had offered her the promise of Tylenol, a drink, and dinner, in that order. She parked beside his vintage BMW in front of a contemporary cedar-sided house with interesting angles and skylights.

"This was Stan's place until he decided to move in with his girl-friend."

"Your dad has a girlfriend?"

"Yeah, she's a great lady. Roxanne. She was there at the show. Real animal rights activist."

Pennie pictured the woman in the red cowboy boots and black hat. "I would have expected that. Seems like your father wouldn't hurt a flea."

"He's got a big heart." Ward led her inside and offered to take her coat.

"How long have you been here?"

"About a year, since my wife and I decided to separate."

"Oh, sorry to hear that." She tried her best to disguise her elation.

"It was the best thing for both of us, believe me. And we're doing what's right for Winnie, our daughter."

The open room was a true bachelor's pad: rustic Ponderosa furniture and large wooden tables, the kitchen and bar and a sunken living room to the right. On the far side of the room, a row of floor-to-ceiling windows looked out onto a deck and large backyard surrounded by dense woods. "Great house," she said.

He thanked her, handing over two Tylenol and a glass of water. "I've got stronger painkillers if you need it." She shook her head, despite the tenderness in her side. "How about a beer, glass of wine?"

She considered her shadow of a hangover. "I really shouldn't. Out late last night for St. Paddy's."

"I think you deserve it after that close call."

"Red wine, if you've got it."

He offered her a stool at the bar. "How's your side feeling?"

"Better, thanks."

"That must've been quite a fall on the mountain."

She paused, thinking about how much to share. "Life changing."

He poured her a glass and popped open an IPA. "How so?"

"I landed a decent job with a vet clinic. But after the accident, I don't know—something made me change my mind, and I decided to work for my uncle."

"That's an interesting career move."

"I guess I never could see myself working for a corporation where animals are just a business. So, a month later, I'm now in real estate."

Ward's lips tightened. "Your uncle's one of the best in the business."

An uneasy feeling rose that she couldn't put her finger on. "We're glad your father called us about your project."

"It's his due diligence, but he'd much rather be running the equestrian center. I'm sure you'll find he's less and less involved as the project moves along." He maneuvered around the kitchen, getting chops from the fridge and tongs for the grill. "Got some homemade sauce here, but then I never even asked you if you eat meat."

"Oh, yeah, I'm a carnivore. Tried to quit once but that was a miserable failure."

"Glad you're as bad as the rest of us." He stepped out the back sliding door and opened the stainless-steel grill cover, his contoured face glowing in the flame. She took a sip of the cabernet, the liquid bringing steadiness. What was it about him that was off? Maybe the separation, that he was now an eligible bachelor. But she sensed a hard edge there, a gloominess masked by his graceful movements.

He came back in and smiled. "I'd invite you out on the deck, but it's still chilly. Maybe I'll light a fire."

She wasn't cold in the least, but content to watch him move down to the living room to crumple paper. "There's a turntable if you want to put some music on."

The old console had built-in speakers and a record collection inside. An album sat on the turntable. "Stevie Wonder?"

"Stan's collection. Came with the house."

Maybe it was fate being here tonight with this strange man. The oak furniture seemed like an outgrowth of the house. "How long did you say your father was here?"

"About seven years. Stan sold the old farmhouse in Gray and moved here within a few months after my mother passed." The fire came to life in the old stone hearth, the chimney reaching through the ceiling beams.

"You must miss her."

Ward seemed to ignore the statement. He didn't stand still for long, stepping up to the kitchen, checking the potatoes in the oven. "What about your parents? Still married?"

She folded the paper napkins, placing them under the forks. "My mother died when I was young, and I don't even remember my father." She took another sip of wine, spilling a little down the side of her mouth. So much for being mature. He moved toward her and picked up a napkin to wipe the drip along her chin.

"Sorry to hear that," he said. "What happened to your mother?"

Hands trembling, she gripped the glass, searching for words. "She fell off Tukey's Bridge during a storm. I don't really know the details, to tell you the truth." She had her own mask on now, wanting to remain hidden inside her own fragile past but also yearning to let go of it. She leaned toward him.

Brushing a strand of hair that'd fallen in her eyes, he kissed her forehead. All the nerves that had consumed her that day—from showing up at the horse show by herself to the trail ride, the spooking of the Appaloosa, and Ward's being there at just the right moment—brought her to an uneasiness.

"Ward, I don't know what I'm doing here."

"Believe me, I'm as confused as you are." He drew her close, so close she could feel the pulse in his neck, could still smell horse on him. They stood like that, in a strange embrace, the fire popping, the music soft. "Sometimes we just need a person to hold on to. You ever feel like that?"

"I don't know if I thanked you for catching me."

"You don't have to." He rubbed her arms until she brought them up to meet his embrace, reaching around him, giving in.

"Promise me something?" he asked. She looked into his smooth, speckled eyes. "Promise me you'll trust me."

She leaned into his waiting mouth. He kissed her very softly, intensely, but just for a moment.

"I don't want to jump into anything too quickly, Penelope. I don't know what it is about you, but you make me feel like myself again." He sighed and moved his rough chin against her forehead. She fell away, her lips wanting from the kiss, and pulled a chair out from the table to steady herself.

He disappeared again and came back trailing the smell of charcoal and barbeque. "Pork chops a la Lewis," he said, placing them on the table.

"What can I get?"

"Nothing, just relax."

It was like she'd moved into another universe for grown-ups. She remembered mealtimes growing up on Pine Street in her aunt and uncle's home where she was usually the one designated to serve others. He piled her plate with steaming food. "Dig in," he said, and they plowed into their plates, trying to maintain manners despite their hunger. It was already past seven. They managed a few words between their shared cravings, cleaning every piece of meat from the bone, wiping the homemade sauce from their chins. "I love a girl with an appetite."

"No problem there. I could stand to lose a little." She patted her stomach.

"Don't be silly. You're perfect. Now what can we have for dessert? Hmmm." He caressed his chin. "I've got some leftover ice cream with freezer burn or perhaps some cookies cemented to the bottom of the cookie jar?"

"I'm fine." She laid her head back, remembering the eerie feeling at the cemetery. "You know, I had the strangest sensation today when Sacajawea got spooked."

"Like what?"

"Like there was something that came out of the woods, like a snow squall sweeping up and around us."

"Sounds like a ghost!" He half-smirked.

"Don't make fun. I'm being serious right now. I've had a lot of these bizarre experiences lately, ever since my accident."

Ward turned sober. "How do you mean?"

"I don't know. Like I saw this guy walking on Baxter Boulevard with this same kind of mini snow squall around him. It was so bizarre. Then I saw that same guy at a restaurant last night and there was a girl sitting beside him that looked like, well, not really there."

"Not really there?"

"Like she was...intangible." She knew how she sounded. "But I did have a few drinks in me."

"Please don't tell me you're going over the deep end. I don't need to jump into another one of those relationships again."

Another one of those relationships? Maybe she shouldn't have said anything. She tried to sound sensible. "It's just that I seem to have this heightened sense of everything around me."

"I've heard people say near-death experiences are like traveling through a dark tunnel toward a bright light."

The memory of Boone's spirit caused the pain in her side to return, flooding her with a dark aching. "No, it was nothing like that." The comfort of full stomachs eased their conversation. But she avoided any more talk of premonitions or her own foolish sensitivities.

THE NEXT MORNING, SHE woke up to the sound of steady rain. Her pulse quickened, remembering the kiss, Ward's whispers still in her ear. *I don't know what it is about you.* Looking out her window onto the park of the Western Promenade, she thought of Boone and the car accident. She fought the urge to pick up the phone and call Ward, to invite him over so she didn't have to be alone in the dreariness.

On her cell was a voicemail from Tita the day before. Irritation rose inside her as she listened. "Hey, sorry about this morning. After you called, I crashed, and I swear I never heard my phone ring. Call me and let me know how the show was!" Maybe Tita really did fall asleep. Besides, if she had gone with her to the show, Pennie never would have had dinner with Ward. She called back.

"Thanks for standing me up."

"Sorry about that! I was so comatose after St. Paddy's."

"Me, too, but I still got my ass out of bed."

"Did you end up meeting up with the hot real estate guy?"

She remembered her conversation with Dani. "Word travels fast."

"Get any action?"

"Are you really going there? Of course not."

"Let's face it, other than the one-night stand with the ski patrol, you've been walking around like a lost soul since Kush left."

"I don't have to have a boyfriend to define myself."

Tita scoffed. "What's that supposed to mean?"

"Nothing." She stared at the raindrops sliding slowly down her window, wondering how she'd occupy herself, get out of her own head. "What are you doing today?"

"Not sure, yet. Teddy, Lars, and I are just watching Netflix."

She pictured them curled up together on her bed in the carriage house studio. "I think I'll lay in bed myself for a while."

Hanging up the phone, she shook her head at Dani for having such a big mouth. She rolled over, her side tender, remembering Ward's arms around her as she was leaning back against him in the saddle. He'd been so attentive. She wanted to hear his voice again but made herself put the cell down on her nightstand. Her camera bag sat on the floor. Forcing herself up, she went to the kitchen to put some coffee on and grab her laptop from the desk. Looking at pictures was like opening a present, the anticipation of secret surprises inside the images.

Hopping back into bed, she plugged the camera into her computer, watching images pop up in rapid succession. The profile of friendly Stan Lewis came up, talking with the woman who reminded her of Bonnie Raitt, Roxanne. Then Ward came into full view, looking right at her, those stonewashed eyes. So confident, traces of gray at his temples, barely visible because of his light-colored hair that was thick and cropped short around the sides. He was certainly nothing like his father.

She canvassed the shots of horses and young riders so proud in their dressage. Then the pictures of the young Mi'kmaq woman on bareback—the first shot a little blurry, disappointing. Pennie remembered Ward standing beside her at that point, disarming her. The next shot was good, though: a perfect handstand on the steady mount, her feet dressed in moccasins pointed straight up.

Ward's daughter, the young petite blonde, came into view, her serious demeanor full of concentration. Those lovely olive eyes passed down from her father, intent and focused. Behind her, the shadow of a horse appeared, the hazy outline of a rider. Pennie's vision blurred. Focusing, she blinked, and the shadow disappeared before reappearing and disappearing again, a soft light flickering on and off. She picked up her laptop and looked at the battery symbol. Fully charged. She went back to the image, but the vibrating shadow had completely disappeared. The next image of red, white, and blue ribbons trailing the horses showed vibrant and clear. Then Ward's pretty almost-ex-wife, her white-blonde hair in a ponytail, looking back at him—a friendly exchange between a separated couple.

Images of the fields around Heritage Acres came up, long dark streaks from the stately pine trees bordering the property creating a ladder pattern in the afternoon sun. Then another blurry frame, and she remembered trying to get the camera steady as Sacajawea started beneath her.

That should have been a warning, but somehow, she kept the camera up to get a shot of the woods, a clear image of trunks of pines and oaks and cedars, a small path to an old graveyard through the trees but no swirl of snow. What had she seen?

She arrowed back to the photo of the entire fifty-acre parcel. Ward was waiting for the town of Fairview to approve the development. She remembered his wide sinewy hands spreading out the blueprint as he expounded on the placement of the three buildings for maximum southerly exposure, a green business complex with a network of trails all around.

Closing the photos, she looked back through her search results, clicking on websites about the Home for the Feeble-Minded, the different superintendents who'd run the place, the judges who'd sent juvenile delinquents and "mental defectives" to work on the hilltop farm or in the kitchen, in the laundry or at the hospital. Often poverty, not retardation, was the reason towns sent people to the farm, leaving them wards of the state, committed by a judge or a physician. It only took one person to hand down a life sentence.

By 1952, numbers escalated to a high of fifteen hundred residents, two hundred employees, only one fully licensed physician, and fifty-one buildings, including a hospital and dormitories, where hundreds were warehoused. Lacking enough staff, they resorted to strapping inmates in at night or using straitjackets, even scalding and beating the patients. The institution eventually lost its accreditation and officially closed in 1996, the residents given rights of self-determination, to live in the community with supports.

The rain had stopped. Through her bedroom window, the sun cast a ray on her screen, on her cold coffee cup. She jumped when her ringtone sounded from under her covers. Pulling it out, Ward's name flashed. She gathered herself and sat up.

"Hope I didn't wake you."

"Oh, no, I've been up for a while." She dabbed the coffee drippings on her pajamas.

"Sleep good?"

"Great. You?"

"Better than I have in a long time. Since the separation really. It's been difficult."

The images of his daughter, his wife, came back to her. "You've been separated a year?"

"Almost exactly. It seems serendipitous that I've met you now."

Her pulse quickened. "I found myself thinking about you this morning." She looked at her screen, the black-and-white pictures of the old institution, a bulldozer destroying one of the old hilltop farm buildings.

"Good thoughts, I hope."

"I enjoyed our dinner last night."

"Me, too. If you're not sick of me already, I wondered if you might want to do something today. I'm feeling a little cooped up. Can I take you to lunch?"

She looked out onto the drenched street and green grass. "I'd love to get out for lunch...and to see you again." A silence like a secret wish fell on the line. Was she disarming him, like he did her? The grave and composed Ward?

"Pick you up in an hour?"

That was not nearly enough time but at this moment she'd do whatever he wanted and rattled off her address before hanging up, her whole body vibrating with expectation. Pressing her hand against the cold window and looking at her broken nails that were starting to heal, her dream of the husky and the necklace resurfaced. What could it mean?

She'd been inside the body of the dog, intently focused on what was buried, digging. Searching for what?

When the buzzer rang, she grabbed her umbrella and purse before checking her face in the small mirror beside the bedroom door. Swiping on some lip gloss, she hurried out and down the flight of stairs to find him on the stoop in the sunlight.

"Let's hope you don't need that." He took the hand holding the small red umbrella.

Pennie's breath caught as he moved toward her and kissed her on the mouth. A soft, insistent kiss. She looked away and up towards the now clear sky. "I hope it stays clear."

He opened the BMW door and she fell into the bucket seat. "Nice car."

"I need to trade up, but I've had this one so long it's hard to give up while it's still running."

"Sounds like me and my VW. We've been through a lot together."

"You get attached to these old friends." He took the wheel and shifted into drive. "This is a great neighborhood. How'd you find the apartment?"

She remembered Uncle Alfie helping to gather her things from the front lawn the morning she was kicked out. They loaded the Karmann Ghia, then he gave her a scrap of paper with this address and a phone number. "My uncle had a client who inherited the building, so I grabbed the open unit. Now I just have to figure out how to keep paying rent."

"Expensive?"

"Let's just say I can squeak by on my meager salary."

He shifted gears through the intersection. "Are you interested in the law?"

The Beemer rattled and rumbled, a loud vibration that moved through her body. "No. It's really just a way for me to avoid the corporate job."

"Where's your heart?"

"I thought I wanted to be a vet, but that dream faded. Now that I turned down a perfectly decent job, here I am, not sure what I want to do with my life."

"Took me until almost forty to figure out that development was my thing."

She considered his age. Maybe about ten years older than her? He parked on the slope of Dartmouth Street, cranked on the emergency brake before turning to face her. "You know, when I graduated from college, I went to law school because that's what I'd always wanted to do, just like my grandfather. But when I got there, I was miserable, so I dropped out."

"How did you get into real estate?"

"Took a job with a surveyor and was happy that summer. But I was truthfully more excited about developing property. Point is, follow your passion."

"I'm not exactly twenty and trying to find my path. I feel like I'm drifting along, waiting for the right thing to hit me. But I will say I love working with my uncle."

He pointed to the brick building beside them. "Want to see the condos I'm working on?" He hoisted out a heavy key ring from his coat pocket. "Office space on the first floor, condos on the second and third."

They walked through the large double front door into a dim dusty hallway, the walls half torn down, the floors plywood. "We're rebuilding the frame. You can't believe the work we've done just to get it structurally sound. Contractors are building out office space next week. Things are really changing in Portland, lots of new startups looking for space. Let me show you upstairs."

The second floor lay wide open, all the walls torn down. A coldness moved through Pennie. The room grew dim as a cloud covered the sun. "Are you cold?"

"Just a chill." She hugged herself.

Putting his arm around her shoulders, he snuggled her. "We don't want that." She leaned into him as he talked about the four condos he envisioned: radiant-heat floors, quartz countertops, and en suite baths. Turning toward another flight of stairs, she hesitated, rubbing her arms to get the circulation back. "Don't worry, the structure's sound, all the stairways are rebuilt."

Taking his hand, she walked up to the third floor—open space with windows facing east toward the occan. "This is what I wanted you to see." All of Casco Bay lay before them, the Million Dollar Bridge to the right, a distant Peaks Island to the left, the whitecaps heaving with a tugboat plowing along.

"This is spectacular."

He came behind, hugging her, willing her to let her defenses down. Still, she stiffened. Why was he so familiar so fast? As he moved his hands along her arms once again, she leaned back against him.

"As soon as I get the other three condos filled, I plan to move in here. Give or take a year, I'm out of Stan's bachelor pad. You wanna see the crow's nest?" Taking her by the hand, not waiting for an answer, he led her up a narrow flight of stairs. When she placed her foot on the first step, another icy chill filled her veins.

He tugged on her hand. "Let's go up. It's perfectly safe."

She followed him up the narrow stairs, then heard a faint noise. Sobbing? "What's that?" she said, following him up.

"What's what?" Surrounded by windows, the sea beyond them an open vista, she grew lightheaded. "I don't hear anything." He took her hands in both of his, like a prayer. "Your hands are freezing."

Again, the muted sound, like a girl crying. Turning, she looked at Ward to see if he had heard it, too.

He focused his stone eyes on her. "Are you okay?"

"Feeling a little woozy."

"Afraid of heights?"

"A little." She had never had any fear of heights in her life but turned to head down the narrow stairway. The sobbing grew louder. She ran to the next stairway on the second floor and jumped every other step until she had her hands on the front door handle.

Close behind, Ward took her shoulder. "You spooked or something?"

"Is there anyone in the building next door?"

"Those are artist studios, so sure, someone could be around."

"I thought I heard a girl crying." She shrugged, trying to put on her brave face and dismiss it for Ward's sake, and stepped outside. "It's a great building."

"As long as we don't have any ghosts up there." He took her hand. "How about a bite to eat? That'll make you feel better."

Looking back up at the cupola, the "crow's nest" as he called it, she recalled the photos from that morning, flickering on and off. Ghosts. Silly superstitions. She wondered if she was making things up in her own mind.

They rounded the cobblestone corner, walking downhill. A group of young Black boys skateboarded toward them, and Ward grabbed her hand to cross the street.

"Why are you crossing here?"

"What?"

"Why are we crossing the street? The pizza place is on the other side."

"Oh, I was just trying to get out of their way." He met her eyes. Pennie shook off the idea that Ward was avoiding, or even afraid of, the boys. She squeezed his hand.

One block downhill, they arrived at the same place she and Dani had shared a pizza on St. Paddy's night. The host sat them at a table near the fireplace. Ward ordered a large pie and two pints of Shipyard Ale. Looking up at the bar, she recalled the man sitting on the barstool and the shadow of a girl beside him. Was she going crazy? Was it too much alcohol? She was completely sober today, but sort of woozy, floaty. Taking a sip of beer, she let Ward's easy way take control, lulling her into his story.

"You know, my father was disappointed in me after I left law school. That was hard on me. We've had a tense relationship, but I've always tried to keep our communication open. He can be very hardheaded sometimes." Reaching for her across the table, he said, "It was especially hard when he took my wife's side in the separation. But she wanted a husband who was home for dinner every night and there for her every day of every weekend. Especially after Winnifred was born. Before then, we seemed to have our own space, you know? I can't help it if I'm ambitious, and I won't apologize for it."

"I think it's important to have your own lives." She wondered if he was a good father. It certainly seemed that way at the horse show, but what did she know of married life and kids? Her only reference was her aunt and uncle, who seemed to have a good balance of home time and away time; Uncle Alfie had his business and friends around town, and Aunt Aggie had her friends and bridge club.

When the food arrived, Ward served her a slice of pesto chicken pizza. "If you don't mind, after lunch I think I'll head over to the office to catch up on some stuff."

"Oh, speaking of, did you send those plans of the development to the office?"

"You should have them on your desk tomorrow morning."

"I wanted to look at the area where you're putting the road in."

His eyes narrowed. "Yes, of course. I'm anxious to get the ball rolling." He forced a smile and she again reached for his hand across the table to soften anything she may have said.

"Let's go on a trail ride again soon." She desperately wanted him to like her.

"You enjoyed yourself?"

"Other than nearly breaking my neck, yes. Good thing you were there to save me."

"Give me the chance." He leaned forward with those washed eyes.

Locking into his gaze, she met him halfway and kissed him.

At the office early the next day, she searched for any information on the web about the Heritage Acres parcel that Ward envisioned for the technology campus. Her uncle showed up around nine with the dogs, a cardboard cylinder under his arm, coffee and pastry bag in his hands. He shut the door with his foot. "How's my bright Pennie this fine morning?"

"Just waking up. You're in a good mood today. Where's Tita?"

He hung his wool coat in the closet. "Not sure, she disappeared after dinner last night. Probably went over to what's-his-name's."

"Lars."

"Anyhow, I'm sure she'll pop in when the moment suits her. You can get the phone until she arrives, I trust."

"Yes, of course. What have you got there?" She pointed to the cylinder.

"Plans from Ward Lewis. Just ran into the courier downstairs. One thing you can say, he's prompt."

Pennie thought of a few other alliterative adjectives to describe him ...perfectly proportioned, powerful, prurient, persistent. "Yeah, he said he was sending them this morning."

"Talked to him over the weekend, did you?"

"He was there at Stan's horse show on Saturday." Doing her best to hide the bubbles rising inside her, she took a sip of coffee. "His daughter rides at the equestrian center."

"Have a good time, then?"

"Absolutely. He even took me on a trail ride." She tried her best to remain nonchalant, unsmiling.

"Who, Stan?"

"No, Ward." She let her voice trail off, watching the familiar scowl come over his face, following him into his office. "He just, um, was polite enough to show me the property, that's all."

He sat with a huff. "Well then, what can you tell me about it? You've seen more than I have." Cassie curled up on the floor under his feet while Fella and Daisy took their respective corners on the couch, all eyes on her, the judge and jury.

"It's a beautiful piece of land, rolling pastures, bordered by a forested area on one side, facing east, I think. I'll have to look at the lot layout."

Jostling the plans from the tube with the dexterity of handling thousands over the years, Uncle Alfie placed a heavy metal ruler on one end and a paperweight on the other to get his bearings. He thumped the right corner with his index finger like he was inserting a puzzle piece.

"This is the area here he's talking about. The woods are on the southeast border and looks like there's a road on the other side, runs parallel to the property."

"Right, that's where he wants to put the access road into the campus."

"Hmmm." He traced a row of markings along the roadside. "Looks like a cemetery right there. That might pose some problems."

She recalled the horse spooking, the swirl of something in the woods, seeing the graveyard through the trees, the headstones. Her skin crawled.

"You okay?"

With a start, she spilled her coffee on the edge of the plans. "Oh, jeez, sorry."

"No harm done." He grabbed a napkin and wiped up the drips, leaving a small stain where Ward had drawn in building number 3 of the campus. Taking a large bite of his lemon scone, he ran his finger along the borderline of another property beside the access road that Ward proposed. "Not too much wiggle room here for a setback. Ward'll need three yards or more between the graveyard and the neighbor's property, which is right along this stone wall here. Unless, of course, he gets permission from the homeowner to move it. But maybe he's already done his homework, has enough clearance. He mention anything to you about it?"

"Not a thing." But it seemed like an important thing, really, the proposed road sandwiched between a graveyard and another property.

They heard the door: Tita. The dogs jumped up, tails wagging, Fella barking. She appeared, flushed from running, her hair wild, peeking into the office. "Hi, sorry I'm late. Had to get gas and drop Lars off at the editing suite."

"Glad you could join us today, Tita Bell." He kept his eyes on the plans. "When you come in for a landing at your desk, give the bank a call. They've got a few foreclosures."

"Okay, sure." She growled at the dogs to move until they trotted back to their places on the couch.

"As I was saying, why don't you call the code enforcement officer over there in Fairview and ask them what they need for a setback here. I'll follow up with Ward."

"That's all I need to ask?"

"Just tell them it's about the fifty-acre development out at Heritage Acres."

She closed the office door and took her seat at the orange desk. Tita was already on the phone getting the information from the bank. Even though she seemed a little flaky sometimes, she was quite impressive on the phone, sounded like she knew what she was talking about. Tita caught her look and crossed her eyes. "Yes," she said, pointing a gun to her head like she wanted to blow her brains out. "Of course. I'll send a courier over to get the documents."

The phone rang again almost as soon as Tita hung up. "Sorry, Mrs. McCarthy, he's on another call. How can I help?"

Tita shot Pennie a grimace before putting on her consoling voice. "Yes, I completely understand, ma'am. He should be free very soon." Pennie waved at her to forward the call. "Would you like to speak to Pennie?"

Picking up, Pennie immediately heard the unabashed fear across the line. The police had been there, had examined the area where the necklace was found and had also found Chloe's bracelet, a horse charm bracelet.

"A charm bracelet?"

"I thought it was strange that that necklace reappeared, but the bracelet? I remember her beautiful little hands together in the casket with that bracelet on..." Scenarios circled Pennie's mind, searching for some logic. It was impossible. "Penelope, I need a good criminal attorney, someone not connected to our family."

She could hear Jack and Ginger yipping in the background. "I'll have my uncle call you as soon as he's off the phone. I'm so sorry, Mrs. McCarthy." She hung up.

Tita stared at her. "You're sheet white. What's going on?"

Uncle Alfie opened his door. "What's wrong with you two? Somebody die?"

Tita sat up. "It was Mrs. McCarthy, she's pretty upset. The police just left."

He eyed Pennie. "You speak with her?"

"Just for a moment. She said the police also found Chloe's bracelet at the same place the necklace was dug up. She said Chloe was buried wearing the same bracelet."

Tita leaned forward. "What? Does she think she was dug up?"

Uncle Alfie scratched his chin. "Maybe some kind of strange coincidence. Anything else?"

"No. No, that's about it. Poor woman. Wants you to recommend a criminal attorney."

"All kinds of nasty things are unearthed in real estate. Other than the property business, it's out of our hands. I'll give her a call."

Turning away so her uncle could not see the tears welling in her eyes, she stared out the window, struggling to fully understand why she was overcome with emotion. It was the girl, something about Chloe and what happened to her. Cassie came to lean against her.

THAT NIGHT, TOSSING AND turning, she fell into a fitful sleep. Darkness consumed her and she found herself on the bridge again. A blurry shape of someone in the distance, leaning over the railing, their long hair a wild tangle. Her own legs, an unrelenting pressure, weighted like tree trunks, moved in slow motion toward her mother's despair. Feeling a low vibration behind her, she turned to see car lights coming toward her, racing by, directly toward her mother, who jumped into the storm.

Chapter 9
Revelations

Pennie and her uncle rode in silence to Heritage Acres to take a "look-see," he said, at the proposed area for the road. She had decided to take a wait-and-see approach with the McCarthy situation. If she said anything more about her "premonitions," he would begin removing her from field work and she'd end up doing paperwork and answering phones with Tita.

He drove with his knee, explaining that Ward had already called a surveyor to come out and double-check the cemetery setback. "He doesn't waste any time."

Pennie knew his irritation, like pulling back an insistent untrained dog. She wanted to say, *You mean he's pushy,* but kept her commentary to herself. When the equestrian center came into view, she craned her neck behind her uncle's balding head, looking for Ward's BMW. No cars around. "I think he's got some great ideas. It's very exciting to think we could have a state-of-the-art technology center right here in Maine."

"Everything in due course, my dear."

"I'm sure Ward wants to do everything correctly to avoid any problems in the future."

He turned onto Gray Road. "Pennie, you've got a lot of trust in this man already. You'll have to forgive me. I've been screwed a few too many times. The cynic comes out." The creases in the corners of his eyes told her to stuff her wide-eyed ideals in a sock. Stopping alongside the road, he parked in front of the cemetery, groups of headstones of all shapes and sizes dotting the sloped grassy area. A dirt road lined with small beech trees and an old stone wall ran along the left side of the graveyard, creating a natural borderline between the road and a neighboring property. She took out her camera.

Uncle Alfie walked along the stone wall, gravel crunching underfoot. "Try to get a few angles between the cemetery and the stone wall." She followed him, snapping shots of the headstones, a mix of shiny speckled granite and small, decaying, cockeyed memorials. She half expected a swirling squall to appear but sensed nothing unusual and remained focused, getting every angle possible. Maybe it was her uncle whistling the Patsy Cline song "Walkin' after Midnight" that kept her hand steady.

At the back of the cemetery, they found another graveyard on the small sloping section toward the woods, six long rows of small mottled gray headstones no larger than ancient Egyptian tablets like she'd seen at the Smithsonian years ago.

"Look at this," he said, pointing to a stately granite monument facing the headstones. Out of the top rose the shape of a carved island in stone, the Malaga Island Memorial. Below was the engraved history:

FROM THE 1860s UNTIL 1912, A COMMUNITY OF LABORERS AND FISHERMEN LIVED ON MALAGA ISLAND OFF THE COAST OF PHIPPSBURG. A CONTROVERSIAL COMMUNITY FOR ITS TIME, WHITE AND BLACK RESIDENTS MARRIED AND LIVED TOGETHER ON THE SMALL ISLAND UNTIL THE STATE OF MAINE EVICTED THEM IN 1912. INCLUDED IN THE EVICTION WAS THE STATE'S REMOVAL OF THE ISLAND CEMETERY TO THE GROUNDS OF THE MAINE SCHOOL FOR THE FEEBLE MINDED WHERE SOME ISLAND RESIDENTS WERE COMMITTED. REMEMBERED HERE ARE THE COMMUNITY MEMBERS EXHUMED FROM THE MALAGA ISLAND CEMETERY BY THE STATE AND THOSE WHO DIED HERE AS PATIENTS.

To the left side were names of the Marks family, who were committed and died at the Maine School for the Feeble-Minded, and on the other side, the names of seventeen islanders whose bodies were exhumed then buried here.

The memory of being here with Dani surfaced. It had to have been at least ten years ago when Dani had shown her these graves, told her about her ancestors buried here. "I think Dani and Mali are related to some of these people."

"I'm not surprised. Sad for that community. Those were different times."

The small headstones jutted from the ground like flat teeth in long rows of twenty or more. "Doesn't feel like it, with all the racism in the world today." She thought about Ward in Portland, crossing the street away from the group of Black boys. She backed up and snapped pictures of the tombstones of three nameless Eason children and two nameless Griffin children, of Jake Marks, Harold Murphy, Elizabeth Darling, Calvin and Laura Tripp—all the same date of November 1912. The same undefined date on each grave marker.

"Penelope, the perimeter's fine."

She kept moving, capturing all of them, stepping across the mossy blanket, drawn to the souls of the islanders exhumed and reinterred. "There's a dark truth in their displacement," she said, more to herself than anyone.

He walked back toward the woods, following the path where Ward wanted to build the road, then stopped. He clasped his hands in contemplation, turning back to look up the slope toward the main road where they had parked. "This is tight. What did that code enforcement fella tell you was the legal setback?"

"Twenty-five feet," she said.

"We'll have to see what the surveyor comes up with. Not sure if the stone wall is on the cemetery side or on the Greenleaf property side. Makes it very tight."

"Do you know if Ward talked to those neighbors?" She pointed to the white Cape sitting back from the road.

"They'd be notified by the town by now. Besides, that's Stan Lewis's girlfriend's place, so I suspect she knows all about it."

Pennie moved her focus away from the lens. "Roxanne lives there?"

"You know her?"

"I saw her with Stan at the horse show. Why didn't he tell us about her property?"

"I imagine she's not happy about this. Stan is trying to do the right thing by hiring us."

Then it sank in. What a strange situation she was in, privy to information that Ward might share with her that she'd feel obligated to tell her uncle, while holding her tongue about anything he might want to know. "Any other options?"

"This is a pretty narrow right-of-way the cemetery association gave him, so unless they own that stone wall and give Ward the approval to take it down, or Roxanne owns the stone wall and gives Ward the okay to take it down, there's no way he'll meet the setback."

Looking into the woods and the pathway to the pastureland on the other side where she and Ward had stopped, she felt the familiar dull throb in her ribs, the eerie sense of something here. She snapped a few more pictures, the same vibrating sensation beginning to rise inside her like a wave of nausea, a slow thrumming. Out of the dense trees flew a large black bird, straight as an arrow toward her, squawking in a panic. Pennie stumbled backward and fell, her head landing inches from a small gravestone.

Her uncle lumbered toward her, swearing. "Jesus, Penelope. Are you alright?"

She wrestled the camera, still strapped around her neck, looking up into the cloudy sky. "Yes, I'm fine. Damn bird. More worried about the camera."

He gave her a hand as she brushed the grass from her ass. "Don't worry about the damn camera. Watch what you're doing."

"I don't know what's the matter with me." The tremor still reverberated underneath her, barely perceptible like the snow squall through the trees she'd seen, warning her either to stay far away or to look deeper.

HER KARMANN GHIA RATTLED at the stoplight. She needed a new muffler but didn't have the money. If her uncle knew, he'd insist on taking it in to his mechanic, but she was determined to be self-reliant, especially after dropping out of grad school. Her student loans—a whopping $1,200 a month— were coming due in July, only four months away, and she didn't know how she would be able to pay along with rent, utilities, gas, and on and on.

Her phone buzzed. Rummaging, she fished it out to see the caller: Dani. Just who she needed to talk to. "Hey, stranger."

"Hey, Miss Moneypenny. Recovered from St. Paddy's Day?"

"Barely. Thanks for staying over."

"Good times with you, as always. Still getting haunted by ghosts on barstools?"

"Very funny. You know me, I've got a big imagination." She didn't know where to begin with that. The spooked horse, the bird diving at her from the woods, the Malaga graves.

"Do you have any plans tonight? Kush is in town and Max invited him over. I don't want to be a third wheel."

"Where's Mali?"

"Accounting class tonight. Thank God she likes the numbers part of this business. They just make my head hurt. C'mon, Pen. You never know, he might be ready to move back to Portland."

"Did he tell Max that?"

"No, but you never know."

The thought of Kush made her glow, but she stopped herself, wondering if this thing with Ward was going anywhere.

Dani sensed her hesitancy. "C'mon, what's the harm?"

"Alright, I've got nothing else going on. Besides, I need to talk to you about a cemetery."

She drove up to the Western Prom to watch the sunset at the spot where Boone had been hit by the car. Sadness overwhelmed her, but it also gave her some peace to stand on the side of the road by the wooden bench where he'd taken his last breath. Closing her eyes, she breathed, in and out, trying to reach a meditative state of calm. The sky was purplish pink and jets soared overhead toward the Portland jetport.

One thing she could use was a vacation far, far away. Maybe she could talk Kush into going on a spontaneous trip, anyplace warm with miles of white sand. They could escape and not think about the future, just a blissful week swimming in a balmy aquamarine sea. The setting sun began to settle something inside her, calmed her scattered mind. There was a reason why Kush was home today, she felt it. He was here to bring her back to reality, before she went headlong into a relationship with an older man she hardly knew. But Kush had left her and moved on, hadn't he? He had left her there and she was now falling for someone else, grasping at another relationship to save her.

She recalled the Saturday mornings she and Kush spent in bed talking about nothing and watching reruns of *Seinfeld*, the characters never seeming to get old, the same jokes a welcome distraction in a chaotic world. One of her favorite episodes was when Elaine fell on the woman in the sauna, only to find out her perfect breasts were real. Pennie laughed out loud at the part where the superbly breasted woman left Jerry's apartment in a huff, saying, "They're real and they're spectacular!"

Why had Kush expected *her* to follow *him*? Wasn't she worth staying here for? Looking at her phone, she realized how late it was getting. No need to change. Other than a grass stain from falling at the cemetery, she looked fine. *What you see is what you get.* She realized she hadn't even offered to bring anything to Dani's place. Too late. Pushing herself up and off the bench, she crossed the road toward her car.

Wheeling onto Congress, she found a parking spot on the street across from their loft, the familiar light on over the tall double-door entryway. Kush's unmistakable figure came into view, tall and slender. A woman was on his arm. Pennie's heart stopped. He looked down at this stranger under the pooling doorway light and they laughed at a shared joke. She had a lovely angular profile and long, straight, dark hair that he smoothed like a ponytail, just the way he used to do with her. Pennie felt herself pulling her own hair back, shocked.

Hunching down behind the steering wheel, she started her car again and backed up, watching them enter the building, her pulse thumping. Dani must not have known or she would have warned her. How could he have a girlfriend already? It had only been a few months! Squealing down Congress, she yelled inside the car, "I'm spectacular! Do you hear me, Kush, you asshole? I'm spectacular!" Veering onto Baxter Boulevard, swerving around joggers in the dark through watery eyes, her own stupid pathetic fantasies began to amuse her in some crazed way. She laughed and cried and laughed and cried until snot came out her nose. "I'm radiant! Do you know that Kush? Just like Charlotte wove in her web, I'm fucking *radiant*!"

The phone rang. It must be Dani, finally calling with a warning for her. She put the phone to her ear to share her desperate moment of misery, only to hear Ward's deep voice. "Hey, you. What are you up to?"

She used her coat sleeve to clear the snot from her nose. "Just heading home, thinking about how poor I am."

"Are you okay? You sound all stuffed up."

"A cold coming on. Could use a Caribbean vacation to get me out of this never-ending hellhole of a winter."

"Well, I can't help you there, not just yet. How about dinner instead?"

She examined her puffy eyes in the rearview, shifted down into second, and turned toward a steady stream of traffic. "I'm pretty tired."

"I made a lasagna last night and it's ready to pop in the oven."

Why shouldn't she give herself this? Didn't she *deserve* this? "How can I refuse your fine Italian cuisine?"

"You simply can't refuse me."

She could hear his rattling BMW starting up. They were clattering car twins. "No, I guess not. Can I pick up a bottle of wine?"

"Whatever you'd like. Meet me at my place in forty-five? I'm just leaving the office."

Hanging up, Pennie's mind moved away from thoughts of Kush and his new plus-one to more promising matters. Ward Lewis, the real estate man who could handle a horse, any horse, and she bet those skills transferred to other things.

Her phone buzzed—a voicemail from Dani and text with their old private code: *Warning. Do not pass go...Do not collect $200.*

"Too little, too late!" she screamed at her phone and threw it in her bag, thinking about picking up wine from her favorite market before heading north to Ward's place.

SHE MOVED BETWEEN THE crowds of hipsters to the stairway down to the basement where the odd little hunched man stacked shelves, the wine-seller in the wine cellar. Without looking up, he said, "What can I help you find today?"

"Hello, Mr., um, Mr.—"

"Snodgrass is the name."

Snodgrass, interesting. "I'd like a Chianti, if you've got anything on special."

"Back right corner. The Ravazzi Borioso is on sale this week."

She moved to the rear, thinking about how much she loved the smell. Like cigars, blackberries, old books, and something ancient she couldn't put her finger on. She liked the soulful music playing in the background. Pulling out the Chianti from the rack, the whirlwind of the day circled her mind. Mrs. McCarthy's distraught voice came back to her, the police, Chloe's bracelet.

"Did you find it?" She jumped, her hand on her heart. "Didn't mean to scare you, Penelope."

How did he know her name? He took the bottle from her and peered down at the label. "Yes, 2019. A nice bottle for the price." She followed him to the counter, and he punched the keys on the old register with the ivory buttons. "Anything else? Port perhaps?"

"No, thank you."

"Did you lose someone?"

Heat rose under her sweater. "Not really. Just my mind."

"Nothing that a good bottle of red won't fix."

"By the way, what is this music?"

"You like it?"

"It's great."

"'I Put a Spell on You' by the timeless Nina Simone. I just happen to have a few albums for sale." He pointed to a stack behind the counter. "It'll be perfect for your Italian tonight."

"How did you—right, the Chianti. You don't miss a trick, do you? Lucky for me, a friend promised lasagna."

"Lucky friend," he said, barely cracking a smile.

Was this funny old man flirting with her? He rang her up and slipped the dusty old album inside the bag. She pictured Stan's old turntable console in the sunken living room. What a coincidence that the wine-seller sold record albums here. She'd never noticed them before.

SHE TOOK A MOMENT to stand in Ward's dirt driveway and breathe in the scent of the lilac bush in his backyard. The side door light came on, and in a moment, he was there in all his assured charm, telling her to come in out of the cold.

"Ah, Chianti, perfect. I'm not much of a wino but I do enjoy a glass now and then." He brushed a kiss against her cheek. "Welcome back to the bachelor pad. I was just working on the bread." The comforting smell of baked lasagna and garlic filled the home. A long baguette sat on the butcher-block counter beside powdered garlic and a stick of butter.

"I'm starving. Thanks for inviting me."

"The lasagna should be done in twenty." He uncorked the bottle and poured it into two stemmed glasses.

She surprised herself by asking, "Do you know this is the third day in a row we've been together?"

"Sounds like the beginning of something."

"You're not tired of me yet?"

"Impossible." He mixed the butter and garlic in a small glass bowl. "Besides, tomorrow I've got my daughter for the next five days. I'm trying to get in as much time with you as I can."

"This is your week?"

"We have a good routine worked out, splitting the weeks and weekends."

Memories of the horse show surfaced. "How's Winnifred doing?"

"It's hard, she still doesn't really understand why I moved out. Of course, her mother blames everything on me, so we always have to adjust for a few days before Winnie warms up to me again. But we're working on it. One day at a time."

"It must have been a very difficult decision for you."

"Yeah, well, my wife—er, soon-to-be ex-wife, forced the issue when I started my new business. She knew my time in the office and out in the field would only increase. Some might say I'm a workaholic."

Pennie appreciated his bluntness, his openness about it. She'd grown up with an uncle who worked sixty-hour weeks and admired a good work ethic. Ward did seem to have his shit together. The dining table was already set with candles and blue woven place mats with matching napkins. His maturity and hospitality touched her, and she pushed memories of dinners with Kush away. That was then, this is now. "Thanks for sending the plans over to the office this morning."

"Gotta keep the ball rolling. Your uncle said you went over to check out the road site."

"We did." She took a sip of her wine and let it linger, crisp and dry. "I didn't realize how close the cemetery was to the road you're proposing."

"The cemetery. Right." He cleared his throat. "They're common in Maine when you're developing pastureland like this. My surveyor doesn't think it's an issue. We've got the required setback to put the road in."

"Did you talk to my uncle about the stone wall?"

"Briefly." He placed a bowl of peanuts in front of her, grabbing a handful and shaking them around like mini dice before popping them into his mouth. "We'll have to iron out those details."

The timer went off. Grabbing the potholders, he took the lasagna from the oven before popping in the foil-wrapped baguette. "We've got to keep the ball rolling, Pen," he said, again. His little mantra.

"I didn't realize your father's girlfriend owns the neighboring property."

"Small world, right?"

She took a sip and swirled it. "Who owns the stone wall?"

He loaded pans into the dishwasher. "The cemetery association. And they see no problem with us removing it to give us the setback.

Pennie took a breath. "Your access road is uncomfortably close to the cemetery."

"I'm sure it's nothing we can't work around." He sat beside her at the bar. "Did I tell you how much I've been thinking about you?" He casually slipped his hand under her hair, behind her neck, and gently kissed her. Pushing away thoughts of Kush, she kissed him back, wanting more of his complicated taste, a harsh sweetness. She was so tired of obsessing about the development, her pathetic single life, memories of Kush, anything instead of just enjoying life in the moment. Their knees pressing together, awkwardly perched on the barstools, she savored his lips, ran her hands along his bulky thighs.

He met her eyes. "You sounded upset on the phone. Everything okay?"

Steadying herself, she realized it was that old familiar Eagles song, "Desperado," playing on the turntable and looked away. "I'm fine. Just a long week." To change the subject, she reached for her bag and grabbed the dusty album, waving it in front of him. "Can I put this on?" She blew the dust while removing the cellophane.

"What, you don't like this?"

It was the song Kush used to sing to her. How she hated it now. "Time to mix it up." She stepped down to the console and barely dragged the needle over the record to replace Don Henley with Nina Simone, her layered voice filling the house. The impulse to buy this was the best decision she'd made all day. Standing up, she moved toward him, took away the serrated knife, and they embraced, body to body. She took his hands, brought them around her, and they rocked back and forth, an easy liquid sway all their own. His palms slipped inside her back pockets, fitting perfectly. Breathing in her ear, he asked, "Are you sure you want this?"

"You never gave me a complete tour of the place."

"That was very rude of me, I apologize." He kissed her cheek and her inhibitions fell away, thawing like a stream in springtime. She dipped her finger in the remnants of the melted butter and slipped it into his mouth.

He never took his stone eyes away from hers. "Mmm, that's tasty."

"That's what I was thinking."

Leading her through the sunken living room, they entered his dark bedroom. When she sat on the bed, the water moved under her, heated. She bounced up and down slightly on the rolling motion.

"Hope you don't mind a waterbed." He moved his hands up inside her sweater, holding her around the ribcage, her tender fracture healed now.

"I wouldn't have known you were a waterbed man. Feels warm."

"Not as warm as you." Lifting her up into the center of the bed, he took her shoes off, then her wool socks, and massaged her toes. Lying down beside her, he shook off his own shoes and kissed her, in search of something. She unbuttoned his shirt, glad to see his broad chest bared, the gray hairs cropping up here and there, and caressed him.

He inched her sweater up and over her head. Pennie lost herself when he wrestled her jeans off. She was helpless, finally at ease, outside of herself with this distraction, this sublime disturbance, and found herself rapturous and at the mercy of this man who knew his way around a woman. Pushing against him, she circled on top to gain ground, and, before she could catch her breath, was releasing with him, like they had surrendered to this a million times over and over and over.

Catching her breath, tears welling in her eyes again, strangely sad and relieved, she fell against him. He moaned in satisfaction. "Wow, didn't expect that. You work fast, Penelope Goode." She hit him hard on his bare chest. "What was that for?" Rolling to face her, he squeezed her small breast, cupped in the same hand that so assuredly was there at the right time to catch her from falling.

"I don't know what got into me. Must be the wine," she said.

"What did you have, half a glass?"

She reached for her bra and sweater, embarrassed. He stopped her. "No need to rush." His stare fixed on her. "You are unusual, Penelope."

Unusual? What does he mean? She rolled away from him. Suddenly, the smell of burning garlic bread filled the room.

"Shit!" He jumped up and threw his pants on before rushing out to the kitchen.

Coming to her senses, she sat up to dress, listening to his cursing, the smoke alarm blaring, the sound of doors and windows sliding open as a cold draft rolled in. She tugged her sweater over her head.

He yelled from the kitchen, "You really know how to distract a guy!"

Flicking on the bedside light, she found a stack of framed photographs on the nightstand. There was his daughter, Winnie, at the beach, just a toddler with her mother, playing in the surf. Popham Beach? Underneath that, a picture of a young man in a cap and gown. She pulled the picture closer; that face was familiar, that lopsided smile.

Oh no.

He reappeared in the doorway, startling her. "Haven't got around to hanging those yet." He picked up the beach photo on the bed beside her and grimaced. "Memories."

Unsteadily, she raised the picture of the graduate. "Who's this?"

"My son, Ethan."

She gulped, horrified. "You have a son?"

"Happened when I was in law school. One night stand. Years ago. We've never been close, but it's not for lack of trying."

She hesitated to ask the next question. "How old is he?"

"Just turned twenty-one. A ski patrol up at Coos Canyon. Why, do you know him?"

Her blood ran cold, her lungs frozen. *That dirty no-good boilermaker.* "No, no, I um, just was curious. Didn't think you were old enough to have a son this...age."

He took the picture from her. "I guess we've never talked about age, have we? I'm forty-three." Taking her chin, he forced her to look up at him. "Hope that's not too old for you."

She stood and forced a smile, backing away from the directness of his stare. "No, of course not. We're only, what, thirteen years apart?" Turning, she slipped into the bathroom.

"Well, that's a relief. Wouldn't want to be robbing any cradles at my age. Don't need that drama."

She felt a slight distaste at his words, an aversion that lingered in the air with the burned garlic, and closed the door behind her.

He spoke through the door. "Despite the age difference, I'd say we're pretty compatible."

Gathering herself, a heavy stone settled inside her. "That we are," she said, trying in earnest to sound cheerful.

What had she done? Was this the same boy from the mountain? With a dull throbbing in her side, an ache that persisted despite her physical healing, she checked the medicine cabinet. Tylenol and a prescription bottle, OxyContin. She slammed it shut and wiped her eyes, mustered the courage to put on a brave face. Finally emerging from the bathroom, she hurried through an apology, avoiding Ward's eyes. "So sorry to do this to you, but I'm suddenly not feeling well. Must be a stomach bug."

Ignoring his protests, she slipped into the kitchen, grabbed her purse, and in a flurry, snatched the open bottle of wine before slamming the door behind her. She ran into the darkness, his pleading fading behind her. *Wait, just wait a minute!* But she was already gone, driving past the dark woods, her aloneness a comforting companion to her regret.

THE NEXT MORNING, SHE woke from a dream, the sun streaming in through slits in the blinds, the daylight holding her accountable for the night before. Closing her eyes, she searched herself to remember the dream, a pleasant one of a little one-room schoolhouse, students of all ages and races mixed together in a room with a young schoolteacher, somber eyes behind black wire-rimmed glasses. She stood at a blackboard in the front of the room near a potbellied stove that roared with warmth. Outside the window, the snow fell steadily, mother ocean in the near distance.

The teacher led them through an arithmetic problem. One of the older students, a girl dressed in a patched homemade cotton dress and wool sweater, raised a dark hesitant hand. The teacher called on her. "Lottie?"

The girl replied, barely audibly, "Yes, Ma'am, Miss Woodman, Ma'am, it's seven." With praise, the teacher ended their lesson and asked them to stand to recite in unison a Bible verse, Revelation 21, she had written on the board: "He will dwell with them, and they shall be His people, and God Himself will be with them; He will wipe away every tear from their eyes, and death shall be no more, neither shall there be mourning nor crying nor pain any more, for the former things have passed away."

Staring out the window, Pennie thought about her aunt and the pamphlets she used to, every now and then, bring home from Catholic Mass with Bible verses like this one. Even though Aunt Aggie was never much of a churchgoer, she ventured out to Mass when times were particularly difficult—when Tita fell during a competition, when her elderly father fell ill, when Aunt Maude came down with pneumonia, and most recently, when Uncle Alfie was hospitalized. Pennie wondered if praying made any difference at all or if everything came down to fate, like with the islanders whose bodies were buried out at the old hilltop farm cemetery or their ghosts who came to her inside her dreams.

Chapter 10
The Wresting Place

SHE ROSE TO LET in the beastly sun. Looking at the time, the clock shone 8:33 back at her. She'd be late, maybe even behind Tita this time. Her head throbbed.

A half hour later, with wet hair, she climbed into the Karmann Ghia and spotted the empty wine bottle on the passenger-side floor. Looking over her shoulder, she promptly grabbed the evidence to deposit in a receptacle beside her building. *Nothing to see here. Nothing at all.*

When she got to the office, Tita was on the phone. "Seriously, Lars? Are you sure this is necessary?"

Pennie waved and Tita pointed to her imaginary watch, mouthing WTF. Hanging up, she tossed Pennie an accusatory stare.

"Like you've never been late," Pennie said. "What's up with Lars? Trouble in the director's chair? Running out of favors to cash in on?"

"Very funny. He needs more footage of me. I'm getting tired of this. Looks like I'm heading to the mountain for the weekend again."

"Any snow left up there?"

"Tons. Over a foot the last two days."

"Better there than here. I'm so sick of winter, I could vomit."

"That's because you're done for the season, wasting your life here on some fantasy real estate man. Hey, speaking of, I heard Kush was in town."

The throbbing returned, as if on command. "Yeah, I heard that." She jumped to the files, pretending to look for a document.

"I also heard he brought a new girlfriend home with him."

Pennie ignored her. Tita was trying to get under her skin. "Oh, yeah? Hadn't heard that. Ward invited me for dinner last night, so I was a little occupied."

"Don't worry. Dani and Mali said she was a pretentious bee-otch."

She picked up a title from Heritage Acres, no idea what she was looking at. "I don't really give a rat's ass what she's like. He's moving on, so am I."

Tita swirled around and around in her chair, getting a hoot out of tormenting her now. "You're right, time to move onto bigger fish. When am I going to meet *Ward*? I've seen pictures of him. Handsome guy, one or two bankrupt companies."

Now Pennie turned, a slow about-face. "Bankruptcies?"

"Pop asked me to do some digging. He had a surveying company, then a property management company. Both tits up, I guess. Oh well, you win some, you lose some."

Pennie wanted to throttle her. But none of this mattered. She wasn't sure about Ward anymore, now knowing (with blinding reality) about the ski patrol. If there's anything her cousin liked, it was some good juicy gossip to make herself feel better about her own stalled life. She would not give her that. "What's going on with the film?"

"Why? Are you planning to tell Mum what a lowlife my boyfriend is again?"

"What gave you that idea?"

"She told me what you said about Lars. That he brought some *baggage* home with him from California."

"I just think you deserve better, I—"

"Spare me. You'd talk to my face and not behind my back if you really cared. And, by the way, it's herpes, also known as a cold sore, and millions of people have it."

They heard Uncle Alfie's footsteps coming up and glared at one another until he entered with his eager dogs. "In my office, Pennie." She was happy to end the conversation with Tita, and hastily gathered some notes on her desk. Inside his office, she closed the door, expecting a lecture about leaving work early yesterday. He stared at her for a long, uncomfortable moment. "You feeling okay?"

She pulled back her hair in a tight ponytail. He could always sense it when she wasn't herself. "I'm okay. You hear anything back from Mrs. McCarthy?"

"Poor woman. The police looked at the surveillance footage from the camera on the side of her house. Caught the culprit that dug up the necklace. A stray dog, they said."

Her mind raced. A stray? Her dream came back in full force, her nails, now healed over, still aching from the memory of digging the frozen mud in her dream. "Really?"

"That's what the police told her. Makes sense. I didn't think one of her little yappers could dig up the ground as deep as that. When we were over measuring the lot, it may have brought up an old scent."

"And Cassie found that old croquet ball."

"Right." He scratched Fella between the ears. "Anyway, they've sent the necklace and the bracelet to the crime lab for DNA testing. Should be a couple weeks, if they can find anything."

Her mind moved to the picture of lovely teenage Chloe wearing the necklace. "How's Mrs. McCarthy holding up?"

"Better. They've got her on sedatives. Too bad her husband isn't alive to help her through this. Sad for her to be alone right now."

Pennie sympathized. She'd had her own fit of sad solo drinking the night before. "Wouldn't they be able to look at old surveillance footage to see who buried anything there when Chloe went missing?"

"Jeannette didn't have the cameras installed until after her husband died."

"Why do I feel like he may have had something to do with this?"

"What, her husband? Seems unlikely. From what I understand, Colin was more distraught than anyone over losing the girl. It maybe even caused his failing health."

"What about the son building the house next door?"

"It does make you wonder. Half of that land was deeded to Chloe before she died."

Pennie's mind swirled. "Now I understand why Jeannette wants her house as far from his as possible."

Alfie reeled her back in. "Yes, well, that's enough conjecture. The police will be closing the crime scene soon, and Jack can get to the property to finish up the measurements. In the meantime, we've got work to do on Heritage Acres." He handed her the cylinder. "Can you drive up to the Fairview surveyor's office today? I need you to look at any old plans for the land and cemetery to help us find the exact plot lines of the graveyard." Cassie barked, as if in agreement.

DRIVING UP THE HIGHWAY, she realized it was April 1st. April Fool's Day. Her phone buzzed with a text from Ward.

Doing her best to keep her mind on matters at hand, she shoved the phone into her purse and took the Fairview exit. At Intervale Surveying, she parked beside the only truck in the dirt lot, an old red Ford pickup. Inside, she waited until a man, maybe her uncle's age, entered the large room, his beer belly protruding like a shelf. Endless wide filing drawers for housing blueprints lined the back wall. "You must be Ms. Goode?"

"Didn't know you were expecting me."

"Alfred called to make sure I had the plans for the cemetery." He turned to a filing cabinet in the corner and pulled out a drawer, thumbing through a stack until he found what he was looking for. With a swift motion, he brought the plans to the counter and laid them out before offering his hand. "Milton Freeman, nice to meet you."

"I'm Pennie, same here."

"You working with Alfred now?"

"Helping him out. There's a developer looking to put in a commercial business development on the Heritage Acres property, about fifty acres. The problem is the access road."

"I heard all about it. Came before the planning board again yesterday. I think they approved it."

"Already? Does my uncle know that?"

"He does now. Talked to him a few minutes ago."

"Are things normally approved this fast?"

"Sometimes. But it first came before the board about six months ago. People around here like the idea of more job opportunities. And of course, the town likes the tax base this could bring in." He directed her attention to the plans. "So, you were wondering about the cemetery?"

"Yes, the Patient's Cemetery in the back."

He ran his weathered hand along the blueprint to the spot. "Right here. From what I understand, the road he's putting in runs alongside the cemetery here—between the cemetery and the abutting property."

"Is there enough setback?"

"I believe so." He produced a dirt-encrusted, 1985-vintage calculator from his shirt pocket and figured out the plot size, based on the plan measurements. "The road's got to be at least twenty-five feet wide, and then you need another twenty-five-foot setback." He punched more numbers in. "Once they remove the stone wall, that'd just about do it. It'd be right up to the neighbor's property line, but it works."

"Looks awfully tight to me, and close to those graves."

"Certainly *is* tight." He ran his crooked finger along the sloping dirt road. "They want to curve it around the backside of the cemetery where the Malaga graves are."

"And there's been no protest from the townspeople?" she asked.

"I believe a few people stood up at the public hearing, some relatives of those buried, and others who used to work at the Home for the Feeble-Minded. And, of course, the abutting owner, Roxanne Greenleaf, is against it. But the promise of development won out. People are all about jobs and more opportunity nowadays."

Outside, the cutting wind of April sliced through her. She hugged herself and opened her car door, placing a copy of the plans and measurements in the passenger seat. She called her uncle and left a message. Driving in a state of numbness, she turned toward the highway before changing her mind and circling back toward Heritage Acres and the cemeteries. When she reached Gray Road, her phone rang. Her uncle. "You must still be at court."

He sounded exhausted already. "Another day fighting City Hall."

"Well, we may just have a fight with the town of Fairview."

"What do the plans tell us?"

"Everything looks legal on paper. You heard it was already approved by the planning board? I can't believe it all happened so fast."

"Funny how Ward Lewis never shared that with us, huh? Made it sound like it was months away from approval."

Pennie pulled over to the side of the road. She needed to think. "What can we do now?"

"Unless we have a case, there isn't much we can do. I'll call Stan."

She stared down the dirt road along the cemetery. She looked at the beech trees to her left and the stone wall anchoring them, knowing the lovely trees would be axed, too. She walked down the sloping road to the older graves in the back and the Malaga headstones she'd taken pictures of days earlier. The ground beneath her rumbled, filling her with a slow steady vibration. A shudder ran up her backside and she moved away, up toward the road until the thrumming lessened. Was she imagining it, or was there an energy pulling her back toward those graves?

Ignoring the strange urge to walk down the slope, she returned to her car and started it up. All she needed was rest, to stop thinking about everything, to pause the constant shifting beneath her feet, to give in to an exhaustion as heavy and formidable as pea soup fog. If she could just get home and away from here, she'd feel normal again.

Driving away, she caught a motion in her periphery. Roxanne Greenleaf, standing in her doorway, watching her.

PENNIE WOKE WITH A start, darkness encroaching outside her bedroom window, the weight of a nightmare still pressing on her. Another dream about the Malaga settlement. It was the same place she'd been before, that island schoolhouse. She was panting like a dog again, only this time she was walking in the woods of the island following a group of men wearing long coats and top hats, accompanied by two women in long dresses and wool coats, rustling along a trail leading to an opening with scattered and subsistent dwellings, tar-paper shacks and modest wood-framed homes, the sturdy little schoolhouse sitting up high nearby on the north end of the island. The officious group waved to a stout middle-aged woman hanging laundry in the windy barren yard, and they stopped to talk to a man hauling traps from his boat on the shore.

Making their way to the newly built one-room schoolhouse, they opened the door and let themselves inside, surprising the group of ten or more students and their young teacher. Startled, Ms. Eveline Woodman introduced herself and welcomed the strangers. When Governor Plaisted introduced himself and his entourage, she asked the children to stand, the boys and girls, ages six to eighteen, commingling, wearing sweaters darned at the elbows in mixed yarns, pants with sailcloth patches, some with fishing twine tied around their boots. The men in long tailored black coats, the women in fine dresses, surveyed the timid students, who recited their ABCs in unison, keeping their bright eyes on Ms. Woodman for direction, for assurance. She led them in Bible verses for the benefit of their unexpected guests: "To love Him with all your heart, with all your understanding and with all your strength, and to love your neighbor as yourself is more important than all burnt offerings and sacrifices," and, "Love one another, as I have loved you."

The strange white men and women nodded gravely. Ms. Woodman, eager to leave their esteemed guests with a good impression, knowing the gravity of the visit, sat at the upright piano to lead the children in a hymn. The song started in timid notes, but gained power and strength as the children sang:

> Let us ever love each other
> With a heart that's warm and true,
> Ever doing to our brother
> As to us we'd have him do.

Kind and loving to each other,
Gentle words to all we meet;
Thus we follow Christ our Savior,
Proving all His service sweet.

When the heart is sad and lonely,
And the eyes with tears o'erflow,
Gentle words and deeds of kindness
Fall like sunbeams on the snow.

Let us help our fallen brother,
Lift him gently by the hand,
Ever speaking words of cheer and comfort,
As point him to a better land.

In this world of toil and sorrow
Many hearts are full of care,
Let us live to serve our Master,
And each other's burdens bear.

Ms. Woodman stood to praise the children and the men clapped with gruff praise and stern nods, commending the song, encouraging them to keep up the good work. The governor then turned on his black polished boots to leave, his entourage close behind.

Outside, the men struck up a conversation with a scruffy, gray-bearded man who stood high on a ladder against the side of his simple sturdy house, telling them about the good fishing around the island, about the mothers and children who tended their own small gardens, planting anything that would grow in the rocky soil or digging clams down in the tidal flats. He spread his arms wide, proud of the community they'd built despite their hardscrabble surroundings; like anyone on the coast, they learned to make do.

The men tipped their hats, and the women lifted their dresses to stomp on through the spruces of the harsh coastal island, back toward the shell beach where they had left their boat, muttering, "Learning despite their tainted blood. Not a bad spot for a hotel." Then they slipped away in the rowboat toward the mainland and Pennie woke.

Sleep still in her eyes and her bones, she looked at her phone. Only 9:00 p.m. She pulled out her laptop and typed in "Malaga Island."

She was drawn into the island's lore. Residents, all descendants of a former enslaved man, Benjamin Darling, had been taken or evicted from their homes between 1911 and 1912. The first to be removed were members of the Marks family, four generations: the father and mother, Jake and Abbie Griffin; three daughters, Lizzie, Lottie, and Eta; one son, James; one grandchild, William; and an old woman, Annie Parker. All were diagnosed incompetent and committed to the Home for the Feeble-Minded in December of 1911 by doctor's order.

After the state took ownership of Malaga in 1912, the remaining families of mixed ancestry, a community of thirty-five or so, were set adrift with nowhere to go. Forced to dismantle their homes and leave, many floated in makeshift houseboats along the coast, without a home, a community, a town, a state they could call their own. To complete the erasure, the state exhumed the remains of seventeen bodies and transported them to the Home for the Feeble-Minded cemetery. In 1913, a newspaper reported the state was "Cleaning Up Malaga Island—No Longer a Reproach to the Good Name of the State."

MEMORIES OF BEING AT the cemetery with Dani years ago came back to her, so she called her. Dani picked up after the first ring. "Hey, Pen."

"Hey, Dan."

"Sorry about that last night. I couldn't believe it when Kush showed up here with the Philly girl."

The memory of the slender angular girl under the streetlight shone dimly. "Oh, that's okay. It's been months. Time to move on."

"You don't sound too convincing."

"I've got bigger things on my mind, to be honest. I wanted to talk to you about something else, a case I'm working on with my uncle that's got me freaked out."

"What's going on?"

"Do you remember that day we went to the Cumberland Fair, maybe about ten years ago, and you took me to an old graveyard over by Heritage Acres?"

"Yes, of course, I do. We're related to a Malaga family buried there."

"I thought that's what you said. Is it the Marks family, the one that was committed there?"

"Yes, that's what my father told us. It only took the order of one doctor and a judge to force them from their home on the island. Most of them died at the institution."

She skimmed her computer screen. "I just read that the entire community was evicted, and then the state dug up the graves of the seventeen people and reburied them at the Patient's Cemetery."

"Oh, I remember. Still makes me sick to my stomach."

"Unfortunately, the saga continues."

"What do you mean?"

"That real estate developer, Ward Lewis, got approval from the town of Fairview to put a business development road in, right beside those graves."

Silence on the line. "All the privileged white people driving over my relatives' dead bodies. All in the name of *progress*."

"I'm hoping my uncle can get some kind of emergency injunction. Are any of those relatives still alive who could help stop this?"

"Not sure. My great-aunt used to live downeast in Jonesport." Dani hesitated. "This may sound rude, but why do you care so much about those graves?"

"You'd have to be heartless to ignore this, after everything these poor families lived through." Still rattled by her eerie dreams, Pennie was afraid to share them with Dani or anyone.

"I'll call my father about my aunt, see if he knows anything."

THE NEXT MORNING, PENNIE woke with another dream about Malaga islanders circling her mind. She was back in the same spruces, on the same rocky path. She spotted a woman with long reddish hair like hers who turned toward Pennie—her own mother! She tried to call out but only a crisp bark escaped, echoing in the woods. She could hear everything: animals rustling in the brush around her, chipmunks scratching underground, birds twittering high in the trees, gulls squawking on the cliff on the other side of the island.

In hot pursuit of her mother, she couldn't seem to catch up until they came to a clearing where two men stood inside a hole in the ground. Another man on higher ground beside five large rectangular wooden boxes told them to haul something up. The men in the dirt hoisted bodies upward so he could drag them into the caskets. The corpse of an old, decayed woman with sparse white hair, the skeleton of a child who couldn't have been more than three, and then what looked like a girl partially decomposed in a tattered dress, dense brown soil falling away from her face, hollow, rotten. The sweating men, huffing and puffing, tossed them up and into the same casket, a few bones falling out here and there, and then three more bodies, half covered in rags, eyes sunken in. They loaded in the bones, the decay, until the box was full, then moved on to the next.

She looked up to her mother standing beside her, tears flooding her flushed cheeks, eyes bluer than Pennie's, arms covered in a handmade shawl. Pennie tried to reach for her, clawing at nothing but a fine mist of a shape. The men filled the last casket with corpses, many preserved by the island's salty glacial soil, then slid on makeshift wooden covers. They loaded the pine boxes into a wagon that they pulled themselves, heading back toward the path in the woods.

One of them spotted Pennie and kicked her. "Damn mutt, get out of here! You get!"

She cowered out of their way as they stomped directly into her mother, passing through her ghostly silhouette, pulling the old wagon with the five caskets toward the shore, the fat man saying, "Well, George, that just about does it."

Those men. The corpses, the caskets. Those were the bodies of the souls out at the Patient's Cemetery, wrested from their island graves and moved forty miles west.

WARD HAD SENT HER numerous texts overnight, ending with:

> Was I really that bad?

Feeling guilty, she texted back:

> Very funny *crying laughing emoji*. Just horribly sick. In bed all day. Call you tomorrow.

How could she trust him after he was so dishonest? Maybe "dishonest" was too strong. Withholding? No, he had deliberately kept the information about the planning board approval from her. She'd ask him straight out why he hadn't told her. What would she say that didn't sound like an accusation? And did she mind accusing him, really?

Outside in the early April chill, her VW sputtered a few times, the ignition being stubborn on her. "Don't give up on me now, baby," she muttered before the engine finally started. Spinning through the familiar blocks to the family townhouse on Pine Street, her vivid Malaga dreams circled in her mind. The islanders and the children, the group of men. Did this really happen in Maine a little over a hundred years ago? Graves dug up, bodies tossed in boxes like trash?

In the warm bright kitchen on Pine Street, she found her aunt and uncle at the table drinking coffee. "Pennie, dear, what a nice surprise." Her aunt extended her hand and Pennie took it, grateful for the welcome. "Why, you're as cold as a corpse. Grab some coffee from the pot."

Uncle Alfie sat engrossed in the *New York Times*. Pouring herself a steaming cup, Pennie wrapped her hands around the mug to absorb the warmth. "Tita around?"

"Sleeping." The clock ticking over the table read 6:33. Goddamn it, more threes. Everything was literally driving her mad. "I had the weirdest dream about my mother last night."

Her uncle dropped the paper down a few inches to peer at her over his reading glasses.

Her aunt shifted in her chair. "What kind of dream?"

"She was out on an island. I think it was Malaga Island. Anyway, she was watching men dig up graves, putting corpses in caskets. She kept crying and there was nothing I could do." She deliberately bit her tongue to leave out the part about her embodiment as a dog.

"Malaga Island?" Her aunt sipped her cup.

Alfie folded the paper. "We've been doing some site work over at the cemetery by Heritage Acres where some of the islanders were buried."

"Sounds more like a nightmare." Aggie folded her gentle palm over Pennie's trembling hand.

"I was reading about the island yesterday." Pennie looked at her uncle. "About the settlement that was exiled, and some even committed to the Home for the Feeble-Minded."

"That's a sad chapter in our history, for sure." He kept his tone neutral. "At the turn of the twentieth century, shipbuilding was declining and fishing stocks depressed. The state started to think about the dollars that tourism would bring in. Unfortunately, some people thought island communities like Malaga were an eyesore."

"You mean they saw it as degenerate and evil because they were mixed race."

"Pennie, you have to remember this wasn't long after the Civil War. Changes in people's thinking about class and race don't happen overnight."

Pennie got up for a refill, trying to control her anger. Why was everybody being so callous about this? "Sounds like you're excusing their horrible actions."

"Not excusing it, putting it in perspective. We've come a long way since then." He stood up to end the conversation, sensing Pennie's tension. "Now, I've got to take the dogs out." They showed up in the kitchen on cue and followed him down the hallway. "I'll see you at the office at eight. We've got a busy day."

Aggie pointed her finger, thumped it on the table. "And don't be dragged down by the past, Pennie. This country has offered a lot to the Blacks."

"I suppose you'd say the same thing about the Native Americans." She walked out before she could say anything more she would regret. There she was again, swimming against the tide.

First thing at the office, before anyone else showed up, she called Ward. He picked up the phone from his car speaker. "Hey, didn't think I'd hear from you till tomorrow."

"Been a little out of sorts. Feeling better now." She looked down on Exchange Street, people hustling to open shops, men and women in trench coats on their way to important jobs, so officious and planned with their lives. "I'm sorry I left in such a hurry."

"That's okay, I forgive you."

She noted a tone of arrogance, and a loathing took hold of her. "I heard your business park road cleared the planning board."

"Yeah, that's right. We thought we'd need to submit a few more rounds, but they must have been in a particularly good mood that night. You never know when the stars will align." He completed his order in the drive-thru, his voice thick with condescension: "No, I said a large re-gu-lar cof-fee, one cream, one sugar."

He spoke into the phone, "No one speaks English anymore. Not sure what this country is coming to."

"Maybe we could start by being more *accepting*."

"Did someone wake up on the wrong side of the bed?" he chuckled.

"I'm not a child, Ward." Her anger rose. "Why didn't you tell me about it the other night when I was at your place?"

"What, the planning board thing? I was going to, but you brought us in another direction, quite to my surprise." He paid for his coffee and closed the window. "To my delight, I should say. Then you left me to my lasagna dinner, all by my lonesome."

"Seems to me the subject of the development came up earlier and you said nothing."

"Pennie, what is this? I thought you'd be happy for me. Your uncle didn't find any problems with the road, did he? From what I know, everything clears the setbacks."

"Your road is right up against the Patient's Cemetery. That's not right. There will be hundreds of cars driving practically over those Malaga graves."

"I think you're exaggerating, Pen. We've got the proper setback. You know I'm limited by the abutting property. I don't make up the rules, and this is the only place I can put a road in."

"Now I understand why your father hired us." She hung up the phone, her hand trembling. She was pulled back to reality by the sound of her uncle whistling Patsy Cline, followed by the commotion of the dogs. He went directly to his office and closed the door.

Tita strolled in behind, coffee in hand. "Happy Friday."

"You're in a chipper mood."

"I saw the film last night. You're not gonna believe what Lars has done. He's a miracle worker in the edit suite."

"I didn't realize it was close to completion."

"He found some incredible footage from the Olympic archives. Great history of women's freeskiing. There's more work to do, a few extra scenes to shoot, but yeah. It's coming right along. Can I talk you into coming up this weekend, maybe help Lars with the shoot? He can always use an extra hand, and you're a natural with the camera. He's used some of the old ski photos you shared with him."

Tita tried her best to butter her up, but her mind was on the development. "I've got too much work to do here."

"C'mon, Pen. You owe me."

Pennie's skin crawled. She hated it when Tita pressured her like this. "What, exactly, do I owe you?"

"It's the least you can do after all the season passes I've given you for ten years."

She was right. Tita's perks, being a spokesperson for the mountain, had trickled down. And Tita loved to keep score.

"Sorry, I really can't go up. I have too much on my plate."

"Like what?"

She lowered her voice. "Like putting the kibosh on Ward's development."

"Sounds like trouble in paradise. What's going on with Mr. Real Estate?"

Her mind swerved to Ward beneath her on the waterbed, then the picture of the ski patrol. Her old familiar self-loathing rose in swells. The last thing she'd do was share all that with Tita; she'd never hear the end of it. "He's trying to build a road practically over an old graveyard. Worst of all, the bodies buried there have already been moved once from their original graves." She gave Tita the *Reader's Digest* version of Malaga and the relatives of Dani and Mali now buried out at the cemetery.

"What a story. I had no idea." She was almost too excited. "You should tell Lars about this. Good material for a documentary." The more Tita was around Lars, the more she sounded like him. What had her aunt called him? An *opportunist*.

Uncle Alfie opened his door. "I don't pay you two to chit-chat. Christina, get the Maine Historical Society on the phone. Pennie, in my office, please."

She grabbed her notebook and followed. He put his phone on speaker, and they listened to a young woman's greeting. Uncle Alfie introduced himself, asking to speak with Liz McClellan. After a few clicks, she answered. "Hi Alfred, how are you?"

"Oh, pretty good for an old man. How about you Liz? Holding down the fort over there?"

She chuckled. "Doing my best. I haven't seen you in the research library lately."

"No, I've got to get back to the family genealogy. Not getting any younger, but I'm calling about a different matter today. My associate, Pennie, and I are researching a business development that's been approved over at Heritage Acres in Fairview. They're putting in a road that runs uncomfortably close to the old Patient's Cemetery, the cemetery with the Malaga Island graves."

"First time I've heard about this."

He raised his eyebrows at Pennie. "No notice from the Preservation Commission?"

"No, nothing."

"I'm not surprised." He leaned back in his chair. "Seems the town pushed it through planning board approval. Not sure they went through the proper channels and thought you might need to get involved."

"Who's the town planner?"

"Jake Boudreau. Been there about six years. Good guy, and I'm sure councilors put the pressure on. They want the tax base."

"I'm sure. But not at the expense of an historically significant gravesite."

"If you could write a notarized letter, I think I can file an emergency stay, but it will have to be done fast."

"Let me double-check with the preservation commission to see if they know anything. I'm surprised the town never sent the proper notice."

He looked in his empty coffee cup and threw it in the trash. "You know how these things work. Local politics."

"You're welcome to search through our Malaga archives, if images or newspaper accounts would help."

"Good idea."

Pennie waved her hands in excitement. He nodded and smiled. "Pennie will be over this afternoon, if that works for you."

"Any time is fine, and I'll get right on this, Alfred. Thank you."

Hanging up the phone, he scratched his chin. "Awful nice woman, always helpful."

Her hands stopped trembling for the first time that morning. "You're a genius, Uncle Alfie."

Chapter 11
Story of Exile

AFTER LUNCH, PENNIE WALKED to the historical society on Congress Street. Housed in the boyhood home of Henry Wadsworth Longfellow, it was a three-story brick building built by Henry's grandfather in 1785—the oldest building on the Portland peninsula. She walked through the iron gate, following a brick pathway on the side of the Wadsworth-Longfellow House leading to the Brown library in a separate building. Inside, a studious young man led her to the archive room out back where she met Liz McClellan, a woman maybe in her forties with a heavy brow and a big smile, dressed in a forest green suit.

Liz had already laid out black-and-white prints for her. Some came from newspaper clippings circa 1900 to 1912; others were contributed by Malaga descendants, librarians, and historians. The first image was from a 1909 issue of *Harper's Monthly Magazine*, a depiction of a dark-skinned family in front of a shack: a boy standing beside a bearded man in overalls wearing a bowler hat and a woman wearing a long dress and apron, surrounded by what looked like three white missionary women and a young girl. The headline read, "The Queer Folk of the Maine Coast." Next to it was a postcard of an elderly Black woman with a boy on her lap, sitting in what looked like a fenced-in pen. "Deuces of Spades," the card read. She flipped to an article from the *Casco Bay Breeze* titled, "Malago, the Home of Southern Negro Blood...Incongruous Scenes on a Spot of Natural Beauty in Casco Bay."

"You can stay as long as you like, Pennie. I'm glad your uncle called."

As Pennie settled in, the library staff and other researchers around her seemed to disappear.

At the turn of the twentieth century, newspaper reports describing the settlement as "not fit for dogs" or "disgusting and pitiable" and "a shameful disgrace" led to the unraveling and expulsion of the community that'd been on the island for several generations, nearly seventy-five years. Myths circulated about Malaga being a stopping point for the Underground Railroad, or a place for sea captains coming from the West Indies to drop off their concubines and illegitimate children before going home to their wives. None of it was true.

The original settler of the colony, Benjamin Darling, was an enslaved man owned by a ship's captain. According to legend, "Black Ben" was granted his freedom and some money to purchase nearby Horse Island in 1794 after saving his owner in a shipwreck. As a free man, he married a white woman, Sarah Proverbs, and they had several children. Eventually, the descendants of Ben and Sarah established homesteads on Malaga, and families grew over the years to include the Darlings, Griffins, Murphys, Easons, Dunnings, Johnsons, Tripps, Parkers, Marks, and McKenneys. Jim McKenney was known as the King of Malaga for his fishing sagacity, and William Johnson was a Civil War veteran, along with Henry Tripp, who served in the 7th and 9th Maine regiments until wounded in Gettysburg. The families were mixed-race—combinations of Black, white, and Native American—and scratched out an existence on the unforgiving ledge of the Maine coast.

During this time in midcoast history, the shipping, wooden shipbuilding, and fishing industries all but collapsed, causing people to leave Maine in droves. The burden of providing for the poor became a stressor on nearly every town budget. The mainland towns near Malaga Island—Harpswell and Phippsburg—argued over who had responsibility for the island and its community.

To increase tensions even more, the eugenics movement took hold at the turn of the twentieth century, extolling the benefits of selective breeding and the purity of the Anglo-Saxon gene pool. The dogma of racial superiority, or inferiority, spread in popularity and Malaga became a target. The December 30, 1905, issue of *The Bath Independent and Enterprise* wrote, "Poor, shiftless and thriftless, the Malagoites make little provision for the coming winter and consequently their sufferings are very keen."

In August 1911, a Boston newspaper article declared, "Their mode of life is not unlike the Indian. The men are shiftless, lazy and ignorant. They prefer to have the women do the hard work and the latter find it necessary to do so if they would subsist without too great a hardship. They go lobstering, clamming, fishing, and hunting for driftwood when the mood takes them. The men have shown a fondness for strong drink and the women crave tobacco and smoke their old clay pipes as regularly as the men. They love sweets and little realize the value of money. If they receive a day's pay, they are likely to row over to the mainland and spend it all for candies and tobacco instead of the necessities of life."

Conditions in other small Maine communities like Frenchboro and Athens were probably worse, but the interracial community of Malaga was seen as different. Because it was inhabited by Black and white people, rumors of incest and corruption were rampant. Malaga grew notorious in New England, but not everyone saw the community as depraved. A missionary couple from Massachusetts who summered on a nearby island took an interest in helping them. Captain George and Lucy Lane started a school for the children and eventually formed the Malaga Association to raise funds to build a real schoolhouse on the island.

Pennie paused. She could picture it. She *had* pictured it. This was the schoolhouse she'd seen in her dream with the young woman teaching the mix of children. Eveline Woodman was the teacher hired by the Lanes. Pennie recalled the group of men in long overcoats and hats, accompanied by two women, touring the island and school. The children recited Bible verses, sang the hymn. A chill ran through her, realizing how her dreams and premonitions coincided with the history that lay in front of her, the newspaper account about the summer of 1911, how Governor Frederick Plaisted and his wife, Secretary of State Cyrus Davis and his wife, and members of the executive council visited the island and the schoolhouse. Impressed with the children, the governor had said that they would not force the Malaga people from their homes but also would not encourage outsiders to go to the island.

She became absorbed in the history and politics of the times around Governor Plaisted. About a year after visiting the island, he lost his bid to repeal Prohibition in Maine. His opponents, driven by the women's temperance movement and missionaries who protested alcohol abuse, paraded the streets of Portland and called him the "Rum Governor." When he lost his battle to make alcohol in Maine legal in 1911, he lost the confidence of his supporters who elected him. His career was ending.

During this time, three parties laid claim to Malaga Island: the heirs of the Perry family, who held a questionable deed; John Griffin, who had received a bond for a deed; and a local physician, H. H. Ferguson, who was issued a quit claim deed in 1888. But none of these men, nor the islanders, ever paid taxes on the island. The state attorney general at the time, William R. Pattangall, proclaimed the Perry family the rightful owners. The Malaga Association, including the same strong-willed group in the temperance movement, began negotiating a price to purchase the island from the Perry family. The family had never cared about the residents living there and so settled on a price of $400.

Out of the blue, without any notice or warning, the State of Maine stepped in to purchase the island from the Perrys for the exact same dollar amount in February 1912. Was this the vengeful act of a governor seeking retribution for his lost battle with the temperance movement and the Malaga Association? Did he make it his personal mission to upend their plans? Or was it merely a thinly veiled political action to take ownership for commercial gain under the guise of ethnic cleansing or moral superiority?

Pennie looked around at the volumes of library history that surrounded her and considered the absolute truth, and how, over time, truth rose like the stark reality of a dead body floating to the surface.

Only months after the state took control of Malaga, the beginning of the forced exile ensued. The state initially took an assessment of the physical, mental, and financial condition of each household. According to the *Bath Independent* newspaper, the Marks family and an elderly Annie Parker—four generations from four to seventy years old—were committed to the Maine School for the Feeble-Minded, forcibly removed by State Agent George Pease, Captain Charles T. Wallace of the Bath Police Department, and Dr. A. F. Williams of Phippsburg under the orders of probate judge James S. Lowell.

With eugenics as their righteous mantra, the council vowed to remove the entire "degenerate" community from their homes and in 1912 they sent the remaining thirty-five islanders an eviction notice. Governor Plaisted said: "I think the best plan would be to burn down the shacks with all of their filth. Certainly, the conditions there are not credible to our state. We ought not to have such things near our front door, and I do not think that a like condition can be found in Maine, although there are some pretty bad localities elsewhere."

Afraid for their lives, the entire colony dismantled their houses for transport, some moving to Phippsburg and others living as castaways along the coast. One destitute family, the Tripps, a mother and father with three young children, could not find a community who'd accept them and so lived as outcasts on a scow tied up in the New Meadows River.

Descendants of Malaga eventually settled in communities throughout Maine, many lying about their ancestry to escape mockery and shame. The slurs continued over the years. If a fisherman caught a dark lobster, he would say that it must have come from around Sebasco near the island on the New Meadows.

Pennie pressed on. She finished reading the transcript of a radio and photo documentary, *Malaga Island: A Story Best Left Untold*, detailing a firsthand history of the island, interviewing locals and descendants. The reporter, Rob Rosenthal, was lucky enough to speak with a descendant whose father was one of the three children of Robert and Laura Tripp—the family set adrift on a scow after the exile, forever without a home. The woman recalled the abuse she and her family suffered at the hands of her tormented father, his angry drunken rages about Malaga.

One local Phippsburg woman even told the reporter, "That's a story best left untold."

NEARLY A CENTURY LATER, in 2010, Maine Governor John Baldacci visited the island with a joint resolution of apology by the state legislature. With about ninety Malaga descendants at hand, he offered the first public admission of "profound regret" for the displacement of their ancestors in 1912. The descendants who were there that day described the apology as spiritual-like, a truth finally whispered in the wind, the sky clearing and the sun shining down on their souls; the first generation to rise above the shame and trauma of the past to declare pride in their heritage.

Pennie thought of Dani and Mali, their stories of growing up with parents who suffered from their own traumas, being forced from the reservation into foster care, displaced against their family's will. It was the incessant desire to control, forcing people of other cultures to adopt the ways of the dominant race.

She put the materials neatly back in the piles that had been laid out for her. The serious young man at the desk, the one who'd ushered Pennie inside, handed her a booklet about the Longfellow House as she was leaving. Walking out in a fog of history, trying to make sense of the past, she examined the plaque on the building: *Wadsworth-Longfellow house has been designated a Registered National Historic Landmark.* She knew Longfellow wrote three epic poems about America's history: "Evangeline," "Hiawatha," and "The Courtship of Miles Standish." It was "Evangeline" she most remembered from her childhood, the poem about the expulsion of the Acadians from their homeland in northern Maine and New Brunswick in the 1600s, a place where they once coexisted in peace with the Mi'kmaq, a band of the Wabanaki. It was another story of exile, the British forcing the Acadians to leave their homeland to become indentured servants.

The wind picked up and the booklet flew from Pennie's hand, falling on the brick sidewalk. Picking it up, a page lay open with a quote from Longfellow: "But happier is he whose heart rides quietly at anchor in the peaceful haven of home."

PENNIE PULLED HER COAT closer, crossing Congress to the city block where Dani and Mali's apartment was. Maine's settlers and descendants grew closer and closer to her heart, as if the Acadian, Mi'kmaq, Malaga Island and other countless ancestors walked the streets all around her. Taking the stairs two at a time, she refused to let the memory of Kush and his new girlfriend hijack her. When she knocked, Dani answered the door with purple ink on her hands. Pennie hugged her, not fully understanding why she was overcome with sudden sadness.

"Looks like I interrupted your work?" she asked, looking at Dani's stained hands.

Dani smiled. "How'd you guess?" Pennie followed her to the industrial work sink and watched her scrub with an old dish towel. "What brings you to this side of town?"

"Just came from the Historical Society, researching Malaga. I wondered if you'd heard anything about your great-aunt."

Dani motioned her to sit. "As a matter of fact, I talked with my father this morning. He said she was still alive, as far as he knew, and gave me her number. Said she was about as pleasant to talk to as an old buzzard."

Pennie sat on the low ottoman. "That's not very nice. Did they have a falling out?"

"My father's family...isn't exactly tight. His parents, and some aunts and uncles, were sent by the state to a boarding school up in Nova Scotia. Really tore our family apart. And later, my father and his brother were sent to foster care."

"I'm sorry to ask this of your father."

"Oh, this is nothing new. Should we call her? Find out if she knows anything about the graves?"

"If you don't mind. She might be able to help us."

Dani plopped on the couch and grabbed a small notebook. Dialing with her thumb, she put the phone on speaker. After five rings, a man's voice said hello.

"Oh, hi, this is Dani Toney. I'm Dana's daughter. He thought maybe his Aunt Eleanor still lived here?"

"Who's Dana?" The man's voice was smooth and kind.

"Dana Toney, my father. His mother was Hannah, Eleanor's sister."

"Oh, well, hello. I'm Eleanor's nephew, Ronnie. You know, seems like I remember hearing about Dana. He was a guide up on Grand Lake, right?"

"That's right! Still is. I don't believe he'll stop until he dies."

"Good to have a job as a lifestyle if you're lucky enough. My aunt doesn't usually take calls, but she may want to talk to you. Give me a sec."

He put the phone down and Pennie pictured an old rotary telephone on the kitchen wall like her aunt and uncle used to have. Through the speaker, the faint thump-thump of a walker grew louder.

A frail but pointed voice came on, loud and clear. "Hello, who's this?"

"Hi, it's Dani Toney. Dana is my father, your sister Hannah's son."

"Hannah's been dead for more than twenty years, hasn't she?"

"Yes, that's right. Cancer. It was very sudden—"

"Well, then, what are you looking for? I ain't got any money if that's what you're after."

"Oh, no, no. That's not why I'm calling."

"Nobody calls me unless they want something."

"This is about Malaga. My father thought you knew about our relation to the Marks family that lived on the island."

She coughed and hacked something up. "Sure, they're cousins. What about them?"

"Did you know some of them are buried at the Patient's Cemetery in Fairview?"

"Oh, I know all about it. The state sent them to live with the lunatics and buried them there, except for Abbie and Lottie. They were the only ones who managed to escape."

"Where are they now?"

"Abbie died a while back, then Lottie, but she made it to 103. She asked to be buried on Malaga, but they don't care, nobody does. I think she's buried somewhere in Brunswick."

Dani stared at Pennie, who prompted her on. "Sorry to hear that, Aunt Eleanor. We just heard that a developer wants to put in a business complex out at Heritage Acres, with a road that runs near the graveyard where Lottie's family is buried."

"What do you want me to do about it?"

"Well, we were wondering if, since we're related to the Marks, you might be willing to write a letter to the court, ask for them to put a stop to it."

"Nothing I've ever said made a lick of difference in the past. Why would it now?"

"I know it must be—"

The phone knocked against the wall followed by the thump of the walker moving away.

"Hey there, Dani." Friendly Ronnie was back. "She doesn't talk to many people."

"I understand. I appreciate you asking her. My friend Pennie works for a law office. And, well, we think a letter from her would sway the court to decide against putting a road in close to the Malaga graves, where some of our relatives are."

A pause fell over the line. Pennie could practically feel Ronnie working up a strategy to persuade Eleanor. "Let me work on her. Give me a few days. I'll see what I can do."

Dani thanked him and hung up. She stared out the window at the dwindling afternoon light. "I can't blame her. No one wants to bring up the past. Most would rather forget about our dark history, families torn apart, exiled, sent to boarding schools where they were abused. All in the name of colonization. Malaga was just another chapter."

When Pennie got back to the office, her uncle came out to see her. "Took you a while."

"I'm still digesting all this information. It's appalling, really. Then I stopped by Dani's. She has a great-aunt who says they're related to the Marks family, the one that was removed from the island and committed to the School for the Feeble-Minded. And most of them are buried at the cemetery. We called her to try to get her to write a letter to stop the road."

"I hope she can write something fast. I talked to the town and the excavation has been cleared to start tomorrow."

"Tomorrow? How did that happen? I don't—"

"Projects can be pushed through, and Ward Lewis has pulled all the strings. You better get on the horn to the Historical Society and see if the director can get that letter to us today. Did you learn anything else?"

She sat down. "Yellow journalism was alive and well at the turn of the century." She recalled the heartbreaking story of the descendant, a daughter of an abusive alcoholic father who was the child of one of the families set adrift with no home on the New Meadows River. "The suffering goes on for generations."

"Good details to make the case," he said, ever practical. "I'll work on the emergency injunction, and we'll see if we can get it filed today." He eyed the clock, then looked at Pennie, still sitting. "What are you waiting for?"

THAT AFTERNOON, THEY RUSHED the paperwork to the courthouse, where Alfie's connections to Judge Ruth Benoit gave them a leg up. Pennie followed him down the halls of the marbled courthouse and descended the stairs to the judge's chambers in the basement. There was no time lost on friendly banter. After a quick exchange, the judge asked her uncle for a quick summary, which he succinctly provided with particulars about the development and the cemetery's proximity to the proposed road. "My associate Pennie here has some information on Malaga from the Historical Society she'd like to share."

Pennie froze for a moment, not expecting to have to speak. Put on the spot, she shuffled in her chair. "Yes, I was, I was over there today and had the chance to look at some photos and newspaper clippings." She cleared her throat, put her hands under her legs to keep from shaking and proceeded to share the encapsulated history of the eugenics movement, the mixed race of the Malaga community making headlines as an immoral, inbred, degenerate colony. The more she talked, the more she felt emboldened, even angry. "But that's not even the worst part. After the island was cleared, including all of their homesteads, the bodies buried on the island were exhumed—seventeen in all—and transported to the Patient's Cemetery in Fairview where they rest today. It's a significant gravesite."

The judge turned to her uncle. "What does the Preservation Commission have to say about this?"

"They were never notified," he said. "Seems they skipped that step."

She shook her head. After a question or two about the development, she swiftly signed the injunction. "Good to see you're still putting up the good fight, Alfred. You'll get notice about the hearing for the temporary injunction. Can't put that off more than a couple of weeks."

"I know how things are. Thanks, Judge. Appreciate it."

Before she knew it, they were on their way out, walking back down the marbled corridors to the outside. Pennie had the urge to embrace her uncle but knew that this was not the time or the place. Instead, she thanked him and tried to hide her exhilaration.

"I'm afraid this might be a losing battle. The road does not touch that gravesite. Close, but it meets the setback."

"But it's so disrespectful to those people, those souls, after all they've been through."

He stopped at the base of the courthouse steps. "You make it sound as though they're still alive."

"Their spirits are alive. I can feel it." She wasn't sure why she'd said it but there it was, sharing her innermost thoughts, her growing premonitions.

"C'mon, birdie. Let's go home and see what Aunt Aggie's got cooking up for dinner."

Chapter 12
Unsettled

AT THE WARM HOUSE on Pine Street, the smell of chicken fricot with dumplings filled her with the comfort of a good, wholesome meal. She scooted the dogs to the big kitchen, Daisy bringing up the rear, and greeted her aunt standing at the stove. She was drinking a gin martini.

"Didn't expect you for dinner, Pennie dear." She recognized the signs of her aunt having a difficult day. Maybe it was the darkness settling in on another cold April night. Spring was around the corner, but Aunt Aggie's mood never stabilized until the last winter breath was sucked into the past.

"Smells delicious. Hope you don't mind."

"You're always welcome here, you know that. Must get lonely living by yourself."

Yes, Pennie knew how much she depended on them, her only family, despite the hurts of the past that only a family can inflict on one another.

Tita breezed in and grabbed a raw carrot from the counter. "Pennie's got a new squeeze, a big real estate man to keep her company during these cold spring nights."

Pennie wanted to choke her for bringing Ward up like this. "It's nothing serious. I'm just getting to know him and don't even know if I like him, to tell you the truth."

Aunt Aggie smiled and held open her palms in surprise, trying her best to sound cheerful. "You'll have to invite him over. What's his name? How did you meet?"

This was the last thing she wanted to talk about. Pennie knew a man like Ward would impress her aunt. "Ward Lewis. He's a developer that's putting in the office park over at Heritage Acres."

Her aunt came over to sit at the table, setting her glass down and pulling up a chair. "That's the road you were telling us about this morning."

"I guess he already has the approval from the town, but Uncle Alfie worked his magic, and we got a court stay today."

As if on cue, Alfie walked in to kiss Aunt Aggie on the cheek and check the pot on the stove. Without a word, he squeezed Pennie's shoulder on the way out to his den to watch the evening news with a glass of bourbon. The dogs followed.

"You can't stop progress, Pennie," her aunt said. "Don't take this personally. A man has to make a living, and if it means building a road close to a gravesite, well, that doesn't seem like such a crime."

Pennie watched her cousin playing on her phone, ignoring their conversation. "You should read about the exile of these poor people from Malaga. It was horrendous."

"I can only imagine. But not the first time and won't be the last."

Pennie recalled the poem about the Acadians. "You know, I thought of you today when I was at the Historical Society. I love that poem 'Evangeline' you used to read to us when we were little. Wasn't that about your own ancestors?"

Aggie paused. "My ancestors learned to keep quiet about that history, living down in Massachusetts. Believe me. Better not to have that bit of business follow you. People can be vicious."

"That's it, don't you see? Your relatives were forcibly removed from their homeland. How devastating that must have been for your family and all the families exiled. Something like five thousand Acadians were loaded on ships to become indentured servants, right?"

"Pennie, dear, I learned a long time ago there are terrible things that come out of war." Now her aunt had something she was uncomfortable talking about. "My father always said, you can wallow in it, or you pull up your bootstraps and move on. There's nothing worse than a victim."

Pennie wanted to say that perhaps sweeping it under the rug, trying to erase history, was even worse. But she didn't have the words. "Did your great-grandparents ever talk about what happened?"

"God, no. No sense in dredging up the past. We were one of the lucky families who survived." She pointed an accusing finger at Pennie as she stood up to check the bread in the oven. "Don't forget, my mother was British. Survival of the fittest, Pennie dear." She sipped her martini.

"Well, I just think we owe it to the dead to keep a road and an office park development far from their burial grounds. We can't change the past, but we can change our actions today."

"That sounds pretty...*woke* of you, Pennie dear." She set the martini glass on the counter with a dissonant *clink*.

Pennie's skin grew cold. A familiar shame was taking hold. Shame. How she was programmed growing up in this household. To hold her tongue lest she get into some forbidden territory and feel sorry for herself, God forbid thinking she had it worse than anybody else.

Tita, never good at handling tense moments, changed the subject. "Pennie, did I tell you that I ran into the ski patrol kid we met on your birthday weekend?"

Her heart pounded. She forced a smile. *Way to kick someone when they're down.* "No, you didn't mention it."

Tita snapped a carrot in half with her teeth. "Yeah, funniest coincidence, his last name is Lewis. Could he be related to Ward?"

"That would be a strange coincidence." Getting up to mask her horror, she grabbed the bottle of gin and poured it into the shaker, added some ice and vermouth. "Want one?' she asked Tita casually, though her face was growing hot.

"Naw, I'm meeting up with Lars after dinner. Looking at the latest footage together."

"How's it coming along? An Oscar-winner in the making?" She did her best to appease her cousin. Tita was probably still pissed that Pennie hinted to her aunt about his "baggage." That's why Tita brought up the ski patrol, just another personal jab creeping into the conversations.

"We need more money for the final cut, Lars says. He's waiting to hear back from the State Theatre about renting it for a fundraiser to show some early footage, you know, generate some buzz."

"That's not a bad idea," Aunt Aggie said. "You have a lot of friends from the ski circuit." Her aunt desperately wanted Tita to succeed, to make something of her life, even if it involved Lars. For now, anyway.

Pennie turned toward her cousin. "Do people do that sort of thing?"

"All the time. And if you stay on the good side of Mr. Real Estate, maybe he'll kick in some funding, become a sponsor. Can you talk to him?"

She gulped the martini, wincing. "Sure, I'll talk to him." Anything to keep Tita from bringing up the ski patrol again.

"Awesome." Tita looked at her phone, excited. "Looks like Lars just heard from his friend at the State Theatre. He's agreed to let us have it the night of May 1st for a grand. That's a steal."

"That's not much time." She wondered how realistic Tita's big plans were.

"It'll have to be enough. This is the only time the calendar's open to do it."

Her aunt scooped out bowls of the steaming chicken fricot. "Aunt Maude and I will invite the ladies in our bridge club. I know their husbands have deep pockets." She chewed her olive and smacked her lips, her mood lightening like a sail catching a switching wind.

DRIVING HOME, EMOTIONALLY EXHAUSTED, Pennie felt her mother's presence in the car beside her. Maybe it was her longing for some connection, some link to her past that would give her a lifeline. She wasn't sure how she fit into this family, other than with her uncle. He was her strongest link, but she suspected Tita was jealous of the bonding going on in the office. While she and Uncle Alfie were out getting injunctions at the courthouse, Tita was at the office taking calls.

A gentle snow was falling, even in early April, making for a slick drive home. She slammed on the brakes when the light turned red, skidding a few yards. The martini and glass of wine made her head spin. Taking the long route, she drove along Casco Bay at night and gazed at the gleaming water under a waxing three-quarter moon. Dani had told her that the original name of this bay was Kaskok, meaning Place of Many Great Blue Herons.

Her mother had asked for her ashes to be scattered out there. Pennie had no recollection of how they were dispensed but knew her uncle had taken care of it for Birdie. The crazy one. That's what Aunt Aggie always said, like her mother was below them, just not right in the head.

Pulling into her driveway, she skidded again and was surprised when she looked up. Ward. There he was on her doorstep. Her heart fluttered.

Goddamn him for being here at her most vulnerable, right after she'd just left the static indifference of her family.

Taking a deep breath for courage, she pulled herself out of the car to face him under a dim light, the silence of downy flurries a testament to their quiet attraction. He had a bottle of wine in his hand. She walked by him and inserted the key in the lock, smelling the whiskey on him. He grabbed her wrist. His hand was icy cold. "Pen, I don't know what I did to upset you, but let me make it—"

Before he could finish, she was on his lips, urgent, needy, desperate for love. He enveloped her with his broad arms, his protection, his bold strength, pushing her against the door until it fell open. Turning, in silence, she took his frozen hand, led him up the stairs, straight to her bedroom where the streetlight shone through slits in the blinds, the quiet of a never-ending winter upon them. They were looking for the heat of each other.

In a moment, they were under the cold sheets, removing every stitch between them, seeking something. Not love, not honesty, not promises of any kind, but only the human touch of someone just as dire for compassion and understanding, a kindness lacking in the daily mishmash of their chaos.

His lips were tender, his torso warm. She shivered and cupped his hands between hers, warming them, warming his heart. Was he under the same spell she was? Would he still be here for her tomorrow, after he found out about the injunction? Somehow, she didn't care inside this moment. All she wanted was to take him, to take everything from him, all his passion and his past, his contempt, and his goodness. It was his attention she wanted, his acceptance. That was it. Without words, only their bodies mingling together, the ruggedness of their sex, the tenderness of their assault onto one another, made her lie back and cry in the darkness afterward, out of breath.

He wiped the tear from the corner of her eye in the dark. "Was it that bad?"

A chuckle rose beneath her. "Yes, it was. You monster. Showing up at my door looking for a booty call, forcing yourself in here."

"Umm, sure, that's it." He ran his soft palm over the outline of her face. "You know you drive me crazy. Showing up at my house like you did, had your way with me and left within the space of an hour. Left me all alone to my lasagna after I slaved over a hot stove."

"You're right, I owe you an explanation." She rolled over and looked at him, thinking about her choices. She was truly a coward at heart. "I had accidentally run across my ex-boyfriend with his new girlfriend that night, before coming to your place."

"Ouch. Why didn't you say anything?"

"The last thing I want to do is wallow in a past relationship. If you did that, I'd hate you for it."

He kissed her shoulder. "I won't do that. I promise."

"Anyway, I'm sorry. Now you know it was revenge sex I had with you."

"I love revenge sex, or whatever you want to call it. You can use me anytime."

Their conversation about the business park at his house that night came to her, but she did not want to ruin the peace between them, the loveliness of the moment, their warm bodies against one another, finally satiated, finally exhausted and quiet. What would he do when the injunction was served? Was he really breaking ground tomorrow?

"Penny for your thoughts."

She leaned into him. "Nickel maybe, but not for a mere cent."

"You got it, nickels galore."

Her mind pivoted and she ran her fingers through his thick light hair, could see the deepening cracks around his mouth, tracing them. "I hope you don't think I'm taking advantage of the moment here, but—"

"Lay it on me, girl."

"I told you about my cousin's film, right? She and her boyfriend, Lars, and the ski documentary."

"You mentioned it. Don't tell me this is about money."

"No moss growing on you." She moved her body closer so he could feel her outline. "They need a few sponsors for the sneak-peek event they're planning."

"And what do I get for this so-called sponsorship?"

"Publicity, I guess. They're planning a big gala at the State Theatre. Lots of people, lots of exposure, and hopefully lots of money raised to finish this thing and market it."

"And what do you think about this movie project? Am I hitching my horse to a winner or a dud?"

"Supposedly it's good. I could ask for footage. Lars probably has some kind of trailer he's put together."

"Sounds like you're not a fan."

"He's a bit much, considers himself a genius. You know the type."

His lopsided grin alarmed her. It was that same grin. The ski patrol. How was she supposed to know they were related? Why hadn't she told him yet? It was her own shame, hanging over her like a cloud.

"I'll want to see some of his movie-making greatness before promising anything. One thing he has on his side is your cousin's reputation on the slopes. I can't believe you haven't introduced us yet."

Breathing in deeply, her heartbeat quickened. She wrapped her arms around him and pulled him close. "Tita's still got it. And she's not afraid to flaunt it. On the slopes, she's still badass."

"I think you're the real badass." He ran his warm hand over her stomach. "Revenge sex." He closed his eyes and in the space of a few minutes, flipped his internal switch and began to snore lightly.

How she wished this kind of shift worked for her. Instead, her mind went to Heritage Acres again, the cemetery, the injunction. How would she ever explain herself? Reluctantly, she fell into a fitful sleep, at odds with herself, falling into the blackness of her mind.

Another dream. She saw the old farm buildings of the School for the Feeble-Minded on the hill, scattered dormitories around. Everything smelled like spring, a bouquet of fragrant wildflowers and pine trees. But there was also something else. Moving toward the pungent scent, she realized she was seeing through the eyes of the dog again.

A group of working women in white button-down uniforms stood smoking outside the nearest building, what looked like a hospital. When they entered the back door, she skulked in behind them. Along corridors sat men and women and children on the floor, half-naked, chained to the wall in their own defecation. A nurse marched toward her down the hall, and she ducked into an alcove. Water pooled on the cement floor underneath her, and looking out, she could see a woman spraying down the patients with a hose.

A man appeared, also in white, smelling like disinfectant. He said to the nurse, "Bring in the Marks girl, Lottie. We're ready for her." The nurse grabbed a girl of about nineteen who was sitting against the wall. "C'mon, girl. Your turn next." It was the same girl from the schoolhouse, the one who answered Mrs. Woodman. Lottie screamed for the nurse to leave her alone, to please let her go. The nurse strapped her to a hospital bed and peeled her clothes off. "This is for your own good." After placing a sheet on top of her, she wheeled her into what looked like an operating room.

Pennie jumped onto a chair beside the door to see, through the eyes of the dog, inside the small window to the room where the doctor covered the writhing girl's mouth with a mask for gas. Lottie's dark eyes stared back at her, leaking a stream of tears, deep never-ending pools of sorrow. Within five minutes, he began the operation, using a scalpel to cut an incision in her abdomen, the young Lottie lifeless, asleep to her forced sterilization.

THE NEXT DAY, SITTING at her desk overlooking Exchange Street, Cassie dozing on the rug beside her, Pennie stared at her phone. Uncle Alfie had told her that the stay order to halt any excavation would be served to Ward that morning before 9:00 a.m. A tight knot rolled around inside her as she thought over whether he meant to hide this truth. Was he that desperate to see this project move ahead that he would deliberately deceive her? They were on two sides of a moral question. It was as simple as that. Her aunt's voice came back to her. *People have to make a living, Pennie.*

Tita strolled in, fashionably late, wearing Ray-Bans and a lined leather jacket, looking like a star of the screen. She was certainly projecting a diva's attitude lately. She and Lars had worked hard on the film and stuck with it, despite their relationship's ups and downs. And from the limited stuff she'd seen of Lars's work, his filming was pretty good.

The phone rang and Tita pulled an earbud out to answer it. "Alfred Goode attorney's office. Let me see if he's available. Can I tell him who's calling?" Pressing hold, she yelled across the office. "Can you take a call from Jack?" It was the surveyor.

"Put him through."

Pennie jumped up to peer into her uncle's office and he waved her in.

"Jack, what do you have for me?" He scratched Fella between the ears, who sat proudly on his lap. "That's interesting. Let me talk to Jeannette and I'll get back to you."

Hanging up the phone, he checked his watch before yelling to Tita. "Call Jeannette McCarthy and ask her if I can come out to see her this morning." He turned his attention to Pennie. "Feel like taking a field trip?"

"Sure, what's up?"

"I guess the police gave Jack the go-ahead to survey the lot next week. He talked to one of the detectives who said they'd gotten the early DNA test back."

"Any leads?"

"Nope, only that the jewelry most definitely was Chloe's. I'm sure Jeannette's a mess."

Tita yelled from her desk. "She's expecting you. She'll be home until lunch."

"Let's go."

Pennie grabbed her laptop and Tita ignored them as they walked out. She said she never was interested in this field work, but that meant Pennie spent a lot of time with her father. She could never really be sure with Tita. Slights were so easily made it was easier to slough it off and let it settle itself.

Outside, the air was crisp. The snow from the previous night had already melted, the cobblestones wet. She checked her phone but still nothing.

"Heard anything from Ward yet?"

She hated how he knew things, and that he was usually right. "Nothing yet."

Cassie, the only dog he allowed on these outings, jumped into the backseat and wagged her tail, smiling, thrilled to be on a mission. Pennie's mind went back to the day they'd measured the lot between the property lines for Mrs. McCarthy. "What will happen now? Are they finished with the crime scene?"

"Pretty much. They'll be pulling out any day now. I'll have to talk to Jeannette about next steps."

"How long do these investigations normally take?"

"Usually months, but I'm not sure they'll have any suspects."

"Can the area still be built on?"

"That's where the criminal attorneys come in. They'll let her know."

The waters of Casco Bay rolled in the distance, a rough dark blue. He cracked Cassie's back window to let the scents in. The day was lovely and brisk, and Pennie absentmindedly checked her phone again. It was almost 10:00 a.m. and nothing from Ward. Would he even call her? Should she call him and explain?

Driving down the long driveway with the wrought-iron fence, the yellow tape around the crime scene beside the mansion came into view. Her uncle steered around the circle drive and parked in front of the grand entrance with white pillars. They stepped out of the car to the salty smell of the bay, and she shivered as they walked to the doorway. Mrs. McCarthy stood just inside, Jack and Ginger at her heels, barking their welcome.

"Hello, Alfie." She smiled, tight-lipped, before turning to Pennie. "Nice to see you, dear." Her kind eyes seemed to have grown older since the first time they'd met, only weeks ago. They followed her into the kitchen where she offered them coffee. Jeannette looked out the window toward her stunning view of the rolling sea, choppy white-caps.

"You've probably heard that the crime scene will be wrapping up soon."

Alfie looked down at the porcelain tile floors. "I'm sorry to hear about all of this. But I hope you get some closure for everything you're going through." It wasn't often Pennie saw her uncle uncomfortable.

Her voice showed her tiredness, sleeplessness. "I'm glad they found the jewelry. Seems almost fate this all happened when we were looking at the property lines."

"Have you found out anything new?"

"No, they won't share anything conclusive with me yet. But they did send me a copy of the surveillance camera video from the night the necklace was dug up. Here, let me show it to you."

She moved to the desk in the corner of her expansive kitchen where she turned on the computer. Clicking through a few screens, she landed on a video file. She opened the video to full screen. They huddled around to look at the darkness of her lawn when a dog appeared, a husky of some sort, who began to dig in the hard wet ground. It was the same spot where they had found the yellow croquet ball, on the far side. Working at the ground with tenacious effort, bits of dirt flying, the dog stuck his muzzle in the ground and pulled back on something a few times before it popped free.

A prickle moved up Pennie's spine. The husky turned toward the camera with the necklace dangling from its mouth and she nearly fell over, grabbing the chair behind her for balance. It was the same dog from her dreams playing out on the screen.

Uncle Alfie placed his hand on her back, staring at the video, the dark, shining eyes of the dog looking through them. He turned to Pennie. "Are you okay? Do you want to sit?"

Fear overwhelmed her. "Yes, I—thank you, I will."

"I know how you feel, dear. I was alarmed watching this, too." Jeannette set a glass of water next to her. "There's no explanation how or why Chloe's necklace was buried here, and...her charm bracelet..." Her jaw quivered.

Pennie gulped the water. "It's just so strange to see that—that dog. Digging it up like he knew it was there."

Uncle Alfie sat in the tall upholstered chair beside Jeannette. "Have you ever seen that dog before?"

"No, never. And I can't believe Jack and Ginger never barked. They always alert me to anything outside. Even the goddamn wind blowing." The Pomeranians lay at her feet, looking up at her as if sensing the accusation.

Her uncle gazed out the window at the wide blue ocean before turning back to Jeannette. "What about your stepson? Did you show him the video?"

"No. The criminal lawyer told me to have as little communication with *Edmund* as possible. Thanks for that referral, by the way. That Leslie is a real pit bull. I'm in good hands with her. The only thing I've told him is that I'm not allowing anything to be done to the property until this investigation is over. Of course, Edmund fought me on it. He was hoping to get his new house started this spring and be moved in by the fall. Well, that won't be happening."

Pennie looked back at the computer, the husky's face and black shining eyes frozen on the screen. She recalled waking from the dream, her nails broken and hands red. Standing up to keep from shaking, she walked to the sink for another drink of water.

Her uncle stood behind her with his cup and saucer. "Jeannette, we'll do whatever you recommend. If you still want Jack to survey the lot, you just let us know."

"I'll talk to Leslie about it. I do want to find out about those property lines."

From the counter, Pennie picked up a framed picture of Chloe, the locket around her neck reflecting the sunlight. Her elderly father stood on one side of her and a middle-aged man with a prominent Adam's apple on the other.

She pointed to the strange man and Jeannette said flatly, "That's Edmund."

Pennie nodded, knowing better than to ask about the stepson. "You said she had the necklace when she died in the accident?"

Jeannette touched her hand with a slight tremble. "Yes, it was her favorite piece of jewelry. Her best friend gave it to her when this picture was taken, on her seventeenth birthday. She never lived to see eighteen."

"I'm sure they'll find out who's behind this."

"More frightening is the unearthing of her horse charm bracelet. It was a family heirloom. I remember putting it on her wrist before they closed the casket." She steadied herself at the counter. "I must be going mad."

Uncle Alfie spoke softly. "Jeannette, did anyone else remember seeing the bracelet on her when she was buried?"

"No, I called the funeral home, but of course, no one seems to remember anything other than how beautiful and peaceful she looked. Even though it was a car accident, and she severed her spine, she looked absolutely perfect lying in that coffin. I even tucked in her riding crop."

Pennie turned to her. "She liked to ride?"

"Oh, yes, Chloe loved it. Took lessons for years over at Heritage Acres."

"What a coincidence. We're working on a case over there." She recalled taking pictures at the horse show, the adolescent girls riding in unison, the image of something coming in and out of focus, of the ghost rider trotting behind them. A rawness seeped into her spine.

"That's not surprising. Hundreds of girls from here to Brunswick have taken lessons there over the years. It was Chloe's happy place."

THE AIR WARMED AS Uncle Alfie drove north on Route 1, Cassie's head out the back window, Pennie's mind still whirling. She pulled up old pictures of Boone on her phone. His lineage—part husky, part Labrador, sometimes called huskador—gave him a beautiful, coarse coat and a friendly disposition. Black and white markings around the face, muzzle, and ears. Penetrating dark eyes.

Her uncle asked her to grab his sunglasses from the glove compartment, startling her. Pulling the glasses out, a picture fell. She handed him the glasses and retrieved the picture from the floor. Her mother.

"Oh, yes, forgot that was in there." He put on the aviators and pointed toward the photo. "Your mum with her dog, Togo."

She stared at the image of her mother with her long auburn hair, the Alaskan husky by her side, her hand on his gray mane. Blue eyes of her ancestors stared back at her. "It's uncanny," she said. "Togo looks just like the dog in the video. Where did this come from?"

"Oh, I've had it forever. Keep it with me to look at when I need some strength. Your mother was always courageous. She and Togo weren't afraid of anything."

She stared at the thick husky coat. "Boone's father."

"That's right." He scratched Cassie, who leaned in from the back seat. "You remember the sire of your pups, don't you girl?"

Her mother wore a long dark brown wool jacket, a gold- and russet-colored silk scarf around her neck pinned with an old brooch. "This is too much of a coincidence."

He crossed the bridge to Fairview. "That's exactly what I thought when I saw that dog on the surveillance video. What do you think it means?"

"I think I'm beginning to get a little freaked out."

He stared ahead. "What aren't you telling me?"

"What do you mean?" She wasn't ready to share any of her crazy dreams with him, or the feeling of Boone's soul hovering over her after the ski accident. He'd never let her continue working with him if he thought she was losing her grip on reality.

"Pennie, you were frightened when you saw that video. I told you this business could get very weird. I'm concerned this is making you a little unsettled."

Unsettled. What he really meant was *unstable*. She hated that word. Maybe because she'd heard people refer to her mother that way. She took a deep breath. "This dog, this husky, came to me in a dream. It was a few weeks ago, even before we knew about the necklace or bracelet in the ground. It's too much of a coincidence. I...I don't know what's happening."

He asked her to put the photo away but before she did, she snapped a picture of it.

"Your mother used to have dreams, too, but she called them visions. I heard enough of them to know that what she saw was indeed a little uncanny."

"And Togo looks exactly like the one on the video we just saw."

He scratched Cassie between the ears. "That could be pure coincidence. There are plenty of huskies around."

She was about to interrupt but he stopped her, his voice more serious now. "Pennie, back when you asked me about working in the office, I told you it would only be temporary."

"But I'm working on the Heritage Acres case."

"You can finish that. The injunction meeting is coming up soon. Once that's sorted out and we have some closure in the matter, you ought to begin transitioning to your career as a vet tech."

Cassie rested her head on Pennie's shoulder. "Okay," she said, knowing there was nothing else to say without digging herself into a deeper hole. "Is that why my mother left home? Aunt Aggie thought she was unstable?"

At first, he didn't say a word, just let the silence engulf them. "You know, that was a long time ago. I'll admit there was tension between your mother and my wife." He chuckled to himself before clearing his throat, becoming serious again. "I loved your mother's strong personality, had grown up with it, but it was trying on the two of us as a young couple. We had our own relationship to sort out."

Pennie knew better than to press it any further, and she also knew he was a good man who loved his sisters. He turned down the road with the cemetery. Soon yellow excavation tractors and trucks came into view. To her relief, the equipment sat dormant, giant metal monsters frozen in time. The front-end loader had begun tearing up the ground for the road and most of the old stone wall but stopped just before the Patient's Cemetery. It indeed looked as if the court order was delivered just in time to halt the digging near those graves.

Stepping out of the car, she immediately felt the slight tremors beneath her again. Her uncle plodded along the border of the cemetery and didn't seem to notice the vibrations. "Looks like Ward got his notice in time." The enormous equipment dwarfed him. "It'll be a miracle if we can keep this one from going through, you know."

The earth trembled with what Pennie knew were the spirits of Malaga, reaching out to her in their unrest. Shoving her hands into her coat pockets, she tried to remain calm. "Yes, I know. All we can do is try."

The wind picked up and swept through her with icy vengeance. Her uncle looked down at the woods separating them from the Heritage Acres property on the other side, the place where she and Ward had ridden the horses, where she'd first felt the aura of the squall.

He looked up at the sky that'd turned gray again, the treetops bending to the stiff gusts. "I hope we don't get more snow. I'm about sick of this winter already."

ON THE DRIVE BACK to the office, Pennie's phone chimed. Her pulse skipped—was Ward calling to confront her? Her heart calmed when she saw it was only Tita.

"Hey, tell Pop to take his phone off silent for a change."

Pennie smiled at her uncle who seemed deep in thought. "What's up?"

"The date of your temporary injunction hearing came in. It's next Friday."

"What, only a week from today?"

Uncle Alfie looked at her with his eyebrows raised. She cupped the phone. "The hearing's next Friday. How will we ever be ready by then?"

"Looks like you've got some fast work to do." He sensed her distress. "Believe me, this injunction hearing is the best thing for both sides. I'm sure Ward wants to keep his construction moving, while we want to seize our chance to have a judge rule against it and stop it immediately."

Tita was in her ear again. "Hey, can you meet me at Mali and Dani's tonight to help make cards? We have a design for the sneak-peek night."

Her mind whirled with all the research she had to do. "They whipped something up already?"

"Sent me some designs this morning, and Lars likes one. We're ready to get rolling. The sooner we get these in the mail the better. We only have twenty-four days. But we've already got Bean's as a sponsor." L.L. Bean as a sponsor, that was saying something about the growing buzz. "They're sending me a check for five grand, so that should cover the expenses. Now all we have to do is sell tickets and find more sponsors. Did you talk to Mr. Real Estate last night?"

"Actually, I did." She stared out the window at Baxter Boulevard. "He said he'd think about it. Wants to see a trailer if you've got it."

"We do, a four-minute piece. I'll send it to you."

"If you don't mind—" Pennie cleared her throat. "I'd rather you send it to him directly."

"Okay, shoot me his email. Tell Pop I have to leave the office early. I'll see you over there."

Even though she knew she should be staying and working late, she was glad for the break. Walking down Congress Street, she looked at her phone and the picture she'd snapped of her mother standing with Togo, wearing a silk scarf around her neck pinned with the brooch, an amber stone to match her hair. What was the universe telling her? Was it leading her down a certain path to some kind of clarity, if only she would just follow her intuition? Was that husky in the surveillance video from her dream? Was it Togo?

Ward had still not called. She was obviously still infatuated with him, despite her best efforts to remain emotionally detached. Was she expecting him to forgive her? If she ever wanted to win the case against him, she had to find out everything she could to stop him.

Tita's Jan Van sat parked in front of the twins' studio. Inside the old building, Pennie immediately sensed the warm spirit of her friends in conversation. Without knocking, she walked in to find the three of them huddled around the large worktable in the middle of the loft, so deep in collaboration over designs they didn't notice Pennie. They all jumped when she said hello.

"My God, you scared the shit out of me." Dani wore a black apron covered in white, burgundy, and gold paint.

Pennie peered between them to see what they were looking at: a large black-and-white ink rendering of a great horned owl's head floating over a freestyler's body with skis pointing out like owl talons, giant curved wings to either side, as if the skier were coming in for a kill. The shadow of the owl fell over the title and tagline: *Freestyle Femme Fatale, Stronger than the Wind, Genius of the Air.*

"Wow, that's quite provocative."

Tita beamed. "Don't you just love it?"

"It certainly makes a statement. Lars likes it?"

"He loves it! Mali came up with the concept and Dani brought it to life. You two are creative geniuses!"

Mali put her hands on hips. "Thank the Cipelahq legend."

Dani smiled wearily. "To be honest, I worry about using one of our legends as a mascot for your documentary."

Mali leaned over the table. "This is an amazing piece of artwork, Dani. Don't belittle it calling it a mascot."

Dani stood straight and took a deep breath. "We're always complaining about cultural appropriation, our customs and history being commercialized. Now, I worry we're doing the *same thing*."

"But it's *our* history. Look around here. This is what we do."

"I know." Dani looked up to the cards hanging on the far wall, her striking Passamaquoddy designs of turtles, hummingbirds, salmon, moose, and bears. "I'm just having second thoughts about Cipelahq being used for a film about a star white athlete. No offense, Tita."

Pennie gently chimed in. "I think I can understand why you'd feel that way. Your ancestors were killed, exiled for trying to keep their culture alive." A shadow passed over her thoughts—the moment of her ski accident, crashing against the tree, sliding down the bank, the great wings passing above her in the bluest sky.

Tita sighed with her palms up, showing her owl tattoo. "I absolutely love it, but I'll leave it up to you."

Mali spread her arms, her own salmon tattoo showing. "Dani, this is your artistic representation of an athlete's spirit. Don't be afraid to share it with the world. You never know where inspiration comes from."

Dani ran her hand over the menacing owl. The loft fell silent. "I do love her. And you were the inspiration, Tita, both light and shadow."

"Light and shadow?" Tita asked.

"Cipelahq represents both the dark side of nature when he stole the maidens away to the other world and also their enlightenment when he gave them special powers to control their own destiny back on earth."

Tita looked out the window. "I guess I can understand that. I certainly have a light and dark side." She smiled, a melancholy passing through her as if she were thinking about the highs and lows of her racing days.

Mali grew impatient at her sister's indecision. "I could really use a cup of tea. Anyone else?"

None of them ever turned down the special tea always brewing in the studio. Dani held up the poster. "Yes, let's celebrate Cipelahq, the superhuman deity, and the freestyle femme fatale!"

Tita clapped her hands in relief while Mali poured the steaming red clover tea into four paper cups. "The very finest china to celebrate the launch of the original femme fatale of the Maine slopes."

Tita took a careful sip. "Lars likes it so much, he's thinking about changing the name of the film."

"Well, now," said Mali. "I think we may be able to negotiate those rights."

Pennie kept thinking about her visions, but she tried to shake off the gloom. She raised her cup to Tita and the film promotion. "From mogul queen to screen queen."

"We've got to print at least a thousand cards," said Tita. "Good thing I have the ski circuit mailing list."

"And we'll need a hundred posters to put around Portland," said Mali.

Tita ran her hand over the design. "Can you make this into an electronic invitation, too?"

Dani sipped. "We can do that. But if you want to mail these things, we'd better start printing. This'll take a while."

Pennie looked around for signs of the guys. "No hubbies tonight?"

"They went to the Great Lost Bear to watch the game. Looks like we get to play with their equipment without them breathing down our necks."

"You mean *our* equipment." Mali walked over to the screen-printing machine to get it fired up while Dani prepared the design for the acetate film to create the stencil. The twins had done this so many times it was second nature and Pennie loved to watch them at their craft. Tita picked out a CD from their eighties collection and inserted it into their stereo system. The voices of Anne and Nancy Wilson filled the loft. Mali found the Pantone Matching System book and they considered ink colors until

Tita landed on a vibrant ultraviolet blue and black. Dani gave the thumbs up.

"Perfect, it'll glow in the dark."

Mali picked out a mesh screen coated with light-reflective emulsion to use for the printing process. Dani laid her sheet with the small image repeated twelve times onto the screen, then laid that on a special machine to expose it to a very bright light to harden the design. Taking the screen to the sink, she washed away the unhardened emulsion to reveal the repeated femme fatale design, three across and four down.

Pennie refilled the paper cups while they waited for the screen to dry. Once ready, Mali lowered it on the printing board while Dani mixed the ink to match the stunning ultraviolet that Tita had chosen. "It's perfect," Dani said, nodding. "Reminds me of the blue hue to the snow in the afternoon light, like it's almost twinkling." She added the ink to the top of the screen and Mali used a squeegee to cover it, pushing the ink through the stencil and imprinting the design onto the pressed paper.

Dani and Mali showed Tita and Pennie how to do it so they could take turns repeating the process with the ink and the squeegee. They soon had ink-covered hands and arms, but they wore the stains with honor, evidence of the spirit of their work. The graphic looked stunning on the white paper and Mali fed them through a special dryer to cure the ink and create a smooth finish that looked and felt raised. Anne and Nancy worked their magic with the music, while Tita and Pennie moved in tandem at the press, Mali on the dryer and Dani on quality control with each finished product. It was as if a spell overtook them. They worked in unison, words barely exchanged in the rhythm of their motions.

After a few hours, they decided to wrap up. The posters would have to be tackled tomorrow. They sank into the couches and bean bag chairs, lighthearted.

"How did it go with the cemetery?" asked Dani.

"The judge granted us the stay, and the excavation actually stopped."

"Unbelievable, Pen. Good work!" They all raised their cups.

"Dani told me you talked to our great-aunt Eleanor," said Mali. "She's a real piece of work, I heard. Not the most warm and friendly."

Pennie recalled the stern, plain-speaking woman on the phone. "I can't imagine the things she has had to endure in her lifetime."

Mali put her feet up on the coffee table. "What all of our relatives have had to put up with." Tita and Pennie both knew about their family history.

Mali asked, "Do you think Aunt Eleanor will help you stop the road?"

"It's a long shot. But her nephew said he'd work on her."

"So, wait," said Tita. "What does this mean for Mr. Real Estate? Now that he knows you're working against him, he'll never want to sponsor the event."

"I didn't want to say anything, but probably best if I'm not involved with that sponsorship-ask any longer. You never know, though. He mentioned a new condo development up at the mountain, so it could be good for his business."

"That sounds like a long shot, too." Tita gathered her full curly mane back in a clip and turned to Mali. "I was telling Pennie that I ran into that hot young ski patrol the last time we were at the mountain. His name is Lewis. You know if there's any connection?"

Pennie felt the blood pump in her ears. "I told you, Tita. Lewis is a pretty common name."

"So the young dude you picked up on your birthday weekend could be related to Mr. Real Estate?" asked Mali.

Pennie shook her head, red in the face. "Highly unlikely."

Dani squeezed her shoulder. "Oh, don't worry about it. Who gives a shit if they're related? Mali and I slept with the same guy before."

"What?" Tita nearly spit out her tea. "Together?"

"No," said Mali, chuckling. "It was by accident and on completely separate occasions."

Dani laughed at the memory. "Remember how horrified you were when you told me you were dating this hot guy, only to learn that he had picked me up at a party a few months before?"

"I seriously think the guy thought we were the same person. Remember how freaked out he was when he saw us together for the first time?" Mali rolled over, laughing.

Dani tipped her head back. "Poor guy, he kept looking at you, then me, like he was seeing a ghost."

"Or shitting his pants," said Mali.

"It feels so good to laugh," said Pennie, getting up to look at the large sheets of glowing owls hanging along the walls, the heroine floating in the air, talons reaching for them, great sweeping wings outstretched, eyes possessed.

Chapter 13

Judgment

THE NEXT NINE DAYS were a blur. From reading the long sobering history of Malaga Island, with conflicting accounts, to trying to reach any descendants on the phone, Pennie's days were saturated with research, reminding her of her days cramming for exams. With the help of the historical society, she pieced together a timeline and it seemed that everything was coming together.

Her uncle warned her about wasting too much time on details of the island's history and not enough on the argument at hand: the importance of leaving the graves undisturbed. He encouraged her to make a trip to the Maine Historic Preservation Commission in Augusta to learn everything she could about the gravesite and introduce herself to Dr. Rachel Goff, the coordinator of historical archaeology.

She drove up on a Wednesday afternoon. Their plans were to review any evidence and testimony that would support the preservation of the cemetery, which the commission considered historically significant. Everything seemed so logical to her, she wondered how anyone could deny a permanent injunction. What was Ward preparing with his lawyers? The same argument about the need for an enormous business park to bring growth to a depressed community? She looked at her phone, expecting something from him, but she hadn't heard a peep since the notice was served. Maybe he would forgive her when this was finished, and he realized the gravity of his plans.

Driving along the turnpike, she passed Freeport and Brunswick, Litchfield and Gardiner, before coming to the Augusta toll booth. It wasn't often she traveled north unless she was headed to the mountains. How she missed the ski season, cut too short for her. She felt a faint twinge in her side from the injury that seemed but a distant memory now that the calendar had turned to April, spring miraculously in the air.

On Western Avenue, she passed hotels, strip malls, and restaurant chains as she made her way to the state capital buildings. The Preservation Commission sat inside a historic brick house with two large bay windows on either side of the doorway. The sign out front read *Capt. Isaac Gage house, c. 1845.*

Maine history runs deep. Benjamin Darling landed here over two hundred years ago, freed by his captain and given his name. A century later, the shipbuilding industry plummeted. What a hardship so many Maine families had endured over generations, from fishing collapses to paper mills closing, the ebbs and flows of the economy like a living pulse of the state's history, a testament to the struggles of its people. Walking into the modest brick building, she felt proud of her heritage, a kinship shared by different people, each with their own personal histories of strife, hardship, and endurance.

Sitting in the lobby with the bright sunlight streaming through the window, Rachel came out from behind an office door to greet her.

"Hello, Ms. Goode, so nice to meet you in person."

"Thank you, Dr. Goff, the pleasure is mine, but please call me Pennie."

"Call me Rachel." She was a stately woman with a pleasant disposition. From their brief phone conversations, Pennie had expected her to be all business, but now she seemed more personable. There was a gentleness about her.

Sitting in Rachel's office, the walls lined with shelves of books and artifacts, from a ship's rigging to an antique brass compass, they settled into planning for Friday's case. Taking out her notes, Pennie asked her if she didn't mind talking about a few things her uncle had suggested. "He wondered about the remains of the bodies shifting underground. As I mentioned on our call, the road they're constructing is only twenty-five feet from the Malaga graves."

"It's been over a century since they were reinterred on the site, so there would only be skeletal remains. Human remains can shift or change position after burial, during decomposition. And, of course, the grave marking was probably not the most exact back then. I think we can safely say that their bones are not exactly where the headstones rest today."

"I'm amazed the town voted to allow this road anyway."

Rachel smiled. "Unless they're your own relatives, people generally don't care that much, and that's a good reason for us to get involved. Cemetery preservation is a way to dignify ancestors, especially the people of Malaga. Even if we did not honor them in life, we can certainly honor them in death."

"That's perfect. Can you please use that in your testimony on Friday?"

"I'll do my best."

They talked a while longer, Rachel fact-checking some of her research about Malaga. Because Pennie had worked so closely with Liz at the historical society, she began to feel more secure. The more she learned, the more pieces of evidence she was able to glean, the more she became obsessed. Now, if everything came together...

Outside, she listened to a voicemail from her uncle, asking her to meet him at Stan Lewis's office on her way back. Driving onto the turnpike, she mulled over the details of the case and wondered what else she was forgetting. What would her uncle ask her that she hadn't already thought of? What would Stan Lewis say about their plan? Uncle Alfie had alerted him about the injunction filed by the historical society before Ward was served, and Stan had seemed okay with it. After all, that's why he had hired her uncle, to uncover any problems with the development before it happened.

Within an hour, she drove down the long dirt driveway with the fenced-in horse corral to her left, the horses trotting around, happy with the spring weather birthing around them, sweet grass shooting up from the wet ground after a long winter of dry hay. She parked beside her uncle's car and let out a heavy sigh, drained from days of research.

Inside the well-kept barn, she passed by the horses in their stalls as they sputtered, tails flicking. She found her uncle sitting in Stan's office, hat on his knee, in quiet conversation. They greeted her with a few pleasantries before her uncle continued. "We're not sure where this is going, but like I said when we made the quick decision to file the injunction, the best move to stay clear of any protests or legal backlash is to defend those graves in the cemetery from any disturbance."

Stan scratched his beard. His eyes mirrored her own tiredness. "You probably know that my phone's been ringing off the hook with the selectmen in town who want this project to go through, along with the locals from the planning board. They all thought they were doing me a favor by voting it through, and now I have to explain our turnaround."

"You did tell us in our first meeting, in no uncertain terms, that we were to represent you and Heritage Acres, not your son's interest. Am I right?"

"Absolutely. I guess I'm worried that I'll have some explaining to do if you lose the injunction hearing. People in this town are real Mainers. They don't like any bullshit." He looked at Pennie and shrugged for a pass on his obscenity.

Uncle Alfie chuckled. "Don't like anyone who's too soft, and they aren't worried about anyone getting their feelings hurt."

"I don't want to come across too liberal around here, or that I'm doing this to protect my girlfriend's property." A nod passed between them. Pennie understood. This was a tight-knit working-class community—everyone knew everyone—and they didn't tolerate anyone leaning too left.

"We'd be making the same recommendation, regardless of who lives next door," Uncle Alfie said. "Pennie's been working on collecting the backstory about the cemetery and graves. Been at it for nine days straight." He turned to her.

She sat up. "There's a long history of the settlement that lived on Malaga, and how they were exiled, how their bodies ended up here."

Stan took a drink from his Styrofoam cup. "I've been reading up on it myself. How are you planning to convince the judge that the road shouldn't run along beside it? From what I've been told, the cemetery would remain untouched."

"It actually might disturb the burial site," she said, her pulse quickening. "Given the haphazard way they moved the bodies, it's most likely they're not within the plot lines on the survey."

"I hope you can convince the judge of that, young lady. My son does not like losing. If there's anything I know about Ward, he'll go to any lengths to win."

Uncle Alfie extended his hand. "We appreciate your time today."

"Good luck tomorrow. If you're going the distance, make it worthwhile. Otherwise, my son will make sure everyone in town thinks I'm a crazy old coot. I don't need any more fuel on that fire."

PENNIE DROVE STRAIGHT HOME in the late afternoon light, barely able to keep her eyes open, making her way through the streets of Portland and finally home to her apartment. She undressed and collapsed on her bed, unable to even feed herself before passing out from sheer exhaustion. She'd done all she could to get ready for the morning. Now it was in the hands of fate. And the judge.

She fell into a dark, fitful slumber. Black-and-white images of the institution's hospital flickered in and out of her dreamscape: men and women in straightjackets being hosed down like animals, dining halls full of sullen women and girls, nurses wheeling young children on cots through echoing corridors, doctors sterilizing girls strapped to metal frames. A young woman stood alone in a doorway, moonlight coming through the window, blurry at first, then coming into focus. The outline of her naked body grew clear and stark, her intense eyes deep, earnest. It was her own eyes Pennie was looking into, staring back at her.

Waking up with a start, the room dark as pitch, she grabbed her phone and looked at the time: 3:33 a.m. A text had just come in from an unknown number. Opening it, there it was, illuminated in the darkness of her room: a photo of her standing naked in the doorway. And then it hit her—this was a photo that Kush had taken of her a year or so ago. It was in the middle of the night, she remembered, and he caught her unawares. But who had sent it?

Now she was wide awake, unsure what was up or what was down. The lines between her dreams and her reality utterly blurred.

WHEN HER UNCLE ARRIVED at the office, she had already been there for two hours, a full pot of coffee finished.

"Morning, Lucky Pennie. Sleep okay?"

"No, unfortunately."

"Hard to sleep before a big hearing. Are we ready?"

She stared at her computer screen, her mind blank. "I'm not sure. I hope you can fill in any missing holes." Cassie walked across the office and nudged her arm.

"I wouldn't worry about it too much. You've got Liz and Rachel coming, right? They'll provide most of the testimony we need."

She still wasn't convinced she'd given her uncle enough to thread the story neatly together. He put too much faith in her, she thought; she was sure to let him down. And now, the photo of her naked, surfacing unexpectedly. Her hands shook and stomach flip-flopped from all the coffee. She felt her face flush and pressed her fingers along the buttons on her high-collared shirt.

He looked at his watch, then at Tita's empty desk. "Your cousin's on time, as usual. The hearing's supposed to start at nine. Why don't you go for a walk, and we'll meet you over at the courthouse? You've got the file?"

"I put everything on your desk."

AT 8:45, SHE STOOD on the bottom courthouse step, thankful to see Dani and Mali walking toward her. Hugging her, the twins immediately sensed her nerves and told her not to worry, that they had asked the spirits of their ancestors to look over them in the courtroom today. Uncle Alfie soon strolled up with Tita and escorted them through the metal detector. They followed him to the second floor, where Rachel and Liz waited outside the courtroom doors.

Long tables on either side of the room faced the judge's bench. Uncle Alfie took the aisle seat, Pennie sitting beside him and Rachel and Liz beside her. Right behind them sat the twins and Tita, their antici-pation palpable.

The defendant's team entered: Ward, walking past without so much as a glance at her, followed by two lawyers in gray suits and another man wearing clean blue jeans and a flannel shirt. They sat at the opposite long table, occupied in hushed conversation. The shorter of the two lawyers, with a neatly trimmed goatee, caught her eye and snidely winked at her. The coffee sloshed in her stomach; she honestly thought she would vomit.

The room fell silent as the judge entered. The officers of the court took names and titles. Pennie sensed a disconnectedness in the room, a low energy.

The somber judge, Ruth Benoit, started the proceedings. "As everyone here has agreed, this is the preliminary injunction and the court trial combined in one hearing. Whatever verdict is reached today will be the outcome of this property development matter. Attorney Goode, please call your first witness."

Alfie began by asking Liz to the stand to provide a brief history of the community on Malaga Island. Beginning with Benjamin Darling becoming a free man at the end of the eighteenth century and buying Horse Island, she described his marriage to Sarah Proverbs, their sons Benjamin and Isaac, and then Isaac's daughters' move to Malaga with their husbands to start the island community in the mid-nineteenth century. She told the story of a healthy working community of different races living in harmony, growing to over forty people by 1900, making a subsistent living from fishing or laundering clothes from the mainland, digging clams, picking berries, and planting small garden plots on the glaciated bedrock terrain of the midcoast region. She wove in the story of

George and Lucy Lane, the missionary couple who took a special interest in helping the poor island community educate their children.

The goateed lawyer tried to object to the relevance of the history lesson, but the judge allowed it.

Liz carried on, describing the difficult economic times during this period in Maine's history, how the newspapers sensationalized accounts of the mixed-race community. Her uncle provided copies of the clippings with shock-worthy stories of Malaga, the "Scandal Island of Maine," and the gross fabrication as "a sort of Skid Row where degeneration, miscegenation, incest and other forms of vice and viciousness too foul to be mentioned in print, flourished like the green bay tree."

Liz finished by describing how the residents were forcibly evicted from the island, beginning with the eight members of the Marks family, who were declared "unfit for society" at the end of 1911. How the family became scapegoats for the eugenics movement and were committed to the Maine School for the Feeble-Minded during a time in the nation's history when race inferiority was a widespread belief. How six of the Marks family members died there and were buried in the cemetery.

Ward's lawyer stood up in a tight, almost ill-fitting suit, giving Pennie a sidelong smile before he spoke. A chill crept up her backside. He began by acknowledging the unfortunate eviction of the settlement and asked Liz if, from a legal perspective, she thought squatters should be allowed to stay on property they did not own. Uncle Alfie objected to the irrelevant question, but the judge allowed it.

"That's a common misunderstanding, Mr. Leadbetter," Liz replied. "There was no official deed of ownership for Malaga Island back then. According to a report by the Town of Phippsburg in 1902, Mr. Eli Perry had a questionable deed, and the state also gave a quitclaim deed to Mr. H. H. Ferguson. Neither party ever made any attempts to enforce their rights or pay taxes. As the town reported, for all intents and purposes, the people living there owned the island."

Leadbetter requested a copy of that town report and Uncle Alfie pulled it from his file, handing it to the judge. The lawyer then asked Liz if she knew about the memorial that was erected at the Patient's Cemetery for the graves of the Malaga residents, and whether she knew that Governor Baldacci had delivered a public apology to the descendants. Of course she did.

"So after these memorials and public apologies, Ms. McClellan, what more can we do?" he asked, almost pleading. "How much is enough? Will these unsettled grievances become a burden on the state's economic progress forever? Or will we be able to move forward together, having learned from our past mistakes?"

"Mr. Leadbetter," said Liz, "the way to move forward, to learn from our past mistakes, is to honor the dead by protecting their graves."

"There's reasonable and then there's unreasonable, Ms. McClellan."

But Leadbetter had no further questions. The judge thanked Liz for her testimony. Uncle Alfie called Dani to the stand. She looked as scared as Pennie. When asked about her connection to Malaga, she explained that her family was related to the Marks family, and that her great-aunt Eleanor knew her cousins Lottie and Etta, the daughters of Abbie Marks. Etta died in the institution in 1925, but Lottie was finally released after thirteen years. She had been a teenager when she went in and left as a woman in her thirties. She never had any children and would never, ever speak of her experience at the institution. Lottie, who lived to be 103 years old.

Uncle Alfie provided the letter from Aunt Eleanor's nephew as evidence, reading the final statement: "While my aunt could not be there for the hearing, she asks the court to please honor her family and do whatever is necessary to keep their graves undisturbed."

Dani left the stand, taking a deep breath. With the judge's permission, Uncle Alfie moved onto the cemetery survey and the evidence against the road construction. He placed an elevation drawing on an easel, showing the survey boundaries clearly marked between the proposed road construction and the Malaga graves. He pointed to the neighboring Greenleaf property line, restricting the movement of the road any further from the burial site. Then he called Dr. Goff to the stand. Introducing her as an archeologist and burial site specialist, he asked Rachel if the proposed plan was any concern.

"From Ms. McClellan's testimony, we know that it's been more than a century since the bodies were moved from Malaga to the current site. Today, these skeletal remains would have shifted from their original position during decomposition. When you take into consideration that seventeen bodies were thrown together in five caskets, and also that the grave markings back then were not the most exact, we can safely say that the remains are not absolutely where the headstones rest today."

Uncle Alfie sat down. The goateed lawyer walked toward Rachel with a slight swagger. "Ms. Goff," he said, conveniently leaving off her doctor title.

"Yes, Mr. Leadbetter." She sat unsmiling.

"Our local surveyor, who has been surveying property in Fairview for over twenty years, has provided testimony to our planning board that we clearly have twenty-five feet between the outside plot lines of the cemetery and the proposed road." He provided a copy of the minutes to Dr. Goff and to the judge. "Are you saying that the bones of the remains have shifted more than that? This seems impossible."

"I'm not suggesting they moved more than twenty-five feet. I'm suggesting that the seventeen bodies were not buried exactly under those grave markers, or within those old plot lines. It's highly plausible that their remains are outside those cemetery boundaries."

He next produced a rendering of the cemetery with an elaborate black iron gate surrounding it, and another fence between the iron gate and the new road. Handing out the colored rending to her uncle and the judge, he smiled.

"Your honor, my client has generously agreed to fully fund the installation of a new cast-iron fence to surround the perimeter of the entire graveyard. In addition, he has agreed to erect a ten-foot-high fence between the new road and the cemetery to fully partition the areas and show respect for the lives of those buried there. We hope, Ms. Goff, you will consider this generous and extensive fencing to respect the graves and meet on common ground."

Uncle Alfie addressed Judge Benoit. "Your honor, this does nothing to address the concerns that the remains are beyond the boundaries of the cemetery. What the defense is suggesting is that they erect two fences over the very cemetery boundary that's in question."

The judge looked at Rachel. "Would you agree, Dr. Goff?"

"Yes, your honor. This is the reason we have a preservation commission, to honor our ancestors, especially those like the people of Malaga who were shown little respect in their lifetime, if any at all."

Ward's lawyer walked back to his table, saying he had no other questions and would like to call his witness. The judge welcomed the older man in blue jeans and flannel up to the stand. The lawyer approached with a folder of papers.

"Dr. Kilgore, please tell the court your affiliation with Fairview."

"Certainly, be happy to. I was born and raised in the town, and my parents, too. I've had a family practice there my entire life. Just retired last year."

"Your family has a long history in Fairview?"

"Sure does."

"So you must be familiar with the School for the Feeble-Minded."

"Yes, my grandmother worked there, was a nurse. She had a special place in her heart for the institution because her brother was a ward there."

"Your grandmother's brother was a resident?"

"Yes. He became a ward of the state back in the mid-thirties. Had a mental illness, diagnosed as schizophrenic. My grandmother was happy they took him in and took exceptionally good care of him."

The lawyer handed Dr. Kilgore a folder. "Can you show the court your family photos?"

He produced two black-and-white pictures of his grandmother in a nurse's uniform, one beside a hospital bed with an old white-haired man, another taken outside with a group of residents in wheelchairs, sitting and smiling in the sun. He showed the judge and pointed out his grandmother and her brother.

Leadbetter continued. "What happened to him?"

"He lived out his days there, working on the farm, and he's buried right in that same cemetery, one of the graves closest to the main road."

"And do you think it would be disrespecting your uncle by building a road for a new office development beside the graveyard?"

"No sir. My ancestors would be happy to see more job opportunities come to Fairview, like this business park. My grandparents grew up during the Depression and they struggled to raise five children. Seeing this kind of opportunity come to town is exciting. I think the fence you're planning seems like a good compromise. And that's something you don't see a lot of these days."

The courtroom door opened at that moment, and they all turned to look. An older, brown-skinned man with wire glasses walked in, and Liz waved to him. Pennie had no idea who he was. The judge asked Leadbetter to continue.

"Dr. Kilgore, did you provide testimony to the planning board supporting the road where it is?"

"I certainly did. It's right here." He proudly gave the testimony to the judge.

Uncle Alfie had no questions for the good doctor—pressing him on his recollections would only risk making himself look petty to the judge.

Ward's lawyer proceeded to present his last piece of evidence, placing a large colored rendering directly on top of Alfred Goode's survey. With a flourish, he used a pointer to show the new road leading to a grand office park, tall white solid fencing between the graveyard and the road that curved a half a mile to the office park in the back lot, with three extensive five-story buildings on a large parcel, complete with nature trails and a recreation facility for the employees. "We think this fencing will show respect for the gravesite while creating an attractive barrier."

When he finished, the judge asked him if he was done. The defense rested, and the judge allowed Uncle Alfie to call his last witness to the stand, the strange man who had walked in late. He introduced himself as Silas Morton Eason.

"What is your connection to Malaga Island?"

"My great-, great-, great-grandfather was John Eason. He was known as the deacon on Malaga and married my grandmother, Rosella Griffin. They had four children, and my great-great-grandfather was the only one who survived."

"What happened to the other three children?"

"They were buried on Malaga and their graves were moved to the Patient's Cemetery at the School for the Feeble-Minded."

Uncle Alfie showed him a picture of the small, mottled headstone, reading THREE EASTON CHILDREN, NOV. 1912 to Silas. "Is this their headstone?"

"Yes." Silas shook his head, looking down.

"Why are you shaking your head?"

"There are a few things wrong with this headstone. First, our last name is spelled wrong. And second, there are only two children buried there."

"What would lead you to believe that?"

"My great-grandfather told me that when they moved the bodies, the remains of one of the children fell out of the boat crossing the New Meadows."

Ward's lawyer stood up. "Objection. Speculation, your honor."

Uncle Alfie said, "It's not speculation if there are verbal accounts, your honor."

"Continue."

"Mr. Eason," said Uncle Alfie. "Did your great-grandfather speak of his ancestors on Malaga often?"

"Hardly ever. They'd been shamed into silence their whole lives. People had all kinds of names back then. Darkys, Malagaites, Malagos. No one was ever proud to be a descendant or related to one."

"What about today?"

"For the first time, I can say I am proud of my family's history on Malaga. Especially after the apology from Governor Baldacci. That seemed to break some long-held taboo. Don't get me wrong, there's plenty around that are still racist, but at least some are willing to take some responsibility."

"Thank you, Mr. Eason. I have no other questions."

Ward's lawyer approached the witness. "Do you mind if I call you Silas?"

He faced him squarely. "Suit yourself."

"With such a formal apology and sincere gesture by the governor and the State of Maine, taking place on the very island of your ancestors, I can't help but wonder if you've considered moving the remains of your ancestors at the Patient's Cemetery back to Malaga, back where they belong?"

Beside her, Pennie heard Rachel gasp in disbelief.

Silas sat up in earnest. "You know, Jeff—you don't mind if I call you Jeff, do you?"

"Not at all." Leadbetter smiled like a cat.

"My ancestors have been disrespected enough. From myths of inbreeding or being morally degenerate and living in squalor to being exiled from their homes and sentenced to live on scows in the New Meadows River, they have had to endure injustices for a long time, even without a final resting place to call home. So no, there is no reason to move them back to Malaga. Their heavenly souls are still there anyway, in the deep rich forest rooted in the granite bedrock, the shell middens of the Wabanaki, and the very saltwater of the New Meadows. And after being out there with the governor for the formal apology, it finally felt like the past was beginning to right itself with the world again. I am ready to let them rest. They've been through enough already."

A quiet swept the courtroom. Before the lawyer could utter another word, Judge Benoit said, "You may step down, Mr. Eason, and thank you for being here." She cleared her throat. "Mr. Leadbetter, do you have any other evidence?"

"No, your honor."

"Mr. Goode, do you have any other information or evidence before the court makes a final ruling?"

Uncle Alfie approached Ward's office park rendering on the tripod, rolled it up swiftly, and gave it back to Leadbetter. Running his steady hand over his survey on the easel, he pointed to an undeveloped area further down Gray Road. "There's a space for a road back here, your honor. I did speak to the surveyor about it. He agreed that it could probably work."

"Your honor, with permission," said Ward, speaking up for the first time, a keening in his voice. "From that distance, and with the ledge in that area, it will cost us over five hundred grand to put a road in there, way over budget for the project."

"Where there's a will, there's a way, Mr. Lewis." The judge paused for a moment, then delivered her ruling. "I hereby rule in favor of the complainant, the Maine Historical Society, for the protection of this historical gravesite." She slammed her gavel before exiting the courtroom.

Pennie restrained herself from whooping and hugging Liz. The other table huffed in disbelief. She kept her head down as Ward walked by without a word. His shorter lawyer, right behind him, dropped something on the floor. Uncle Alfie picked it up to hand it back. To Pennie's great shock, it was an 8 x 10-inch glossy photo of her, naked in the dim light of her bedroom doorway, the one from the mysterious text that morning.

The lawyer accepted it back, in slow dramatic fashion, waving it in front of her uncle. "Oh, why thank you, Alfie. It's so interesting what you can *dig up* on the internet when researching a case."

Chapter 14

Synchronicity

She'd never seen Dani, Mali, and Tita more animated than when they left the courthouse. Liz and Rachel were just as exuberant, standing beside a subdued Silas Morton Eason, their unsung poet, who'd driven down from New Brunswick to give his firsthand testimony. Uncle Alfie believed his account prompted the judge to act so swiftly and decisively. He explained the possible appeals by the defense, which sounded rather doubtful given the way the verdict was handed down.

Her uncle offered to buy everyone lunch. Liz and Rachel, their new-found compatriots, had to get back to their jobs and Silas had to get back to Canada and his children and grandchildren. They promised to keep in touch about next steps for preservation of the cemetery.

Pennie was anxious, though, the courtroom victory overshadowed by the revealing photo in Ward's possession. She walked alongside the twins, Uncle Alfie, and Tita, making their way to F. Parker Reidy's on Exchange Street. She was as hungry as a bear.

Tita checked her phone. "Lars wants me to meet him for lunch." She looked at Mali. "It's with the State Theatre people. Can you come?"

Mali beamed at the thought of helping organize the gala. "I'd love to."

Tita said, "What about you, Dani?"

"I think you and Mali have this covered."

Tita looked at her father. "Mind if I go?"

"Suit yourself." He kissed her on the cheek. "And take the after-noon off."

"Thanks, Pop. You're the best!" She turned to Pennie and hugged her. "Great work today." She sounded almost sad but perked up and waved before leaving with Mali.

Inside the mahogany-paneled restaurant filled with mingling business sorts, the waitress set pints of Harp on the table. The three of them toasted to the trial being over and how impressed they were with all the testimonies, especially Silas's. His late entry into the courtroom seemed like fate. And finally, like a coup d'état, Uncle Alfie's solution of another road further down seemed to seal the deal. How Ward and his lawyers had bristled with contempt at the thought.

Pennie finally drew up enough gumption to address the elephant in the room. "I should have told you about the picture this morn-ing," she said to her uncle.

Dani looked up from the menu. "What picture?"

He sat back and smiled in a way that said everything was going to be alright, but Pennie was still anxious. She looked at Dani. "The picture that Ward's lawyer dropped on the floor was of me. A…revealing picture from about a year ago."

Uncle Alfie scratched his chin. "Where did it come from?"

"I don't know how he ever would have gotten it. Kush took that picture of me at least a year ago when we were dating. We never shared it with anyone."

Dani looked puzzled. "Wait, there was a risqué picture of you? Naked?"

Sometimes her friend's bluntness could still surprise her. "Like I said, it was a personal moment."

Her uncle took a long swig of beer, thinking. "You said you should have told me about the picture. Did you know it was out there?"

"Last night I got a text with the photo from an unknown number."

Dani asked, "Did you try reverse look-up?"

"That's the first thing I did this morning, but it's unlisted, of course."

"Send me the number," he said. "I'll see what my sources can find out."

She never asked about his sources. He was an attorney, after all. "I'm so embarrassed."

"It's only to intimidate you, Birdie. The photo will have no bearing whatsoever on the case. Let's just hope, for your personal sanity, Ward and his lawyers get tired of their little charades and don't send it to anyone else." He waved the waitress down and ordered a second pint.

She felt a stomachache coming on and ordered only the French onion soup. Luckily, Dani changed the subject and kept the conversation lively, peppering Uncle Alfie with questions about the trial and why things had happened—and what might happen next.

"There's always a chance they'll appeal," he said. "But that takes a long time and probably isn't worth the cost of the legal team. My hunch is that the matter is dead, so to speak."

AFTER LUNCH, PENNIE DROVE toward home in a daze, determined only to become one with her couch. But her phone rang as she turned onto the Western Prom, an unknown number. She couldn't resist picking up. "Hello?"

"Hi, is this Penelope Goode?'

"Yes, who's this?"

"Fred Humiston, reporter from the *Tribune*. Mind if I ask you a few questions about the trial today?" It was the small local newspaper.

A moment of hesitation came over her before she yielded cautiously. "No, I don't mind."

"Great. My editor put me on the story this afternoon, and I'm playing a little catch-up. I heard that Dr. Kilgore from Fairview testified today on behalf of Ward Lewis?"

"Yes, that's right."

"Did he say anything about his relatives that lived at the institution?"

"Why, yes, he did, that his great-uncle lived there, was buried at the cemetery."

"In my cursory research, I haven't been able to find any Kilgore family connection with the School for the Feeble-Minded."

"Really? You know, I wonder how much he made up. And he said his mother was a nurse there."

"That's interesting."

She thought about the nasty little lawyer conveniently dropping the photo of her. "You never know what lengths people will go to, to win."

"Real estate development, right? What a bit of business."

"You can say that again."

"Thank you, Ms. Goode."

"Oh, thanks. It was really all my uncle, though."

SHE FINALLY SHUFFLED INTO her apartment to lie down on her couch, completely wrung out. It had all worked out in their favor, a better outcome than she could have expected for such a harried process, but she was still troubled by a suspicion that things were not quite finished. And then there were her dreams. Were they just random, coincidental?

Maybe in her delirium last night, she'd subconsciously seen the text pop up on her phone with the photo, invading her dream. And when she woke up, it was there.

Picking up her phone, she searched her contacts for Kush. There he was. Before she could talk herself out of it, she pressed his number, and it began to buzz. After four rings, he picked up.

"Pennie?"

Her chin trembled. "You still have my number in your phone."

"Sure I do. Why wouldn't I?"

She pictured him in his work suit, looking sharp, cool as a cucumber, quick with a joke. "I don't know…wasn't sure how you'd feel after all these months. If you were still mad."

"I'm not mad, Pen. I was upset you didn't want to move to Philly with me, but I'm okay now. I just needed to transition, that's all. Start a new life. Change can be hard."

A new life. He never said anything about missing her. "I miss you." Her brokenness gave her away. Even though she hated him for jumping into a new romance, for maybe even leaking the provocative photo, she missed him terribly. She was pathetic, she knew. Anyone else would be angry.

"Oh, hey, I miss you too!" He was trying for her. He might as well have said, "Keep your chin up, bucko!"

Taking a deep breath, she jumped right in. "Do you remember that photo you took of me, the night after the show?"

"Um, you'll have to give me a little more."

She lowered her voice to a whisper. "The night we took mushrooms before the concert at Merrill. I couldn't sleep and got out of bed to grab some water. I stood in the doorway naked, and—"

"Yeah, I remember." His voice turned soft. "The light coming through the window lit you from behind and I couldn't resist."

She took a deep breath. "Did you send that to anyone?"

"No, of course not. Just to myself."

"What do you mean 'to yourself'?"

"I used your phone—it was on the nightstand—and then sent it to myself. And you know I wouldn't share that with anyone. What's this all about?"

"Someone texted me the photo from an unknown number."

"Does anyone have access to your photo drive?"

"My photo drive?"

"Yes, Pennie, your Google photo drive."

She hated it when he talked down to her. "No, I don't think so."

"That's about all I can think of. And I'll check my cloud storage, too. Wouldn't want Loralee to accidentally come across it."

Her heart fell to the pit of her stomach. "I heard you had someone new."

"She's really great, Pennie. You'd like her. Sorry you missed meeting her when I was home a few weeks ago."

"Me, too." The vision of their silhouettes under the streetlight in front of Dani and Mali's place moved across her mind. That same deep sadness sank inside her.

Kush spoke to someone nearby: "Be right there." Then to her, "Well, I gotta get back to it."

"Of course." Silent hot tears rolled down her face.

He hung up and she wondered if he had to get back to her, to Loralee.

Taking out her laptop, she opened her Google Drive. The last time she'd looked here was after she'd taken the pictures of the horse show at Heritage Acres, the ones she'd sent to Ward. Her own stupidity began to sink in. She thought she'd sent him just the link to view the photos, but she must have given him access to her entire drive. If there was ever a moment when she felt like an idiot, it was now.

She scrolled down through the photos from the day at the cemetery, the small Malaga headstones and woods behind them. Then the photos from the horse show, of Stan and Roxanne and Ward and his ex-wife, of the talented Native American rider, and then the high school girls in flawless formation, and then—the flickering again, the faint image of the ghost rider, just like before, the blurry outline of a rider on a horse following the rest of the girls.

Before she could get a good look, the flickering was gone. She was losing it. Hadn't Jeannette said that Chloe took lessons out there? Was it possible that her spirit still lived in that arena?

Continuing to scroll, she came across ski pictures, she and Tita, Mali, and Dani taking on the slopes, carefree and beaming at the top of the mountain with the lake behind them. Then photos with Kush from a year ago, dressed up and ready to hit the town. Then there she was, staring back at her, standing naked, her pupils as large as saucers. She pulled it up and trembled at her own exposure before deleting it and emptying her trash. But it was too late. It was already out there for the world to see, thanks to Ward. She despised him more than she'd ever despised anyone. Getting up, she opened a bottle of wine and poured herself a glass, then another, and another, dulling the anger that fired inside of her.

THE NEXT MORNING, SHE woke, delirious, to her phone ringing. It was Dani.

"Morning, public defender. Did you see the paper today?"

"It's nine a.m. on a Saturday morning. I haven't even gotten up yet."

"There's an article about the trial. I didn't know you were interviewed!"

She sat up. "A reporter called me on the way home."

"You might want to look it up. You're quoted as saying a few unkind things about the good doctor."

Turning on her laptop, she opened the *Tribune* to read the article. Dani chatted on. "How do you know that he never had a great uncle at the institution? I mean, I believe you that he could have made it all up."

"The reporter said he couldn't find any history of his family at the School for the Feeble-Minded, and well..."

Skimming the article, she found her quote, just like she remembered it: *I wonder how much he made up. You never know what lengths people will go to to get their way.* Her uncle was not going to be happy. "Thanks, Dani. I gotta go."

When she arrived at the townhouse on Pine Street, her hair still wet, the dogs greeted her at the door. Cassie licked her hand and Teddy nudged her with his block head for a scratch. She could smell the coffee and nearly walked by the dining room before catching her uncle in her periphery, working on another puzzle. The newspaper lay open on the end of the table. "Morning, Pennie." He kept his head down in concentration, fiddling with a piece of blue ocean or sky, the two seeming to blend together in the backdrop of the three-masted schooner.

"I don't know how you do these things. I think I'd go mad trying to figure out which blue piece goes where."

"Takes my mind off other things. Helps me relax." He thumped a piece in place. "Catch up on your sleep?"

"I, um, yes, thanks." Her head slightly ached from the wine.

Her aunt walked by, said hello. She was on her way out the door to meet Tita over at the State Theatre. They were in full event-planning mode. Pennie wished she could escape with her. Maybe Uncle Alfie hadn't seen the article yet.

No luck. He waved to the paper. "Interesting article today about the trial."

"Yeah, I know. Listen, I'm sorry. That quote was out of context. The reporter said he couldn't find any history of Kilgore's great uncle at the institution, and—"

"No comment."

"No comment?"

"Yes, that's the general rule of thumb for a response when a reporter calls, whether you win or lose. Especially if you win."

She sat down in one of the captain's chairs. Fella came out from under the table and hopped up in her lap. "I know. I'm sorry. He caught me in a moment."

"How's the job search going?"

Her heart sank. She was hoping he'd consider her staying on, given the success of the trial. "I was going to start on that today."

"No time like the present."

"Should I do anything, you know, about the article?"

"We'll have to wait and see if Kilgore responds. Not much to be done right now."

Fella nuzzled against her until she scratched him behind the ears. At least this one still loved her.

THE LAST THING SHE wanted to do was sit down in front of a computer screen and search for a job, so she drove to the nearest coffee shop and ordered an extra-large with two espresso shots. Her car sounded worse than ever, coughing and sputtering whenever she started it up. Thinking about her dismal checking account balance ($109), she wondered if she would ever get her shit together. The bills for the ambulance ($1,500) and hospital ($30,000) had arrived and were due immediately. She didn't know where to turn. The only option was to somehow find a job as a vet tech with health insurance, maybe call the job she'd turned down? She remembered the terse exchange with the woman who had hired her when Pennie finally shared the news that she was turning it down. How had things come so unraveled? If her car died on her, she would be in even worse shit.

Driving over to Dani and Mali's, she circled around the Congress Street block three times before finding a parking spot. Up in their loft, Dani and Max were busy trimming posters for *Freestyle Femme Fatale* on the giant automatic paper cutter, waving to her when she came in. Pennie wondered how they managed to add new equipment all the time and where it came from. They had a niche operation, enough custom silk-screening work from local businesses and schools to keep the twins and their husbands employed. Mali sat at her desk in the corner working on the books. No doubt she kept all the finances in order, running a tight ship. How she envied that ability. "Got any job openings?"

Mali looked up from her laptop. "We could use about ten more hands around here. Do you come cheap?"

"Depends how desperate I get."

Dani looked over at her. "I'm guessing it didn't go so well with your uncle."

"That's a nice way to put it. He's at the end of his rope with me."

Max jogged a stack of posters together. "We could use a hand distributing these around town. Where's your cousin?"

"At the State, meeting with the manager."

Mali stood up and stretched. "Oh, that's right. Your aunt seems to be really into this."

Pennie helped Dani and Max put the trimmed posters into even stacks. "Helping her get out of her winter funk, I suppose."

From the hundred-plus posters, they each took a stack and decided to break up their distribution by the east, west, north, and south sides of the Portland Peninsula to cover every laundromat, coffee shop, book shop, hardware store, pizza place, pub, and grill in the area, to blanket Portland with the flashy blue and black silk-screened posters sporting the crossed ski-talons of the Freestyle Femme Fatale. They all headed in opposite directions, Pennie taking her own area on the West End, glad to lend a hand and take her mind off the news story about the trial, and the photo of her that was God knows where. Maybe if she called Ward she could reason with him, plead for some kind of reckoning so that he would never ever share that photo again.

Every place she popped into was happy to let her put a poster up; nearly everyone had heard of the famous freestyle skier Christina Goode. Pennie found herself either surreptitiously removing posters to make room for her own or taping right over others. No one seemed to care. The posters had a QR code people could scan that would take them to the event's Facebook page. They already had over two hundred followers, and it was picking up speed. Now that it was finally warming up, people were looking for things to do, to get out and about and catapult into summer.

Her last stop was her favorite wine and cheese shop. After getting permission from the manager, she found a center spot for the last poster on the bulletin board by the doorway leading down to the wine cellar. She couldn't resist descending the stairs to the brick-lined vault filled with wines and a few old books and classic albums. It was still early in the day and the eccentric old man was nowhere around, to her disappointment. Something about him comforted her. Thumbing through the albums, she came across the Eagles. "Desperado" played in her mind and her thoughts went to Kush, then to the night at Ward's when he played it on his old turntable in the sunken living room.

"There's nothing like an old album to bring back memories."

She jumped at Snodgrass's voice from behind. He had a book in his hand. "Is there a particular artist you're looking for?"

"Just perusing." He stared into her eyes until she spoke the truth. "Actually, I could really use something uplifting, you know?"

"Precisely. Let's see, you like cassette tapes for your car, right?"

"Why, yes, that's right."

This old man with the uncanny intuition walked over to a desk and opened a drawer to pull out *Greatest Hits* by Aretha Franklin. "Aretha. She always puts me in a good mood."

She looked at the tape with "You Make Me Feel like a Natural Woman" and "Respect" and "Chain of Fools" on the case. *How appropriate.* She refrained from buying a bottle of wine, a first for her, and paid at the register. The total came to $12.34. She wondered out loud: "That's funny. One, two, three, four."

He handed her the paper bag. "Sounds like the universe is telling you to follow your intuition. Keep going."

When she got to her car, she checked her phone. The time was 3:45. Bizarre. Taking the tape from the bag, she found a small book underneath. The funny old man must have dropped it in without her seeing. The worn hardcover with overlapping blue and green circles, eyes at the center, filled her with curiosity. *Synchronicity* by Carl Jung. Synchronicity? Her phone rang and she jumped, again. It was Dani looking for her.

They were all at their favorite Korean barbeque place in the Old Port waiting for her.

On Monday morning, it was after nine by the time she got to the office. Tita looked up in expectation when she walked in the door.

"Have you checked your email this morning?"

"Good morning to you, too. What's the matter?"

Tita drummed her fingers. "Kilgore's attorney sent you a message."

"So you're looking at my emails?

"No, he copied Pop, and I get all his emails."

She sat down at her desktop to open her inbox. The message was sent at 6:00 a.m.:

Dear Ms. Goode,

I am writing to you on behalf of Dr. Grey Kilgore. He is retaining legal counsel for defamation in the article published by the *Tribune* on Saturday, April 10. Are you aware that you have accused Dr. Kilgore of lying under oath in trial? Your alarming accusations have put his character into question where none existed before.

Dr. Kilgore is distressed by your blatant false accusations of him. What caused you to question whether his relative lived at the institution? We request that you retain all records regarding this matter and notify your legal firm's insurance carrier. We also request that you immediately prepare a retraction and apology for our review. I am making this request out of our duty to mitigate damage caused to Dr. Kilgore's reputation.

This matter will be turned over to a national defamation legal expert team. For now, please respond to my requests.

Regards,

D.B. Leadbetter, JD

How could she have been so stupid to talk to that reporter? Ignoring Tita's concerned look from across the desk, she walked into her uncle's office and closed the door. "I am sick about this. What should I do? Send in a retraction?"

"Calm down, Pennie. First, a legitimate legal action threatening a defamation suit would more likely be sent via certified mail than email. Secondly, what you said to the paper about the doctor would be a hard sell in terms of qualifying as libel. Libel, in its most basic definition, is a harm to reputation. Leadbetter is blowing smoke about your comment. You never said anything factual about Kilgore one way or another, just speculating about what he might have made up."

She sat down. "So, you're saying this isn't a legitimate concern?"

"Your intention was not to question Dr. Kilgore's statements in the hearing."

"What about the reporter? Should we do anything?"

"I don't see any reason to take it any further. These types of things happen all the time. Let's try not to give this flame any oxygen."

"Do you think Kilgore may have made up any of it?"

"I don't think Kilgore would be on the warpath if he did. But it makes you wonder why the reporter led you on like that. I smell something fishy."

"What do you mean?"

"Like the reporter set you up."

"Why would he do that?" She contemplated how she'd confront him.

"Nothing like a juicy story." He ate the last bite of his cheese Danish. "Let's let the firestorm settle for now."

She was completely ashamed to have to bring up the photo again, but had to know something, anything. "Were you able to look into that unlisted number that sent me the photo?"

"Nothing back yet. Don't get your hopes up. People create aliases all the time."

Looking out the window, she knew it was Ward anyway. After such a victory over him in the courthouse on Friday, how quickly things changed. She'd made a mess of everything.

Uncle Alfie's flip phone vibrated with an incoming call. He ignored it. "I talked to Stan Lewis on Friday, and he sounded happy with the outcome of the trial. Why don't you give him a call and find out if he has any questions?"

What she really wanted to do was call that reporter and give him a piece of her mind, but her uncle was right. Let the firestorm settle. At her desk, she looked up Fred Humiston. He was an older guy, maybe in his forties with a full beard, reddish hair, wire glasses. Had been at the *Tribune* for less than a year. Before then, it looked like he worked for a paper down in Woburn, Massachusetts. That wasn't a surprise. Just a jerk-off from away.

Chapter 15
Dark Truth

As the days marched on that week and into the next, her hopelessness intensified. The photo surfaced on Facebook. Someone had posted a link to her revealing picture on the Freestyle Femme Fatale event page with the caption, "Penelope Goode, researcher at Alfred Goode Esquire, shown in action doing evening field work," and it had been shared widely before Dani and Mali discovered it. Apparently, the link was disguised under the fan comments. By the time Tita alerted Mali to take it down and block the user, the damage had been done, and it would take an act of Congress to get Facebook to respond.

She had a sick foreboding sense when she walked or drove around town that all eyes were on her, judging her, condemning her. The worst part was that her family knew about it. When she walked to her aunt and uncle's house for Sunday dinner, she prepared herself to face the shame she had brought upon her family. Walking down the brick path to the front door, she caught the stare of old lady Payson scoffing at her, her judgy cat at her side.

The dogs met Pennie at the door, tails wagging, ignorant of her desperation. Inside, at the kitchen table, Tita, Dani, and Mali were in a lively conversation with Aunt Maude about the number of tickets sold. Tita greeted her exuberantly. "Hey Pennie! Where have you been?"

"Well, if it isn't the star of the show," said Aunt Maude, lightly, as if there was nothing to worry about.

"Pennie's got the spotlight," said Aunt Aggie, sipping a martini. "It's all my ladies' bridge club can talk about."

"Oh, Aggie, don't give her a hard time." Aunt Maude squeezed Pennie's hand. "We've all had embarrassing moments, dear." Aunt Aggie continued to stir whatever was on the stove.

Dani pulled out a chair for her and smiled. "Pop a squat, Pen. We're making plans for the big night."

Tita said, "I'll give you a pass for hogging the spotlight because our ticket numbers are soaring."

Mali added, "We were slow going, with only maybe 250 registered, but after that picture of you, things took off."

"Oh c'mon," Pennie said. "How could this help your ticket sales?"

"Beats me, but within a day, the numbers started to tick up steadily." Mali beamed.

Tita jumped in. "It's like Lars said, any publicity is good publicity. You know what they say about word of mouth. Maine is small state, and, well, it's strange but true."

Pennie looked at Mali's computer screen. "How many have you sold?

"Over nine hundred. It's wild!" said Mali.

"Over nine hundred tickets sold?" Then she realized, with a slow sinking depression, just how many people really had seen the photo.

"Yes, and at sixty-five bucks a ticket, we'll reach sixty grand or more!"

Tita vibrated with excitement. "Lars is coming out of his skin. We had thought maybe we'd be lucky to raise thirty grand. Now it's twice that. Oh, and you're not going to believe this, but Ward Lewis came on as a sponsor today."

All the blood drained from her face. "Ward?" She could hardly say his name, she was so incensed by his audacity. "But why?"

Mali jumped in. "I guess he's moving forward with that condo development at the mountain, and the buzz of the event is really spreading. Everybody's talking about it. It's the place to be."

Pennie grimaced. Sensing her stress, Dani took her hand. "Don't worry. We haven't seen your photo appear again. We've been watching it."

"It's all the other private sharing I'm worried about," said Pennie. "God, I feel like all of Portland has seen me naked."

"All of Maine, you mean," said Aunt Aggie. "My brother Jerold up in Brunswick called me. Wanted to know what line of work you'd gone into. And what was up with your eyes, anyway?"

She wanted to crawl into a hole.

"Chin up, my dear," said Aunt Maude. "That Jerold is nothing but a dirty old man. I'm not surprised he'd get a copy of it, the likes of people he associates with."

"You never liked Jerold," said Aggie. "Not since he beat you in that bridge match."

"Aggie, everyone knows your brother is nothing but a cheater." It was rare to hear Maude stand up to her, especially in this house. Pennie felt a warmness settle in and smiled at her mother's sister.

"Okay," said Tita. "We've got to plan the sequence of the night. Lars said the sneak-peek footage is about thirty-five minutes long, so we have time for raffles, and I've got some great stuff that the mountain donated for the silent auction."

While they chatted about the line-up, Pennie could feel the heat of judging Aunt Aggie behind her. Maybe she should not go to the event, not subject herself to the gossip and stares she was bound to face. Besides, it was Tita's night, and the last thing she wanted to do was take away her moment in the limelight.

When she got back to her apartment, she pulled up Facebook, something she usually avoided after so much stupid teenage gossiping and pettiness in high school. She had an old account with an outdated profile image from her twenties wearing ski gear and plastic yellow sunglasses. Young and innocent. She searched for Ward Lewis and found his page almost immediately. He had a professional headshot, and most of his feed was filled with development updates, including the new one planned for Coos Canyon: *Reserve your mountainside condo for next season now!*

Scrolling down, she looked over pictures of grand openings and happy hour events. Then she stopped. A guy with a reddish beard was standing with him inside what looked like a pub. It was him—the heavyset reporter with the wire glasses. Enlarging the photo as much as she could, she had no doubt it was the same guy: Fred Humiston drinking a pint, Ward's arm over his shoulder, very chummy. Old pals.

THE NEXT MORNING OVER coffee, she opened her laptop before she even left her apartment. The last thing she needed was another surprise waiting for her at the office. About three messages deep was one from Dr. Kilgore addressed to her uncle:

Dear Attorney Goode,

I am writing to inform you that I have retained representation to seek damages against your law firm for Ms. Penelope Goode's misrepresentation of me in the *Tribune* article published on April 10. I am deeply disappointed and mortified by her unprofessionalism in slandering my reputation.

Ms. Goode's remarks questioning my testimony under oath at the trial have permanently smeared my name in my community and in the state of Maine.

As a well-respected physician in family practice for over 30 years, serving the community where I was born and raised, I am dumbfounded by Ms. Goode's unkind insinuations that I may have fabricated my relatives who worked and lived at the School for the Feeble-Minded. My uncle Roy Levy was a resident there for nineteen years until his death in 1942. Records of his residency, his burial, and our lineage have been provided to my attorney.

I have no recourse but to take swift action to repair the unkind characterizations and prejudicial fabrications that Ms. Goode has bestowed on me and my reputation.

Signed,

Dr. Grey Kilgore

Slamming her laptop shut, she faced the sunless day out her window. If Kilgore wanted her to feel guilt and shame, he knew what he was doing. Her uncle's voice came back to her from that St. Paddy's night: "Your mother had an unusual sixth sense. I think that's what made her so ill. She could never seem to tame her own thoughts. I would never want you to end up like that."

Her phone read 36 degrees with an air quality index of 33. What was the book that the quirky Mr. Snodgrass had given her? She pulled it out of the front pocket of her backpack: *Synchronicity*. Something beyond her comprehension pushed her on and she instinctively dialed the number for Liz at the historical society. If anyone could find out about Kilgore's family history, she could.

Liz picked up the phone. "Pennie, I've been expecting your call. I saw your interview in the *Tribune* after the trial."

"You're a perceptive historian *and* a mind reader."

Liz chuckled. "Not sure about that, but I do like to dig into the weeds. I did a little preemptive research on Kilgore, and it turns out he did indeed have a great-uncle who lived at the institution, and his grandmother worked there as a nurse. But the interesting thing he didn't mention is that his grandfather was also a doctor there at that time."

"Why would he leave that part out?"

"That was the time they were performing sterilizations on patients. Could be very possible that one or more of the Marks women had the operation. And, well, he was the presiding physician."

"Are there any records?"

"Unfortunately, they didn't keep good records. Maybe by design. And unbelievably, tubal ligations were common all over the country at this time, from the 1920s through as late as the seventies. Not surprisingly, more women of color were involuntarily sterilized than any other group."

"That's sickening."

"And not that long ago. But it doesn't do you any good with Kilgore. He does indeed have the relatives he said he did in court."

"Thanks for researching that, Liz. I appreciate the favor."

"I'm happy to do it. You and your uncle were the only thing between those graves and the development."

Pennie went to her car. After three tries, the old girl finally started up, rattling. Normally she would have called her uncle to make an appointment with his mechanic but she'd more than troubled him already. Driving onto I-295, she headed north to Fairview to pay a visit to Stan Lewis. If anyone could help demystify Ward's behavior, his father could.

At Heritage Acres, she eased her way down the long driveway bordered by the split-rail fence, and spotted Stan at the far end of the enclosed pasture. She parked near the post-and-beam barn, glad she'd worn her comfortable field boots. At the gate, she let herself in and walked over to Stan, who seemed pleasantly surprised to see her on the cloudy morning.

He ran his steady hand soothingly along one of the horse's flanks. She realized it was Sacajawea, the spirited horse she'd ridden that day on the trail with Ward.

"To what do I owe this surprise visit?" he asked. "Aren't you busy helping your uncle put the real estate puzzle together?"

If there was ever a day she appreciated his joviality, it was today. "Any excuse to come out here to see the horses." Sacajawea nudged her in familiarity with her soft velvet nose.

"They're amazing animals. Especially this one. She came to us about five winters ago, nearly starved to death." He patted her healthy rump. "She's got some kind of sixth sense about people. Can tell she likes you."

"I've ridden her before. The day I came out here for the show in the arena." She hesitated. "Ward took me out."

Stan grew serious. "Wouldn't be the first time he took a woman for a ride. A trail ride, that is."

She turned crimson and wondered if he had seen the photo. This would be her life from here on out: wondering, embarrassed, regretful. "He does have a certain charm. But I am sorry to hear about his separation."

"What separation?"

She felt hot under the collar again. "I thought his wife left him."

"Not as far as I know. Just had dinner with them last week. Can't go for more than a week without seeing my granddaughter."

The whole thing had been a lie. She began to simmer inside, twist and boil. "I thought he'd said something about living apart but staying friends for the sake of Winnie."

"He'll never leave his wife. Her family has deep pockets, and she's bailed him out of more than one business failure. They may not be the most loving couple, but they manage to keep it together somehow."

Her head felt like it might melt under this hot awareness but she knew she had to save herself. She didn't want Stan to think she was a complete moron. "I must have misunderstood."

"The one thing about Ward, and I don't like to say this about my son, but he isn't the most straightforward character."

She could feel his stare but kept her eyes on the horse. "I'm really here to talk about Kilgore."

"Oh, yeah? What's that old rattlesnake up to?"

Now she looked him straight in the eye. "Why do you say that?"

"He and Ward are pretty chummy. Have known each other for a long time."

"You probably know about my misstep with the reporter."

He nodded. "I did hear something about that. What, is he suing you now?"

She gazed up at the shifting clouds against a gray sky. "You're not surprised."

"He's known for stirring up trouble." The Appaloosa nuzzled his neck.

"According to Kilgore and his attorney, he's got a stellar reputation to maintain."

He laughed. "Yes, he's as pure as the driven snow. I hope you're not worried about all this. Like I told you, Ward doesn't like to lose. Now you're caught in the middle."

She sighed and ran her hand along Sacajawea's healthy speckled girth. "He's bringing a suit against me, and my uncle's firm by default, since I was representing the firm."

Stan scratched his beard. "No good deed goes unpunished. What can I do to help?"

"Nothing really, just wanted you to know."

He took off his baseball cap and scratched his head. "My sister in Florida is very happy with the decision to protect that cemetery. We need development, but responsible development."

She smiled, grateful for the acknowledgement. "Ward can always put a road in further down."

"Remains to be seen, I guess. For now, you've done a good thing."

Sacajawea whinnied for more attention, and Pennie rubbed her long, strong white neck, looking into the white sclera of her eye. "There's one more thing I wanted to ask you."

He smiled on one side, that lopsided smile so exaggerated on Ward. "What's on your mind?"

"That's a loaded question." She laughed. "Did you know Chloe Mc-Carthy?"

"Why, yes, she rode with the high school team. Good kid. Sad what happened in that car accident. My granddaughter and she were good friends. It took Winnie a while to get over that." He squinted at the stocky mustangs grazing in the distance. "Did you know Chloe?"

"No, but my uncle and I are working with Mrs. McCarthy on a property deed. She mentioned that Chloe rode here."

"Well tell Jeannette I said hello the next time you see her." He whistled to the horses to come, heading in for the night. "I know she's also had some trouble with that stepson of hers next door, Edmond."

"You know about the property dispute?"

"Oh, yes. He's another one known for stirring up trouble. He went to high school with Ward, too." The chestnut mustangs, Lewis and Clark, walked up behind Stan. "These types band together."

She realized how closely connected everyone and everything was. "Somehow, I'm not surprised."

"The more people you get to know around here, good and bad, the more you know." He bid her a friendly goodbye, walking toward the barn with his troupe of horses. She wondered about all the locals he had taught to ride in his lifetime, the interconnectedness of people that crossed paths day in and day out in this barn, this pasture, this life.

TAKING A LEFT ON Gray Road, she headed toward the cemetery on her way out of town. Pulling over next to the side of the road, she was relieved to see all excavation equipment gone from the site. The only evidence left was the toppled stone wall and grass dug up along the dirt road stretching to the Patient's Cemetery.

Pennie stepped out of the car and immediately sensed a difference. The ground vibrations were quiet, peaceful. She ran her hands over the small mottled white gravestones, the immense solemnity.

WILLIAM MARKS, 1909–1928

ETTA MARKS, 1897–1925

JAKE MARKS, 1892–1912

LIZZIE MARKS, 1886–1921

ANNIE PARKER, 1853–1916

JOSEPH E. ROLLINS, 1894–1914

LEONA V. BALLARD, 1894–1913

HAROLD MURPHY, NOV. 1912

GEORGE GRIFFIN, NOV. 1912

HANNAH MARKS, NOV. 1912

ELIZABETH DARLING, NOV. 1912

CALVIN & LAURA TRIPP, NOV. 1912

FIVE CHILDREN OF H. GRIFFIN, NOV. 1912

ROXANNE & ELLEN GRIFFIN, NOV. 1912

LUCY G. JOHNSON, NOV. 1912

THREE EASTON CHILDREN, NOV. 1912

A breeze shuffled through the pine trees, the mighty pointed tops swaying in the wind. A feeling of anguish moved her. November 1912, the faceless day the governor's men shamelessly wrested the remains from Malaga and reburied them here—exiled, dispersed, displaced, even in death. A child's body lost, rolling from the top of the heaped casket, falling against a gunnel, and slipping into the depths of the saltwater eddy, the small bones and brittle tendons rolling and tossing. Under the weight of grief, a profound grasp of human depravity, Pennie fell to her knees, onto the still and quiet ground, and wept.

IF THERE WAS EVER a time in her life when she felt utterly compelled to confront a situation, to try to make sense of the senseless, it was now. In what seemed like a snap of fingers, a forward thrust of time, she found herself parked in front of Ward's real estate office. Only one month earlier, on St. Paddy's Day, she had stood in this lobby with her uncle, nervous as a schoolgirl at the prospect of being on her first call with her uncle and meeting Ward Lewis. So much had happened since then. She was not the same person.

The elevator lights descended, coming from the fifth floor where Ward's office was. Bracing herself, she waited for the doors to open. Holding her breath as they parted, a man's fine-groomed head appeared, looking down, texting. When he looked up, she was stunned to come eye to eye with the attorney, Leadbetter, and his neatly trimmed goatee. He

set his jaw and glared, walking toward her, leaning in her path. "Cunt,"
he muttered.

Catching her breath, she tensed against his uttered assault, stepped
inside and hit the button. She leaned against the elevator wall and hugged
herself to keep from shaking. The last thing she wanted was Ward seeing
her losing her shit. She came here to confront him, to call him on his
insidious lies. When the door opened to the lobby, the young assistant
broker looked up from the front desk.

In a moment, he realized who she was and stood up. "What do you
want?"

"I'm looking for Ward." Her voice shook.

"He's not here." Before losing her nerve, she walked down the hall
with his voice calling behind her, "You have no right!"

To her disappointment, Ward's pristine office with the glass doors
was vacant. The rain slashed against his window overlooking the city.
Turning on her heels, she returned to the lobby. The polished associate
was on the phone, undoubtedly calling Ward.

Instead of waiting for the elevator, she took the stairway, running
down.

The streets were showered in an icy dismal April rain. People passed
her on the cobblestone sidewalk, seeking cover from the unpredictable
elements. What was it that had made her so trusting, so completely
vulnerable? It began to pour even harder. Looking up at the sky, she
let the rain fall on her face, washing over her until she was completely
drenched, accepting what a fool she had been.

She drove through the streets of the Old Port, heading toward the
West End, thinking about sitting in front of a warm fire at her aunt and
uncle's house—the home where she wondered if she was even welcome
any longer—when she spotted Ward's BMW parked outside his condo

on Dartmouth Street, the place he had taken her on their first lunch date. She slammed on the brakes, then swerved to park.

Across the street, a tall thin man in a dark canvas jacket walked away from the building, shoulders down. When he disappeared from sight, and before she lost her courage, she crossed the street and ran up the steps, opening the door to the vestibule. The studded walls were halfway covered with Sheetrock—not much progress since the last time she'd been here. She walked toward the stairway and heard his voice coming from the next floor. "I just need a little bit more time and you'll get your money. Don't bail on me now." His voice lowered. "Yeah, well fuck you, too!"

Ascending the stairs, she looked up toward the cupola, the crow's nest, where they had kissed, where she'd felt a presence, heard the young woman crying.

He nearly ran into her in his hurry toward the stairs. "What the hell are you doing here?'

She'd never seen him angry before and realized just how little she knew about this man. "I was driving by and saw your car."

"Why don't you get back in your little shit box and keep driving?"

She wasn't sure what else she'd expected. "You lied to me about your wife. The whole thing has been a lie, hasn't it?"

"You had to stick your nose in where it didn't belong. Don't tell me you give two shits about those people buried over there, Pennie Goode. This has all been about impressing your uncle, showing him how fucking smart you are after flunking out of school and refusing to get a real job, to work for a living."

It stunned her, this downright hate. "So you resort to sharing nude pictures of me, of sending that vicious asshole Leadbetter after me? Is that how you deal with the women in your life who don't *behave*?"

"Don't act so sweet and innocent, Pennie. I know all about you sleeping around."

"What are you talking about?"

"I'm talking about my son. You don't think I found out about your whoring around up on the mountain? You knew I was his father and decided to come after me, to play your little games with me. Or was it your uncle's idea? Has he got you working on your back to keep his office doors open? Takes a dimwit like my father to call him."

"I don't like what you're insinuating. You told me you were separated, almost divorced from your wife. And I had no idea about your son."

"Little innocent victim Pennie Goode, right?"

She stood firm. "I'm no victim and I'm certainly not pure. But I am honest, which is more than I can say for you. Even your own father says you'll go to any lengths to win, even threatening my uncle's business by coming after me. I know all about you and that reporter. You and Humiston are quite the old pals, aren't you?"

"Get the fuck out of my building."

"Not until you promise me that you, Leadbetter, and Kilgore will drop this lawsuit. This is insane."

"Why? So you can come after me for the development at the mountain? That'll be the next thing. Pretty soon you and your uncle won't have a business or a reputation to stand on."

"Ward, you can't be serious about this."

"I told you to get the fuck out of here before I have to throw you out." He raised his arm, threatening, his face shaking with rage.

She turned, running, numb to the tips of her fingers. Somehow her legs brought her down the stairway and across the road and into her car where she sat, bleak, terrified, and alone.

A knocking on her passenger door window startled her. It was the thin man in the canvas jacket, and the same man from the restaurant sitting at the barstool with the floating apparition beside him, the man from Baxter Boulevard with the ghostly squall. She rolled down the window.

He stood soaking wet, his face devastated. "I saw you leave that building. I don't know who you are, but please, please stay away from that man." She looked back at Ward's building for any sign of him. The gaunt man gripped her door, his knuckles white. "A few years ago, I saw a young girl about half your age leaving this same building crying. She had a big welt on the side of her face. So I went inside to ask Ward what happened, and he said if I ever said anything about that girl being here he'd never pay me. That asshole still owes me thousands."

She hesitated, afraid to ask the next question. "Do you know what happened to that girl?"

"She died in a car accident on the turnpike. It was the same day. I've never forgiven myself for not helping her." He looked through Pennie. "I feel her unrest every day." He walked away, down toward the waterfront, a steady drizzle following his steps.

So, this was it. Ward had turned the tables on her for something he most hated about himself, berating her for sleeping with his son, knowing he had seduced a girl much younger and more naive, a teenager. He'd used his own dark perverse truth as a weapon.

Instead of going over to sit by a warm fire at her aunt and uncle's place, she went straight home to a hot shower. She crawled into bed while it was still light out, the pouring rain signaling a shift from a relentless winter into spring. She fell into a heavy sleep.

In her dreams, she found herself running in the dark fog on a vacant highway, looking through the eyes of the Alaskan husky, panting. Running alongside her was Chloe, her desperate sobs echoing in the night. On the other side was Lottie, her eyes full of terror, as dark and deep as an ocean of pain. Sensing something behind them, she turned to see bright headlights nearly blinding, chasing them. Running from it, the pavement vibrating and shaking under them, she knew it was a matter of survival. They were being hunted, pursued by an unknown evil. Crossing a bridge, she saw Back Cove underneath them, the place where her mother had jumped. Hearing squealing tires from behind, the full force of the automobile rushing toward her in hot pursuit, she leapt out into the blackness, midair—before wrenching herself out of it, out of that ending, fully awake in the pitch darkness of her room.

Chapter 16
A Night to Remember

FOR THE NEXT TWO weeks, they went through the motions of work at the office without hearing anything more from Kilgore, Leadbetter, or Ward Lewis. Uncle Alfie never mentioned anything, just continued like things were normal. The silence drowned her a little each day.

Tita, on the other hand, grew animated and anxious, making the final preparations for the documentary screening with Lars, who had spent hours upon hours in the editing suite working on final tweaks to the preview. Their ticket sales were up to 1,300 and counting. They'd received a major sponsorship from Salomon, the brand of Tita's old racing skis, and about thirty silent auction donations thanks to Aunt Aggie and Maude's bridge club. The affair was billed as semi-formal, so they expected a crowd dressed to the nines.

Tita tried to get Pennie out of her funk by talking about what they'd wear, but Pennie was not motivated to go dress shopping. Her bank account nearly empty and job prospects mirky at best, she pondered the situation, the lacking wardrobe in her closet. "I'll go to Goodwill to find something."

"Are you serious? You can't wear something used. Come shopping with Aunt Aggie and me. I bet she'll buy something for you."

"I don't want her buying anything for me."

"Sometimes you can be so stubborn, Pennie. You can always move back home if you need to." There it was, Tita again trying to mend things back together. Pennie knew it was the right thing to do, to remedy things with Aunt Aggie, to move on for the sake of the family, but she was tired of trying to please for the sake of peace. "Are we having this conversation again?"

Her uncle popped his head out and asked Pennie into his office. At least she'd been rescued from the conversation. She closed the door behind her. "Have you heard anything from Leadbetter or Kilgore?" she asked.

"Not a word, thankfully. Jeannette called me, so I thought you'd like to jump on the call." She pictured the thin dark man leaning in her car window, defeated. He dialed Mrs. McCarthy's number and put the phone on speaker. "Jeannette, how are you? I'm here with Pennie."

"Not bad, Alfie. Nice you both could call. I just got the final DNA results from the lab yesterday afternoon."

"Good or bad?"

"Depends on your perspective, I guess. The only conclusive DNA they found on the necklace and bracelet was mine."

Pennie pictured the husky staring back at the security camera with the sterling locket necklace in his mouth. Her fingers ached from the dream of clawing at the cold, frozen ground. Uncle Alfie stared at her, continuing his conversation over the speaker. "I'm sorry to hear there isn't more evidence, but I'm not surprised."

Mrs. McCarthy's voice over the speaker quavered. "My dear Chloe. Maybe she was trying to send me a message that things are the way they are, that I just need to move on."

"Sometimes there's no rhyme or reason for tragedy." He scratched Fella, who lay sprawled across the floor beside his desk. "I'm sorry."

Over the line came a bone-deep sigh. "You let me know when your surveyor can come back to finalize those plot lines."

Listening to her uncle, his gentle voice, Pennie was inclined to tell him everything she knew about Ward Lewis, but it still did not add up to enough to incriminate him. There was no definitive link between him and Chloe.

At the end of the day, she took Cassie home with her. The last thing she wanted was to be, or to sleep, alone. Fear of spiraling into another dream where she was falling to her own demise scared the hell out of her.

Pulling in to her driveway, she found a package the size of a boot box on her stoop. Someone had written "Penelope Goode" on the top in black marker, no address. Someone had just dropped it there. Cassie barked at her to let them inside. She checked her mailbox and pulled out two bills with PAST DUE in red across the front.

Setting everything on her coffee table, she grabbed a glass of wine and contemplated the brown cardboard box. Could it be a bomb, or something laced with poison, arsenic? What lengths would Ward go to? She turned on the television and absentmindedly listened to the news to give herself something else to focus on: another riot in another city, another school shooting, another politician paid off, another racially motivated killing. She thought about the souls buried at Fairview. As she stared at the box, Cassie pawed it, flipping in onto the floor. Whatever it was, it wasn't heavy. How dangerous could it be? Cassie whined at her and scratched at the box.

"What, you want me to open it?" She picked it up. "This doesn't smell funny to you?" Sniffing it herself, she set it down to grab a knife. "Okay, this is your fault if we blow up." Cassie whined at her again and sat down, wagging her tail.

With a swift motion, she cut through the duct tape on the seam and found another white rectangular box inside with a note taped to the top. Hesitating for a moment, she opened it: *Make it a night to remember*, the note read, neatly printed in blue pen.

Sitting on the couch, she opened the white box. Inside was a gold sequined dress.

Unfolding it, she let her companion sniff it. "You like it? I don't know, it's pretty risqué." Cassie barked in approval.

Although short, it had a high neckline with spaghetti straps and a tasteful A-line silhouette. Her mind went to Ward, of course. Was he, again, trying to get her guard down? "Well, it does look like my size." She went to the bathroom to slip it on, and to her surprise, it fit like it'd been tailored for her. No doubt it was from someone who knew her well. But then again, most of Portland knew what she looked like without clothes.

Her phone chirped with a text from Tita. She and Aunt Aggie were out dress shopping and she'd sent a picture.

Should we pick this up for you? Super cute, right?

It was an Audrey Hepburn-esque retro cocktail dress with a high neck and black polka dots. Something her aunt would pick out for her, especially now.

All I need is a corset to go with it.

LOL, it's actually sweet. And you need to wear something special for the big night!

I found something today. I'm all set. Thanks!

Tita sent her some pictures of long Oscar-looking starlet dresses she was trying on. Pennie gave them all a thumbs up. Instead of shying away from this challenge, she would meet it head on, a fierceness like a fire growing inside of her. Intimidation would not get the best of her, and she felt herself changing somehow, coming to terms with her shame, her anger, herself. Instead of wallowing in humiliation inflicted by men like Ward, she would try on this newfound power of just being herself in her own nakedness, regardless of others' expectations and judgment. Looking in the full-length mirror behind her bedroom door, she pulled her hair up and asked Cassie what heels might work best.

THE REST OF THE week floated by in a blur until the big night finally arrived, the weather turning warmer in time. She'd found a black silk scarf to cover her bare shoulders in the gold mini-dress and wore her hair up, a few strands loose around her face. It suited her, the slightly messy, wild look. A newfound courage bolstered her as she started her sputtering Karmann Ghia, her shit box. Ward. She never knew just how charmingly low he could be. But she was recognizing his way of wielding power over women by shaming them, by using his own vile behavior to turn the tables.

Waiting out front on Congress Street, she rolled her window down to let in the early evening sounds of car horns, the movement in the air, the vibrations of the city moving through her. Dani and Mali came out wearing form-fitting satin dresses with long slits up the sides. Dani strutted in yellow, the dress hugging her waist and chest just right, the top straps tied around her long neck. Mali floated along in black with a plunging neckline and chiffon skirt, catching the warmer winds of May. Individually they were stunning, but put them together and they stopped time. Every eye in the early evening city rested on them when they crossed the street to her car.

"Thanks for picking us up," said Mali, climbing in front.

"I got my marching orders from Aunt Aggie. Thank God she's organizing this whole affair. Tita's a nervous wreck." Pennie pulled on the hem of her dress.

Dani leaned forward from the back. "We'll buy her a cosmo or two."

She downshifted, driving along Congress toward the theater. "Careful, we don't want Tita stumbling at the premiere."

Mali rolled down her window. "You look amazing by the way. Where'd that little number come from?"

"Thanks, you clean up nice, too," she said, dodging the question. "I don't think anyone will notice I'm alive with you two stealing the show."

Dani said, "I wouldn't count on that."

Pennie sat up straight, mustering the courage to face the crowd, as they pulled into a parking spot in front of the State. Lars carried boxes from his van, looking tall and dapper in his vintage black tux.

She stepped onto the pavement and slammed her rattling door shut. Running to grab the door for Lars, she could feel his anxiety bubbling at the surface. "Here we go, Mr. Director!" He barely smiled, his wall of fear firmly in place. They followed him up the platform to the long grand hallway where Tita had arranged the silent auction. She was there, wearing a shapely long red Armani number. She argued with Aggie and Maude about the placement of the displays for the oil paintings, autographed album covers, and concert tickets.

Tita's makeup was the most impressive Pennie had ever seen on her—crimson lips to match the dress, her dark eyes outlined in black, strikingly seductive. In her platform heels, she came up to Lars' shoulder. They looked evermore the power couple, and the high energy in the theater grew by the seconds. Lars's film buddies carried in sound equipment, eyeing Pennie up and down. She drew herself up, masking her unease.

The State had been completely renovated a few years prior, and the Art Deco style of old Hollywood made it a perfect backdrop for a film screening. Even though she hadn't skied in competition for eight years, Tita was still as athletic as she was when she was a teenager, her arms toned and her thighs taut, years of still taming the slopes apparent against the red dress.

Aunt Aggie did her best to keep her only daughter from blowing a gasket over nothing. "Christina, why don't you get yourself a drink and Maude and I will finish setting up?"

Mali and Dani took their cue and whisked Tita away toward the bar. Pennie followed, anxious to calm her own jumping nerves, and checked her phone: only one hour until the doors opened. Caterers rushed around, setting up white linens on long tables with shrimp cocktail, cucumber canapes, golden puff pastries, and bottles of champagne on ice. Mali made herself at home behind the fully stocked bar, helping herself to the vodka to make drinks for Pennie and Tita, only soda water with cranberry for her and Dani. They each took a glass and admired the glorious old theater with the red cushioned seats facing the main stage, flanked by ornate ivory pillars, a stately gold crest and a Scottish coat of arms above. Small balconies sat along the walls on either side for special patrons, the main balcony on the floor above them.

Pennie sidled up beside Dani to clink glasses. "What was the final count of tickets sold?"

"I think just under 1,500. They'll make a killing."

"They've worked on this thing for three years. I hope it's as good as Tita says it is."

The star of the night walked brusquely away to meet Lars onstage at the podium, making sure they had their evening choreography in sync. Lars controlled the giant screen, cuing the projection booth to test it one more time. The grainy home video footage of Tita as a little kid in ski school, her front teeth missing, appeared briefly on the big screen. Pennie's own heart skipped in anticipation, holding herself back from a wave of emotion, from the effervescent memories.

Aunt Maude appeared by her side. "Looks like these two are actually pulling it off."

Dani beamed. "I can't wait to see it!"

"Now if we can keep Aggie and Tita apart, we'll probably have a successful show."

They shared relieved laughter, watching Tita ordering Lars around and Aunt Aggie directing the theater people where to stand. The idea was to keep the seats roped off until the screening. The first hour and a half everyone would congregate in the upper and lower hallways around the bars and silent auctions. Then guests would be invited to take their seats for the grand sneak peek.

In the dim theater light, Pennie caught the glimmer of Aunt Maude's brooch, a bright amber yellow stone. "That's a beautiful pin. I've never seen it before."

Her aunt looked down at the sand-dollar-sized brooch on her collar. "You know, I just found this old cairngorm brooch. Used to belong to Grammy Goode. I thought it had been lost forever, but I found it in my garden after the snow melt. Must have dropped it there at some point." The picture of her own mother, the one with Togo, came to Pennie. Her mother was wearing the silk scarf and a brooch just like that one.

Her uncle's voice came from behind her. He took a seat at the bar in his best navyblue three-piece suit, his favorite cufflinks brandishing the Goode crest. Despite what she'd put him through over the last few weeks, he looked well and rested. Aunt Aggie joined him by his side, wearing her own charcoal suit with a three-quarter-length skirt, looking very regal with her hair up and dark lipstick on. Everyone in town knew them or knew about them, a formidable couple. He kissed her on the cheek, and she brushed his shoulders before walking toward the stage, yelling to the front. "Christina, are you ready? The doors open soon."

Tita looked at Lars expectantly and he retracted the screen and shut off the mic. It was showtime.

A kinetic swell took over the theater. Pennie tried to keep her thoughts away from Ward as early guests began to trickle in. There was Jeannette McCarthy and the surveyor, Jack, greeting Uncle Alfie at the bar, Aunt Aggie watching them like a hawk from the hallway. Lanky Peter shyly stood beside Mali and burly Max firmly planted himself beside Dani at a silent auction table. Tita and Lars stood in the hallway, facing the front door, greeting the swarm of people as they entered, a veritable hive of excitement. Coaches and old friends from the ski teams and even a few celebs from the Olympic team were showing up. Then, to her great dismay, Tracy Bayer walked in with Ethan Lewis, Ward's son. Her legs wobbled.

She could feel Dani from behind and turned to her. "I just saw who walked in."

Her best friend smiled and raised an eyebrow. "Your two favorite mountain men. Decisions, decisions."

"Very funny." She tried to stop herself from breaking out into a cold sweat as she dealt with the sinking realization that Ward and his son would be in the same place.

"Let's go." Dani looped her elbow and literally dragged her over to say hello. Probably the best approach—face the situation head-on. She gushed, "Hey, Tracy and, um, Ethan, is it?"

"Hey!" Tracy said, so baked, eyes so slitted you could blind him with dental floss. "What's up, Dani? Pen? Wow, you both look amaaaazing." He eyed them shamelessly up and down.

Ethan wiped his sweaty palms on his army green suit jacket and stuck his hand out to her. "Hey there." Pennie took it, awkwardly, wondering if they were both undressing her with their eyes. He stared at her, awestruck. "You look fully recovered."

Right, the ski accident. It seemed like a year ago, but it'd only been a few months. "Oh, yeah. Completely healed. Back to normal."

"That's a relief." His tender face full of attention, and there it was, that lopsided grin. "Where do you get a beer around here?"

Dani, seeing the bar in the lobby already three lines deep, led the way. "Follow me."

Working their way through the crowd and around the silent auction tables, they all trailed behind Dani up the grand winding staircase to the second floor where only a few others had found the second bar. The four of them ordered a drink, taking in the majesty of the grand old theater. Dani's design, the devilish owl, was displayed on the big screen, with the main sponsor logos underneath: Salomon, Coos Canyon, L.L.Bean, and Ward Lewis Properties.

"Cool artwork," said Tracy.

Pennie hugged her best friend for dear life. "Dani's magic."

Ethan took a long swig of beer. "I bet we could sell T-shirts with that design up at the mountain."

"It'll cost you," said Dani, taking on the business sense of her sister.

He laughed. "I'll get my father to fund the first shipment."

Trying her best to melt into the floor, Pennie stepped toward the balcony. Tracy leaned against the railing beside her. His easygoing nature comforted her. "How've you been?" she asked.

"You know. Thinking about getting a real job now that the mountain is closed for the season. I just moved to Portland."

"Really?" She held her breath, trying to hide her elation.

"Yeah, took the plunge and moved in with my girlfriend."

Bam. Just like that, her anticipation fell. "Well, good for you. Gotta settle down sometime, right?" She gulped her drink.

"What about you? You can't be single with that bod."

Her face grew hot, the dress feeling shorter, transparent. "Nah, not me. Well, I was in, um, something, but it didn't last."

"Maybe we can go on a double date?" He looked at Ethan.

She tried to keep herself from wincing. "Not ready for that yet. Taking things single for a while."

"Roger that." He chatted it up in his best boarder-dude persona, then suddenly, she felt a shift in the air of the theater. The energy changed from a high hum to a low thrum in the space of a few moments. Looking up, she saw a black owl and its shining eyes upon her from a high perch. Following the great horned owl's gaze down, she saw him there—Ward standing by the stage with Lars and Tita. Ethan, deep in conversation, hadn't noticed his father yet. She watched the top of Aunt Maude's head following the owl's flight soaring across the theater, over the outline of the tall thin man from outside Ward's building, who was standing in the footlights beside a smaller hunched balding man with glasses, odd Mr. Snodgrass from the wine cellar. The owl disappeared in the eaves. The low frequency in the theater moved through her.

"Be right back." She wandered through the growing crowd on the balcony floor and found the ladies' room down the hallway. Facing herself in the mirror, taking a deep breath, she realized with a newfound clarity that she was not the same person she was just a few months ago. That was someone consumed with self-doubt, scared of uncovering the truth. The past weeks had been a slow turning. Her blue eyes that had once betrayed her emotions to the world now emboldened her with a new awareness.

Dani walked in. "There you are."

"Yeah, had to pee."

"Did you see Ward?"

"Sure did." She went through the motions of washing her hands. "Let's go see if Aunt Aggie needs anything."

"Hey, are you okay?" Dani looked over her shoulder, concerned.

She talked to Dani in the mirror. "I found out that Ward is not separated."

"What?"

"His father told me. And Ward knows I slept with his son."

Dani narrowed her dark eyes. "How do you know?"

"He told me. He called me a whore and few other choice names."

"That motherfucker."

"That's not the half of it." The image of the desperately thin man in the drizzle outside her car door drifted across her mind.

Dani was saying something, but she'd already turned to escape out the bathroom door. Pennie practically ran into Max at the top of the staircase. She waved and slipped around him, anxious to get away, in search of her uncle for his calm composure in all things.

At the bottom of the stairway, she came face-to-face with Jeannette McCarthy. The stylish Southern belle, dressed in floral, reached out her hand. "Just the person I was looking for."

"Oh, hello, Mrs. McCarthy, so kind of you to come tonight." Was it a coincidence she ran into her as these thoughts about Chloe and Ward nagged at her?

"I love a good gala. Can't wait to see the sneak peek. But I wanted to thank you for all your help this summer."

"I didn't do anything, really. Just there to support my uncle."

"I think you did more than meets the eye." The gold horse charm bracelet dangled from her delicate senescent wrist.

Pennie said, "It's the bracelet."

"Yes, I think Chloe wanted me to find it. Still not sure how it ended up in the ground, but I believe it's a sign from her, reaching out."

Pennie thought about her aunt's brooch, the same one her mother wore, the one that'd been lost. Jeannette opened her pink clutch and drew out a necklace. It was the necklace from her dream. Dangling the sterling silver locket, Jeannette fanned the chain out. "I'd like you to have this. Do you mind if I put it on you?"

Pennie could see the triskelion design etched in the front. She felt her own bare neck. "Why, I—I don't know what to say. This is something so personal, you should keep it."

"Chloe came to me in a dream last night. It's the first time since she died." Her sagging eyes grew teary. She looked off in the distance for a moment to gather herself. "Anyway, she was sitting on a blanket on the front lawn, gazing out at the calm seas, and you were there beside her. Then Chloe unclasped this necklace from her own neck and handed it to you. You were smiling at one another, the wind mingling your hair."

Pennie took Jeannette's shaking hand in hers.

"Even though it couldn't save my dear Chloe, it's a link to her."

She bent down for Mrs. McCarthy to secure it on the back of her neck. Tears came to her own eyes. "I don't know what to say." She caressed the silver etching and opened the locket. Inside was an inscription: *Make it a night to remember — W.L.*

A small gasp escaped as she absorbed the script, the same words that had been written on the note to her. "Who's W.L.?" she asked.

"Winnie Lewis, her best friend. They took riding lessons for years together. This was from their junior prom night. Neither had dates, so they went together." Mrs. McCarthy looked into some invisible silent ache. "It was the night before she died in the accident."

"Right..." She held back who the real W.L. was. What good would ever come of it, to share this with a mother grieving a never-ending loss?

She took Pennie's fingers in hers. "Now, it looks like your hands are empty. Can't have that at a party."

They found the bar, the low thrumming growing louder. On the other side was Ward Lewis, holding court with his admirers encircling him: Bethany from his office next to the young front-desk gatekeeper, standing beside foul-mouthed Leadbetter and the infamous Edmund with his prominent Adam's apple. All gave their full attention to Ward in his tailored tux, his hair curled in just the right wave, his lopsided grin that captivated women day and night, that allowed him into the room and around the table where deals were made. How he reminded her of the politicians who claimed Malaga Island for financial gain, using power over humanity. These men who used oppression for possession, who doctored stories and lives to suit their insatiable greed.

A higher vibration hummed from across the hallway. She turned to see Stan and the sturdy no-bullshit, white-haired woman in cowgirl boots, his girlfriend Roxanne, bantering with her aunt and uncle. Roxanne hugged Uncle Alfie in gratitude, Stan watching on with his wizened eyes.

From behind her, Mali grabbed her arm. "Help me gather the silent auction bids. It's almost time." Looking at her phone, it was 8:08. They grabbed the clipboards as Lars's deep voice came over the loudspeaker, directing everyone to take seats. The hallway slowly emptied out, the energy moving into the grandiose theater.

Pennie helped Dani and Mali pack all the items back into the boxes and stuffed them under the table as if they had done it a million times over. Finally, the last to enter the now full theater, they found Pennie's aunts and uncles up front, their eyes on the stage. Looking up and around, she spotted Ward and his wife sitting with Ethan and Tracy in the balcony, the black owl perched stealthily over their heads. The room hummed, penetrating her very core. With keen eyes attuned to the darkened space, she searched in vain for the thin man and wine-seller, but they had disappeared from the footlights.

Tita sat at the end of the aisle; her gaze was fixed on the stage. Lars walked to the podium as the theater grew silent. "Ladies and gentlemen, welcome to the premiere of *Freestyle Femme Fatale*." The crowd clapped in polite applause. In the dim light, Aunt Maude's dazzling amber brooch shone. She squeezed Pennie's hand and whispered, "That locket brings out the light in your eyes."

The director thanked the sponsors and gave a brief history about the making of the documentary around the history of women's freestyle skiing, featuring the light of his life, Christina. She sent him a kiss with both hands, cuing the lights to dim and the film to light up the screen.

The story unfolded before their eyes, chronicling the rise of women's freeskiing and Tita's own rise to the Olympic stage. From the time she was a baby, she was a child of the mountain. Pulled in the sled by Aunt Aggie, riding in a backpack behind Uncle Alfie while he skied, taking the chairlift with Pennie when they were little sprites, and racing through the gates at the age of five, born to ski. Even before they had a mogul competition for girls, Tita was skiing and jumping against the boys—the only way for a girl to compete back then. When she finally won her first competition against them, she was disqualified; automatically negated from the race because none of the judges had realized she was a girl until she took her helmet off.

The sound of Joan Jett singing "Bad Reputation" filled the theater, shifting to her days of winning competitions around the country and her rise to the Olympic team, leading to the mogul run of her life, the first jump a triple twist in the air with a solid landing, speeding over the top of the bumps to her final backward twist, buoyed by the molecules around her. The thirty-minute sneak peek moved toward a close with newspaper headlines: "Goode Makes History on Slopes and at the Afterparty" and "Goode Disgraced, Trying to Keep Up with the Boys."

As the very real headlines sunk in, sober reminders of Tita's public downfall, the theater fell silent. The final image of Tita standing high in front of a group of admiring young female athletes made the theater bust open with applause, a standing ovation. Tita sat motionless. Pennie was proud of her cousin and glad that Lars had left out the part when Tita had assaulted the cameraman on that night of revelry.

Aunt Aggie gathered Tita together to help her to the stage where she thanked her mother and father, and especially Lars for bringing her story to life. She promised the crowd that this was just a taste of the entire documentary coming to theaters around New England later in the year. Aunt Aggie joined her to announce the winners of the silent auction and then raffled off the ski tickets and equipment. Pennie left her seat to find Dani back at the tables getting the boxes out for the winners. Mali counted the money in the lockbox, examining the receipts.

"Did they make a killing or what?" Pennie asked.

"Lars won't have to worry about finishing his documentary."

Soon the crowd filled the bar and hallway once again. The twins bestowed the auction items on the winners, flush from the preview and the buzzing crowd and the drinks.

A low thrum rattled her again. Turning, she watched Ward leaning over her uncle's shoulder, slurring, mouthing something about Uncle Alfie's practice closing for good, spitting his words. Her uncle replied, with exaggeration, "Maybe it's time for you to go." Ward laughed hysterically before he spotted her.

To her own surprise, she didn't move. The frequency dropped an octave as he approached her, grasping his whiskey on ice. At first, he merely smiled, but then motioned to someone across the room. It was his wife who walked toward them in her immaculate white dress, tall in her heels, nearly matching him.

"Pennie, I don't believe I've introduced you to my wife, Rosalind." His words ran together in a mushy cadence.

Rosalind stuck out her diamond-studded hand. "Nice to meet you, Pennie."

"Same here. Ward has told me so much about you."

"And he's told me all about you, too, dear. Please call me Roz. Ward says you're quite a whiz in real estate investigations." The stately blonde, features sculpted on her stern face, emphasized each syllable of "investigations."

Pennie tilted her head toward Ward. "And your husband's lawyer is quite an *investigator*, too."

He opened his mouth but closed it, thinking better of himself, as drunk as he was. "Pennie here is dating Ethan."

She bit her cheek, hating how he used his own son as a weapon against her, grasping for anything to take down with him. "No, we're just friends, met skiing at the mountain."

"Oh, I heard it was more than *friends*," he slurred, eyeing her up and down.

Roz turned to him. "That mountain scene is full of hook-ups, isn't it?" She raised her eyebrows at Pennie's hemline. "Girls just throw themselves at young men these days." She looked at her watch. "I called a car. It's out front."

He kissed his wife. "I'll walk you out." They turned to go, and he leaned down to whisper, "Glad you decided to wear the dress, perfect fit. Maybe I'll drop by later to take it off." He then grabbed the locket around her neck, pulling her forward and she gulped in horror until he let go and backed off. Her spine crawled and she clung to the locket. For the first time, she was afraid for her safety.

Alfie touched her on the shoulder. "What was that all about?"

Composing herself, she put on a brave face. "Introduced me to his wife. That's all."

Aunt Aggie drew up next to them. "Ready, Alfie? I'm beat."

He put his arm around his wife, his eyes still on Pennie. "You going to be alright?"

"I'll be fine. Heading out myself."

"You be careful tonight, Birdie." It was barely audible, but she heard it, his concern, a lingering charge in the air.

She found Dani and Mali with their husbands talking to Tita and Lars. "Amazing what you've done, Lars," she said. "I can't wait to see the whole thing."

Tita took his arm. "He's remarkable, isn't he? I guess the trip to California was well worth it." She wobbled, blurry-eyed and half drunk, her sarcasm beginning to slip out. "We're going out to Zootz to dance and celebrate."

Out of the corner of her eye, Pennie caught sight of Leadbetter and Ward at the bar, deep in conversation. "I'll pass. I've got to go home and sleep." She was exhausted from the low frequency in the room.

Dani tried to talk her into going, but Pennie hugged and kissed them goodbye. Trailing the steady stream of guests leaving the theater, she stepped into the cool of the spring night, the air fresh and foggy. Under the streetlight, she ran into Tracy and Ethan, both now slightly drunk and very high.

"Hey, Pen," said Tracy. "Where you headed?"

"Straight home to collapse." She walked toward her car.

"Can you give us a lift?"

The two looked like little boys ready to thumb a ride across town. "Where's your apartment?"

"Washington Ave."

"Sure, hop in."

Tracy joined her in the front seat, to her relief. "Cool ride," he said as she turned the engine over once, twice, and the lucky third time, finally sputtering to life. "Sounds a little rough."

"My life is rough. This is the next thing on my list, as soon as I have more than $50 in my checking account." Looking in the rearview, she saw Ward getting into his BMW, Leadbetter joining him in the passenger seat.

Ethan piped in from the back. "My father says you work with your uncle. I didn't know you were in real estate."

She wanted to say, *And I didn't know your father was a flaming asshole.* "I only started working in my uncle's office a couple months ago. Your grandfather hired us to look into your father's development, to make sure everything was copacetic. I'm sorry things didn't work out for the office park."

"I don't care about him. My father just uses people to get what he wants." At a stoplight, she looked back and saw the old round headlights of a BMW a few cars back.

Tracy lit a joint. "Wow, that's a lot, man. You want some?" He passed it to Ethan in the backseat, who took a long toke and passed it to her. She waved it away as they drove on the north ramp to I-295 in the fog, the BMW's lights right behind them. They reached the bridge before Washington Ave. The bridge. Tukey's bridge. The dream came back to her—of being chased, of falling.

She rolled her window down. "Your grandfather seems like a very nice man."

"Yeah, Stan's the best. Taught me how to ski."

Turning off the exit, she scanned the road for the BMW, but any sign of its lights had disappeared in the fog. Trying her best to stay calm and focused, she shifted down, following Tracy's direction. She pulled in front of a rundown three-story building on a side street, trash cans out front, broken shades in the windows, shadowy characters walking around. "Thanks for the lift, Pen."

"Wanna come in?" asked stoned Ethan, trying to charm her.

This was tempting. Maybe go in for a half hour, just to lose Ward if he was following her? She checked the rearview again, scanning the streetlights and debris and empty, cracked pavement. She weighed her options but didn't have the energy to give Ethan excuses about her disinterest in him. Her arms and legs felt like lead pipes. "Sorry, I'm wiped. Catch you later."

They left her car, now reeking of pot, and she turned around in a dark driveway before making her way back to the southbound exit, her eyes flitting from the road to the rearview. Sleep could not come soon enough. When the light turned green, her car sputtered ahead toward the interstate and chugged, surging, and slowing, then petered out. Right there on the on-ramp, her Karmann Ghia rolled down the hill under the underpass before coming to a slow rolling stop. The car had finally died.

Dropping her head on the steering wheel, she thought about her options as drivers whizzed by, honking around her, angry. Dense uncertainty settled inside her. She couldn't see anyone coming up from behind. Ward and Leadbetter must have continued north. There was no way she could stay here. She stepped out in her heels, purse under her arm, and realized she'd forgotten her wrap at the theater. Careful to ease herself out and around the car without getting nailed, she walked uphill until she came out of the underpass into the cloak of the fog again. Taking her heels off, she tucked them under her arm and marched on the sidewalk as dim headlights came out of the pea soup.

When she reached the bridge, she checked her phone. It was 11:11. Looking around, Baxter Boulevard and the basin of Casco Bay below her, the tide undulating, she gripped the railing, feeling the vibrations of cars in her hands and feet, shaking her insides. Back inside her dream, she heard Chloe crying and saw Lottie's terrorized eyes penetrate the darkness. She heard her mother now, screaming in the night. Pennie looked out to the other side, across the bridge where her mother stood on the railing, hair a wild tangle, waving her arms high in the air, frantic. Without hesitation, Pennie jumped into the road to run to her, to rescue her, when she felt the rumbling of tires. Ward. His BMW coming from behind. She turned around to face the oncoming car, staring at Ward's headlights that rushed toward her.

At the last moment, a furious reflex, he swerved to miss her, breaking through the railing, out like a bullet into the dark envelope of Casco Bay and the deep basin below. The night fell silent, eerie. She peered down to watch the trunk submerge, swallowed by the rolling waters of a powerful high tide. Pennie turned around to find her mother in the darkness, but she was gone.

A deep aloneness sank inside, but the thick fog, a comforting blanket, kept her warm and protected and hidden in her new reality. Her new awareness led her away from the scene, leaving the bridge behind but carrying forward the memory of her mother and Chloe and Lottie, of every threatened child, woman, or mortal soul. She walked and walked barefoot, without a chill or a shiver or a rumble along the streets and busy intersections of Forest and Park Avenue, up the hill toward Congress and the West End, where she finally reached her apartment. Inside, she collapsed into a deep forgiving slumber, the triskelion locket still around her neck.

Chapter 17

Goode Vibrations

SHE WOKE UP TO the sun peeking through the slats in her blinds. She had voicemail from the Portland Police Department. Her car had been towed and they had questions about an incident last night. Calling back, she spoke to the captain who asked if she knew anything about the accident on the bridge. She pulled on the cord to raise her blinds to let in the sun.

"First I've heard about it, officer," she said.

More well rested than she'd been in a month, she recalled the vibrations on the bridge, her mother screaming for her and how she had jumped out to face oncoming lights. She knew Ward was dead, both him and his attorney. An unsettling coldness moved her, realizing she had done something out of pure instinct. Her mother had been with her, inside of her when she jumped in front of the oncoming car. It was the first time she'd felt her mother's essence.

In a state of a constant hum, like the world was falling into sync, she walked to her aunt and uncle's place, knowing someone would give her a lift to the station and her car. Inside, Mama Cass was the first to greet her, tail wagging and sniffing her up and down for the good vibrations that Pennie could not contain.

Tita sat at the kitchen table with Aunt Aggie and Uncle Alfie, wearing a weary mask of triumph, and red eyes, nursing her coffee. Pennie helped herself to a cup. There sat the *Tribune*, the picture on the front page of the Tukey's Bridge railing busted through with the headline: "Two Dead after Car Falls into Casco Bay."

Uncle Alfie glanced her way. "Hear about this?"

"I talked to the police this morning."

"They called you?"

"My car broke down on the Washington Avenue exit after giving some friends a lift home."

Tita lifted her head, too hungover to ask any questions. Aunt Aggie eyed her with suspicion. "You were on the bridge last night?"

"I know, it's a strange coincidence. The last thing I remember about Ward was how drunk he was. Too bad to hear he went into the bay like that."

Tita scratched her aching head, trying to comprehend the whole thing. "Where's your car?"

"The police towed it to the station because it was so close to the accident scene." She looked at her uncle.

"They've probably searched it thoroughly," he said, sipping his coffee, scratching his gray stubble.

"They can search all they want. Hopefully, those potheads I gave a ride home last night didn't leave anything behind."

He gave her a half-smile. "That's all we need."

Her aunt took coffee cake out of the oven and brought it to the table, the smell heavenly. "How did you get home last night, dear?"

"Walked. It was a nice night."

She pressed on. "And you didn't see the accident?"

"I heard a loud noise, but it was pretty dark and foggy. Thick as pea soup. It's no wonder he crashed."

Tita said, "You're lucky you weren't hit."

Aunt Aggie delicately placed the pan on a trivet in front of her. "You know, that's where your mother...well, you know..."

"I was thinking about that last night when I was there." Pennie scratched Mama Cass's head under the table.

Uncle Alfie put an arm around her. "I'm sure she was there with you, Birdie."

She took a piece of hot steaming cake and wolfed it down, ravenous. Tita stood up, found her sunglasses on the counter, and walked out the back door.

Aunt Aggie poured Pennie more coffee. "She's awfully glum this morning after such a big night last night." Pennie knew that this was her cue to find out what was wrong.

Out back, she sidled up beside Tita on the stone bench in front of the vacant birdbath, the same bench they'd sat on together as kids, sharing secrets. "I heard you made a killing last night. Mali said you'll clear over a hundred grand."

"Great turnout. Lars is pumped."

"I'm surprised you're not with the man of the hour."

"Had a fight. Something stupid."

Pennie had the feeling Tita didn't want to talk about it. "You two always seem to patch things up. And you've got an unbelievable documentary you made together. You should be so proud, Tita."

Her cousin folded her arms together. "I still can't believe Ward Lewis's car went off the bridge last night. Uncanny."

"It's so strange the feeling I had this morning when I woke up, like the world was more aligned somehow."

"That's one way to look at it."

"After what he put me through, I can't say I feel remorse. The threatening emails from his lawyer, lying to me about his wife, the photo."

Tita put her head in her hands.

Pennie turned toward her. "What? Don't tell me you feel bad for him."

"No, it's not that, it's just—" Tita took a deep breath. "Lars and I fought last night because I found out he posted that link with your picture on Facebook."

She felt all the blood drain from her face. "The naked photo of me? Lars posted that?"

"He was kind of desperate to get the buzz going. I'm not even sure how he came up with that idea. I only found out about it afterward."

She struggled to control her anger. "How long have you known?"

She shrugged. "A few weeks, I guess."

"How did he get it?"

"Remember you gave me access to your drive for those ski photos? Well, I shared it with him and he, well—"

"That's creepy. Why didn't you tell me? I thought it was Ward and his attorney!"

Tita pressed her lips together. "They did help spread it around, you know."

Her picture was infamous now, but it didn't matter anymore. She knew that Ward and his attorney had helped spread it far and wide, using any piece of intimidation they could get their hands on.

Tita picked up a pebble on the bench and threw it into the birdbath. The pool rippled in widening circles. Pennie began to chuckle, staring up at the cloudless sky.

"What?" Tita asked.

"You have to admit, Lars is a hell of a marketer."

Tita tried to laugh. "God, my head hurts."

Uncle Alfie opened the door behind them. "Can I take you down to the station?"

"Sure." She nudged Tita, standing up. "You mind if I borrow the Jan Van today?"

"Keys are on the hallway table."

UNCLE ALFIE ACCOMPANIED HER into the station to talk to the officers. Other than the timing of possibly being near the bridge when the car broke through the railing, no one had seen Pennie in that area. She explained she'd heard something that sounded like a crash after she walked over the bridge, but that was it. There was no sign of foul play at the scene and her car was clean. The police thanked them for coming in. She was free to go.

On the ride back to Pine Street, Uncle Alfie called the tow company to have her car brought to his mechanic. They rode in silence, only the sound of the road under his winter tires until he interrupted the quiet. "Life is full of synchronicity."

She thought about the small book the wine-seller had dropped in her bag. "How do you mean?"

"Oh, you know, being on the same bridge as Ward and Leadbetter last night or dreaming about people and places you've never seen before."

She looked out the window toward Casco Bay, instinctively reaching for the triskelion locket about her neck, thinking about Ward and Chloe, the necklace and the dog, her mother, Lottie and Malaga. "I know what you mean. It can be kind of scary."

"When you take signs seriously, you can begin to understand their gravity, their power."

"I'm not sure how I feel about Ward and Leadbetter going off the bridge. To tell you the truth, I woke up kind of lighthearted and numb, almost nonfeeling. Does that make any sense?"

"I'm not quite sure how I feel about it either. But sometimes it seems like the universe moves in meaningful and unexplained ways. You've been through a tremendous amount these past few months. Give yourself some time to come to terms with everything."

She was afraid to share that moment on the bridge, instinctively jumping into the road when her mother screamed out. He turned in to the driveway and parked in front of the old carriage house where she'd seen the owl. "You headed to Malaga?"

"How did you know?"

"I had a feeling. Nice day for it." He turned off the engine. "When you go back generations, we're all descendants of good and bad, the persecutors and the persecuted. The important thing is to recognize the past to change for the better."

"Do you think my mother was depressed? Is that why she jumped?"

"No, I think it was the opposite. She was full of life and that's what made her so vulnerable. She had this uncanny ability to empathize with others, to feel other people's pain, and to help them. But there is a dark side to empathy."

"How do you mean?"

"She too readily took on the pain of others. It was her intense struggle. She could be overwhelmed by selfish people, become too deeply involved because her emotions ran so high and deep."

"There are selfish people everywhere."

"That's right. And there are good people everywhere. You just have to keep your balance, Birdie."

Chapter 18
Ghosts of Erasure

THE RED JAN VAN sputtered, rough and loud. Pennie shifted the tall spindly stick from third to fourth, thankful for the VW bus. She wished Dani and Mali were joining her, but they were journeying up to Jonesport to visit Aunt Eleanor. Maybe it was better to be alone for this soul-searching trip anyway.

She cranked the window down, letting in the warm sea air of Casco Bay, crossing Tukey's Bridge, gazing out onto the calm light blue sea, the dancing glitter of sun bouncing with the swells, twinkling. Clicking on the radio, Sinead O'Connor's voice filled the cab once again, "The Lion and the Cobra," drawn out in spectral sonorous tones—a higher frequency than most could bear—the beautiful, brutal truth.

The familiar coastal route took her through Brunswick and up to Bath, out toward Phippsburg, the Popham Beach State Park signs along the winding narrow road. Ski equipment rattled in the back with every turn. The GPS led her to the little fishing village of Sebasco, and she shifted down, coasting the steep incline, looking out to Malaga Island, over forty acres of pristine undeveloped beauty, just across the river about four hundred feet away.

On the waterfront, she parked in front of Anna's Water's Edge Restaurant, a one-story red clapboard building next to a small brown cottage. A middle-aged woman with thick yellow hair piled on her head in a clip sat on the ground pulling weeds underneath a sign in the cottage window: HOUSE FOR RENT. Pennie tentatively approached her. "Hi, um, sorry to bother you, but I'm looking for a way over to Malaga."

The dubious local looked up from her work, squinting in the sun. "Have you got a kayak?"

Pennie considered the boathouse wharf stacked with traps behind the cottage. "No, I didn't bring a boat. I was wondering if the tide went out low enough to walk over."

"Nope, impossible. You could swim, but it's a little chilly this time of year." She coughed, low and scratchy, sitting in the grass.

Even though the day was mild, unseasonably warm, Pennie imagined the water temperature and shuddered. "Do you happen to know anyone with a boat? I've done some research on Malaga. Was hoping to walk the loop trail."

She waved to the area downriver beyond the restaurant. "Best bet is to drive over to the acre lot. There's a public dock. Somebody's bound to show up and give you a lift."

"The acre lot?"

"You've never heard of the acre lot? What kind of a researcher are you?" She stood up from her weeding, a sturdy long-legged woman, dusting off her T-shirt.

Pennie stepped closer. "No, sorry to say."

"That's the lot the town gave to those islanders when they kicked 'em off."

"Terrible what happened to them."

"You'll find people all around here related." She pointed toward the hill Pennie had just driven down. "You go back up and then down the hill to the main road, take a right, and look for Ridge Road. That'll take you to Baker's Wharf Road." She motioned up, down, and over with her broad hand. "You can't miss it."

Pennie repeated what she'd heard to make sure it stuck. Instead of reaching for the stranger's gloved hand holding the trowel, she nodded. "Thanks so much. Really appreciate the help."

"Just be nice. Somebody will give you a ride if you're nice about it."

She smiled, grateful for the advice. "Yes, of course. Thanks, again." Hopping in the van, she turned it around to drive back up the hill, watching for the road signs. In about five minutes, she came upon Baker's Wharf and turned onto the dirt road to see a handwritten sign in the grassy spot beside the wharf that said ACRE LOT.

An acre. An acre in exchange for an island.

Old graying steps led up to a long pier that stretched over the granite shore and seaweed. She stepped carefully along the weathered planks, down the long runway to the working dock, directly across from the rocky shore of the island. The warm sun sparkled off the murky, greenish-brown water of the New Meadows, dotted with fishing boats tied to moorings. A group of three men hauled a net onboard a fishing trawler from a skiff.

As if summoned, a small inflatable Zodiac pulled alongside the dock. A slim dark-haired girl, no more than seventeen, steered the small motor, her hand on the throttle, a black Labrador sitting at her feet. "Hi," said Pennie. "I'm looking for a ride to Malaga. Any chance you could give me a lift?"

Quiet eyes set apart, the dark girl motioned her to get in the boat without a word. Sensing familiarity, Pennie stepped into the bow carefully, sitting on the floor of the inflatable dinghy beside the graying black dog who edged his way over, missing one of his front legs. Pushing from the dock, the girl motored around a few moorings to the north side of the island and over a seaweed forest floating in the cold saltwater, coasting up to the white shell beach with a woosh.

The old dog stood up in anticipation and Pennie offered her navigator a $10 bill, but she only smiled and waved her away. There was something about this girl. Then it hit her. She looked like the girl in her dream, the teenage girl in the schoolhouse, the one on the stretcher at the School for the Feeble-Minded, her eyes dark pools of sorrow. She looked just like Lottie.

Her eyes were soft and kind like the waters of the New Meadows. Pennie thanked her and took off her sneakers to straddle the inflated sides and step into the frigid water. She jumped along, wading up onto the craggy shell beach near the lobster traps piled high. Her feet were numb, but the sharp shells made her step with trepidation. "I won't be long, maybe a half hour." The Lottie lookalike turned slowly to back out of the small cove with her smiling three-legged companion. Somehow Pennie knew she didn't have to worry about getting a ride back to the mainland.

Millions of shell pieces and fish bones underfoot, a midden left from the days when the Wabanaki settled on these shores, an awareness of time sunk in, of life and death throughout the thousands of years of human history on these coastal islands. Making her way over the sharp remnants, she stepped up on the north end where the fishing community had settled, thousands of years after the Indigenous Americans had been here.

All the artifacts from the archaeological dig appeared in her mind's eye, evidence of the past—bones, nails, buttons, fishhooks, coins, pipe stems, teacup fragments, a spoon, a belt buckle, a rusted heart-shaped lock, a key. A child's opal ring. She clutched the locket around her neck, thoughts of Chloe drifting through her mind. A raven soared overhead and roosted in a tall spruce tree at the edge of the quiet woods on the ridge.

Brushing off the sharp pieces of iridescent shell from her tender feet, she put on her sneakers and made her way up the trail along the northern ledge, admiring the signs of old homesteads, foundation holes overgrown with shrubs, grass, and wildflowers—the homes of the McKenneys, Markses, Griffins, Easons, Murphys, and Johnsons—marked by numbered posts, these sites of fishers and laborers, diggers and planters, tailors and menders, preachers and seekers. The moss-lined slope on the east side led her past the hops and lilac bushes, past milkweed pods and wispy cocoons, prickly thistle, huckleberry, raspberry, juniper, cordgrass, and tender ferns of bright green, leading toward the deep forest that sheltered most of the island. A tangled web of tree roots grew over the glaciated bedrock, an exoskeleton protecting the heartbeat of settlement that once lived there, a collective soul.

The steep rooted trail led her to the site of the old schoolhouse, high on the bluff. The ghostly sounds of children's voices filled her with peace and harmony, the innocence of youth, the contentment of life, home, and family. Sweet, hungry children of all ages, together in a melting pot of learning, trust, and survival.

Deeper into the spruce woods, the green moss grew more emerald, vibrant, glowing along the trail. A feather drifted down and landed on her arm, a single brown striped feather, downy tufts on one end and barred on the other. The spirit of Cipelahq moved above her, high overhead, hiding in the deep hole of the spruce tree, watching.

A rumble of thunder rolled in the distance, the sky growing darker. Gazing out onto the sixty-foot cliffs of Bear Island across the river, she fell into a vision. A scow tossed in the rough current, hawsered to a tree on the island. The air electrified with lightning, a slow low rumble vibrating through her, and the deathly silence was broken by a loud crack and a deluge of rain. Under darkness, a man in the scow lowered a frail sickly woman into a rowboat in the drenching rain. Carefully, he stepped down with her and, one by one, helped his three children into the small dory, rocking in the storm. Their cries of fear echoed from the cliffs, and he picked up the oars, rowing with everything he had, carrying his family around the island, the chop and wind nearly capsizing them. The dory filled with water and the children hovered over their dying mother. Finally, making it to shore, he hoisted the rowboat alongside a shallow gravel bed only to realize his wife was gone, the children clinging to her in frightened devastation.

The rumble subsided, the rain stopped, and the clouds slowly moved overhead, clearing to sunlight again. She could smell the organic forest, could see the glowing richness of emerald moss, the bright yellow of enchanted mushrooms, the glossy wintergreen, the immovable boulders, and red spruce branches. Above the crowns of balsam fir trees, a breeze whispered, the warblers twittered, and the terns dipped amid the resilient salt marshes in homage to the souls departed, the very heartbeat of the island, Malaga, the place where bodies were removed but the grave souls remained deep in the holy wood. She could almost hear the wind exhaling the names of the Malaga inhabitants: Harold, George, Hannah, Elizabeth, Calvin, Laura, Roxanna, Ellen, Lucy, Rufus, Harry, Timy, Gyrard, Mary Ellen, Silas...

The loop trail of bedrock ledge and sinewy root meandered through the trees and the tangled grasses, witch hazel and poison ivy, until coming around to the pocket beach of nightshade, sea rocket, and bladder wrack, back to the shell fragments of razor clams and quahog, the stacks of traps going upriver. The fishing boats rocked in the tide, a testament to the lives of the industrious working community, this coastal rock that had once been envisioned as a tourist destination, now sacred undeveloped land, a paradise preserved.

She knew what she had seen. The visions stayed with her, made her shudder deep inside for the families living in scows, forever drifting without a home. The visions of bodies removed, of a small child slipping overboard, disappearing in the New Meadows, the ghosts of erasure, the sound of those children's children echoing on the island for their very souls. Lives wrested, eviscerated for generations, oppressed by society and trauma, a tenuous thread back to their ancestors' souls sown on the New Meadows, insistent, lingering, and deep-rooted on the rocky ledge called Malaga.

Notes

Chapter 4: Cipelahq

46 **"Have you ever heard the Passamaquoddy…"**: "A Passamaquoddy Story of Leux," AccessGenealogy, https://accessgenealogy.com/native/a-story-of-leux.htm.

Chapter 6: Sixth Sense

68 **"In the early and mid-1900s"**: Stephen T. Murphy, *Voices of Pineland: Eugenics, Social Reform, and the Legacy of "Feeblemindedness" in Maine* (Charlotte, NC: Information Age Publishing, 2011), 109–110.

Chapter 8: Crow's Nest

109 **By 1952, numbers escalated…:** Richard S. Kimball, *Pineland's Past: The First One Hundred Years* (Portsmouth, NH: Peter E. Randall, 2001), 45–46, 74–79.

Chapter 9: Revelations

124 **From the 1860s until 1912…:** Malaga Monument at Webber Cemetery, 1375 Intervale Road, New Gloucester, Maine.

Chapter 10: The Wresting Place

148 **Let us ever love each other...**: William J. Henry and Luella B. Henry, "Love Each Other," Timeless Truths, circa 1900, https://library.timelesstruths.org/music/Love_Each_Other/midi/.

150 **Residents, all descendants of...**: Pineland Case Files, Digital Public Library of America, https://digitalmaine.com/pinland_case_files/#:~:text=In%20December%201911%2C%20the%20State%20of%20Maine%20committed,small%20island%20community%20off%20the%20coast%20of%20Phippsburg.

150 **In 1913, a newspaper...**: William David Barry, "The Shameful Story of Malaga Island," *Down East*, November 1980, https://downeast.com/history/malaga/.

Chapter 11: Story of Exile

161 **The headline read...**: "Malaga Island Residents with Missionary, 1909," *Harper's Weekly*, circa 1909, https://www.mainememory.net/record/23859.

161 **Next to it was a postcard...**: Postcard, Maine State Museum Collection, circa 1908.

161 **She flipped to an article...**: Lauris Percy, "Strange Scenes on a Strange Land," *Casco Bay Breeze*,vol. V, no. 16 (August 24,1905): 2. Chronicling America, Library of Congress, https://chroniclingamerica.loc.gov/lccn/sn95068036/1905-08-24/ed-1/seq-1/.

162 **At the turn of the twentieth century...**: Steve Mitchell, *The Shame of Maine: Malaga, the Story behind the Pictures* (Brunswick, ME: S. Mitchell, 1999), 4.

162 **According to legend...**: John P. Mosher, "No Greater Abomination: Ethnicity, Class, and Power Relations on Malaga Island, Maine,

1880–1912" (master's thesis, University of Southern Maine, 1991), 29–32.

162 **Eventually, the descendants of...**: William David Barry, "The Shameful Story of Malaga Island," *Down East*, November 1980, https://downeast.com/history/malaga/.

162 **During this time in the midcoast...**: Mosher, "No Greater Abomination," 63–64.

163 **The December 30, 1905, issue...**: Mosher, "No Greater Abomination," 85.

163 **In August 1911, a Boston newspaper...**: Seth Goldstein, "A Window on the Past—Malaga Island," *Portland Press Herald*, November 23, 2022, https://www.pressherald.com/2022/11/23/a -window-on-the-past-malaga-island/.

163 **Because it was inhabited by...**: Miriam Stover Thomas, *Flotsam and Jetsam* (Maine: private publication, 1973), 87.

163 **Captain George and Lucy Lane...**: Mosher, "No Greater Abomination," 116–121.

164 **Impressed with the children...**: Deborah Dubrule, "Malaga, Revisited: On a Casco Bay Island, a Shameful Incident in Maine's History Comes to Light," The Working Waterfront Archives, August 1, 2005, http://www.workingwaterfrontarchives.org/2005/08/01/malaga-r evisited-on-a-casco-bay-island-a-shameful-incident-in-maines-histo ry-comes-to-light/.

164 **About a year after visiting...**: Rob Rosenthal and Kate Philbrick, *Malaga Island: A Story Best Left Untold*, audio documentary, 58:38, http://malagaisland.mainememory.net/page/5126/dis play.html.

164 **During this time, three parties…**: H. H. Price and Gerald E. Talbot, *Maine's Visible Black History: The First Chronicle of Its People* (Gardiner, ME: Tilbury House, 2006), 73.

164 **The state attorney general…**: Thomas, *Flotsam and Jetsam*, 87.

165 **According to the *Bath Independent*…**: Mitchell, *The Shame of Maine*, citing December 16, 1911, *Bath Independent*.

165 **Governor Plaisted said…**: Katherine A. McBrien, *Malaga Island: Fragmented Lives*, Augusta, ME: Friends of the Maine State Museum, 2013, accompanying a past exhibition about Malaga at the Maine State Museum by the same name. http://www.mainestatemuseum.org/exhibits/malaga_island_fragmented_lives_-_educational_materials/

166 **One destitute family…**: "The Death of Laura Tripp or the Tragedy of Malaga Island," *Casco Bay Breeze*, March 6, 1913, Maine State Museum Archives.

166 **Descendants of Malaga eventually…**: Rosenthal and Philbrick, *Malaga Island,*

166 **She finished reading…**: Rosenthal and Philbrick, *Malaga Island: A Story Best Left Untold.*

166 **Nearly a century later…**: Rob Rosenthal and Kate Philbrick, "Joint Resolution Recognizing the Tragic Expulsion of the Residents of Malaga Island, 124th Legislature, April 7, 2010," *Malaga Island: A Story Best Left Untold*, supplemental text, http://malagaisland.mainem emory.net/page/5130/display.html.

166 **With about ninety Malaga…**: Dennis Hoey, "Troubling History of Malaga Island Takes on Added Significance a Century Later," *Portland Press Herald*, February 2, 2023, https://www.pressherald.com/2023/02/02/troubling-history-o f-malaga-island-takes-on-added-significance-a-century-later/.

Chapter 13: Judgment

209 **Her uncle provided copies…:** Fred Hunniston, *Portland Sunday Telegram*, April 11, 1965.

209 **According to a report…:** "Report on Malaga Island, Phippsburg Maine," presented at Phippsburg, Maine, town meeting on April 1, 1902, Alfred F. Totman Public Library Archives.

210 **Etta died in the institution…:** Stephen T. Murphy, *Voices of Pineland: Eugenics, Social Reform, and the Legacy of "Feeblemindedness" in Maine* (Charlotte, NH: Information Age Publishing, 2011), 79, 91.

Chapter 15: Dark Truth

244 **WILLIAM MARKS…:** Gravestones at the Pineland Patients Cemetery, 1375 Intervale Road, New Gloucester, Maine.

Acknowledgments

An earnest thanks to my patient and generous editors, Mark Athitakis and Kellyn Eaddy. I am not sure how I was lucky enough to find you both, but you have made all the difference in the evolution of this story. Mark, your developmental edits shaped the novel in fundamental ways; Kellyn, your sharp DEI lens and exacting notes helped me realize what a skilled copy editor really is. For the stunning cover design, I was fortunate to find Mi'kmaq artist Marissa Joly.

The inclusion of Wabanaki characters in this tale of and about Maine and our unique coastal heritage makes the story whole. Thank you, Maria Girouard, executive director of Wabanaki Reach, for offering kind and vital edits and insight into these characters. Your Indigenous spirit has left me feeling a deep sense of honor to know and work with you. And thank you to Esther Anne, policy associate at the University of Southern Maine (USM), for introducing us and for sharing your ideals on truth and reconciliation.

Through my ties with the Stonecoast MFA Creative Writing Program at USM, I am lucky enough to know Robin Talbot, the longtime associate director and champion of all writers who continue to pass through the program annually. Robin, thank you for introducing me to Libby Bischof, executive director of the Osher Map Library and professor of history at USM, who read early drafts of chapters and offered valuable expertise.

Thank you, Libby, and all the research librarians I met in my travels around the southern and midcoast area, helping me locate any historical articles and records of Malaga, including Katie Alleman at the Maine Historical Society Brown Research Library, and the staff at the Patten Free Library in Bath and the Albert F. Totman Library in Phippsburg. And thank you to Joyce Mongeau and author Jaed Coffin who recommended these resources and others.

The people who were kind enough to read early drafts not only helped me get my arms around the story, but also offered ideas and encouragement when I most needed it. Thank you, Rob Rosenthal, for your early critique and extraordinary radio documentary, *Malaga Island: A Story Best Left Untold*; and Julia Bouwsma, for your kind advice and poignant book of poems, *Midden*. And thank you to lyric poet Kristin Rieff, for your encouragement, your friendship, and for composing the resonant opening poem, *New Meadows*.

The path to publishing has been long and winding, but despite the years since I graduated from the Stonecoast program, I often think back to the patient mentors who shaped my early writing. Thank you to authors Jack Driscoll, Clint McCown, Elizabeth Searle, Brad Barkley, and Ann Hood. Also, thanks to writers Monica Wood and Sarah Carson, faculty at the Iota Short Forms Conference, and to the late Daniel Menaker at the Key West Writer's Workshop. Your mentorship has been invaluable.

I would not be the writer or the person I am today without my writer's group over so many years. Thank you to Pauline Briere, Cal Armistead, and Pamela McKenney. You and only you can understand our common suffering, of writing endless drafts and sitting through rounds of critiques, remaining steadfast in our pursuit of mastering the art of fiction. Your collective voice is my writing companion.

Finally, and most importantly, thank you to my best reader, my best friend, and my husband, Jonathan Safford. You read the first novel I ever wrote, and everything since. Thank you for keeping my head above water and giving me the strength to continue along the path of this writer's journey. I could not have completed this novel without you. And to my children, Isaac, Ana, Claire, and Sam. I burst with gratitude for you.